Recent Titles by Anna Jacobs from Severn House

CHANGE OF SEASON
CHESTNUT LANE
THE CORRIGAN LEGACY
FAMILY CONNECTIONS
A FORBIDDEN EMBRACE
AN INDEPENDENT WOMAN
IN FOCUS
IN SEARCH OF HOPE
KIRSTY'S VINEYARD
LICENCE TO DREAM
MARRYING MISS MARTHA
MISTRESS OF MARYMOOR
MOVING ON
A PLACE OF HOPE
REPLENISH THE EARTH
SAVING WILLOWBROOK
SEASONS OF LOVE
A TIME FOR HOPE
TOMORROW'S PATH
THE WISHING WELL
WINDS OF CHANGE

Short Stories
SHORT AND SWEET

Anna is always delighted to hear from readers and can be contacted via the internet:
Anna has her own web page, with details of her books and excerpts, and invites you to visit it at http://www.annajacobs.com
Anna can be contacted by email at anna@annajacobs.com
If you'd like to receive an email newsletter about Anna and her books every month or two, you are cordially invited to join her announcements list. Just email her and ask to be added to the list, or follow the link from her web page.

TOMORROW'S PATH

Anna Jacobs

This first world edition published 2015
in Great Britain and 2016 in the USA by
SEVERN HOUSE PUBLISHERS LTD of
19 Cedar Road, Sutton, Surrey, England, SM2 5DA.
Trade paperback edition first published
in Great Britain and the USA 2016 by
SEVERN HOUSE PUBLISHERS LTD.

Jacobs, Anna author.
Tomorrow's path.
1. Novelists–Fiction. 2. Divorced people–Fiction.
3. Man-woman relationships–Fiction. 4. Romantic suspense
novels.
I. Title
823.9'14-dc23

ISBN-13: 978-0-7278-8558-6 (cased)
ISBN-13: 978-1-84751-667-1 (trade paper)
ISBN-13: 978-1-78010-721-9 (e-book)

All Severn House titles are printed on acid-free paper.

Severn House Publishers support the Forest Stewardship Council™ [FSC™],
the leading international forest certification organisation. All our titles that
are printed on FSC certified paper carry the FSC logo.

Typeset by Palimpsest Book Production Ltd.,
Falkirk, Stirlingshire, Scotland.
Printed and bound in Great Britain by
TJ International, Padstow, Cornwall.

One

Jessica Lord had been waiting for this television programme for two weeks and had even refused an invitation to the cinema, because her favourite author, Jivan Childering, was going to appear on Sally Mennon's ***People in the News***. It was a rare opportunity to see a writer who normally went to extreme lengths to avoid publicity and who was becoming famous for his tangles with the press.

She tied her hair back, cleaned her spectacles and got ready to enjoy herself. After pouring a glass of wine, she got out the box of chocolates she'd been saving for a happy occasion and curled up in the corner of the couch with her feet up. It was Saturday night, after all.

She looked down at her book with its author photo. Childering was one of the most handsome men she'd ever seen. Or else the photo in the book had been touched up.

As the programme began and he was introduced to the studio audience, she sighed. No, it hadn't been touched up. He really was gorgeous, with his straight blue-black hair and dark eyes. Just as the newspapers said, he seemed to have inherited the best from both parents, the height and clear-cut aristocratic features of his English mother, the graceful carriage and olive skin of his Indian father.

Until he opened his mouth. And then this brilliant author, whose latest book had hit the bestseller lists within days of being published, turned wooden and uncooperative, answering the interviewer's questions with monosyllables. From the way the two of them looked at one another, they were not on good terms.

The wine remained untasted on the table beside Jessica, and when the unopened box of chocolates slid to the floor, she didn't bother to pick it up.

Sally's questions were tactless and deliberately provocative, but Childering wasn't handling them well. She was trying to get him to talk about his childhood and how badly his mother's family had treated him. She didn't mention his mixed race specifically, but that was clearly what she meant when she called him 'the cuckoo in the nest'.

His wooden expression was replaced for a moment by anger at the phrase, then he said, 'Is my childhood relevant? I was told you wanted me to talk about my latest book tonight.'

'Yes, of course I do. And later on we'll have the viewer segment. We've picked three questions for you to answer. So . . . tell us about your new book, Jivan. What does your intrepid hero get up to this time?'

Just as he opened his mouth to reply, Jessica's telephone rang.

'Oh, no!' For a moment, she debated leaving it, but she could never bear to do that, so picked up the phone. 'Yes?'

'Is that Jessica Lord?'

'Yes.' Quick, she thought, whoever you are, tell me what you want and go away! And you'd better not be trying to sell me anything. She continued to stare at the television screen, trying to follow what Childering was saying about his book.

'Jessica,' said an unknown voice, 'your question has been picked for use during the Jivan Childering interview tonight.'

'*What*?'

The voice repeated what it had said in a bored tone. 'Would you like time to fetch your question?'

'No. I can remember it.'

'Then if you'd like to hold the line for two or three minutes, we'll connect you to the studio and you can speak to Mr Childering. Oh, wait – can you just turn down the sound on your TV first? We're getting a bit of echo.'

She did as he asked, then waited, trying to control her nervousness as she held the phone to her ear and listened to the programme through it.

'You're through,' said the voice.

'Good evening, Jessica Lord from London.' Sally was smiling across at her from the screen.

'Good evening, Sally and Jivan.' Jessica was pleased that her voice had neither wobbled nor risen nervously at the end of the phrase.

'You have a question for tonight's guest, I believe. Go ahead.'

'Jivan, I've read all your books, and loved them.' She paused, expecting him to smile or say thank you.

He did nothing except incline his head slightly. His face was expressionless again and his eyes were glazed with what looked suspiciously like boredom.

She persevered. 'I'd like to ask you why the women in your last book had such minor roles? Your other heroines were so real, I could almost see them walking down the street, but in *Swift Justice* the women seem very colourless, fading into the background . . .' Whoops, had she gone too far? But this defect had haunted her, because even his minor characters were usually vivid.

She watched the television screen and saw his face grow tight and shuttered, which surprised her. Surely a famous writer would be used to all sorts of questions and not get angry?

'In the book you mentioned,' he said slowly, as if speaking to a half-wit, 'the story focuses on the male characters and it's they who carry the action, so the women *are* unimportant. One has to be true to one's story, you know.'

'But Laura's intervention marked a crucial turning point in the action. Surely a man whose life she'd saved, who had just gone to bed with her, wouldn't have walked out and left her without a word afterwards.'

Jivan sighed audibly. 'It's very true to Sam Shere's character for him to walk away. We can't have him in a permanent relationship, you know, or how would I get him into his next adventure?'

His tone was so patronising Jessica felt insulted. 'How can the female character be unimportant? You wouldn't even *have* an ongoing hero without Laura.'

She could see the amusement building up on Sally Mennon's face.

'Laura saved Sam's life by mere chance,' he insisted.

'And by some quick thinking, not to mention bravery,' Jessica insisted.

'Look, this discussion is getting us nowhere. *Nowhere*! If you feel you can do better yourself, go ahead and produce a bestselling story dominated by women.'

By now, Jessica was angry enough to shout back, 'That would be as unbalanced as your last book.'

'Then go ahead and write a *balanced* tale.' His voice was dripping with sarcasm and he was glaring at the cameras.

Sally was smiling openly.

'I will. In fact, I've written one already.' She'd entered it in a writing competition but it would be a while before she found out the results.

He made a visible effort to control his anger. 'Then as fellow writers we'll just have to agree to disagree, won't we?'

She opened her mouth to reply, but—

'Thank you, Jessica,' cooed Sally. 'And good luck with your own writing. Now, our next viewer should be on the line. Are you there, Paul Jones from Taunton?'

Jessica put down the phone and walked back to the couch. Turning up the sound, she sat through the rest of the interview and found it as bitterly disappointing as the first part.

The other viewers asked innocuous questions like: 'How do you start writing a new book?' and 'Where do you get your ideas?' Jivan gave brief and unrevealing answers.

The undercurrent of animosity between him and his host was quite obvious and in Jessica's opinion was unprofessional on both sides. When the show ended, he got up and strode out of the studio before the credits had started playing across the screen.

'And that concludes our interview with the famous writer, Jivan Childering,' Sally's tone was mocking. 'A rare treat.'

Another voice took over. 'Next week's guest will be—'

Jessica switched off the TV set, but didn't move. She was disappointed and still angry.

After a few minutes, she went into the spare bedroom and switched her computer on, muttering, 'I *will* get my novels published. If not this one, then the next. And it'll include strong men *and* women characters, thank you very much, Mr Childering.'

The following weekend, Jessica read an article about Childering's acrimonious break-up and forthcoming divorce in the Sunday papers and saw a photo in a scandal rag showing him with a bandaged head where his wife had thrown a vase at him. That must have happened soon after he'd been on the Sally Mennon show.

If his marriage had been going sour, no wonder his female characters had become either unsympathetic or pale shadows.

But he still shouldn't have talked to her like that.

The phone rang and when she picked it up, it was her father.

'We've . . . um, got a bit of bad news, love.'

'What's wrong, Dad?'

'Your mother's got breast cancer.'

'Oh, no! What stage is it at?'

'It's early days, so she stands a good chance of recovering, but I thought you should know. Perhaps you can get home more often at weekends. She'd like that and we have to keep her happy.'

'Of course I will. I'll come up tonight.'

'No, don't do that. She'll think she's worse than they've told her. They said she stands a good chance of recovering, thank heaven.'

'I'll come up to Lancashire next weekend then.'

'Don't be anything but positive. Don't even hint at . . . anything else.'

'I won't, Dad. How are you coping?'

'I'm doing fine. No one needs to worry about me.'

When she put the phone down she had tears in her eyes.

Cancer! She couldn't bear the thought of it. She'd have to go home far more often now. She *wanted* to go, to keep an eye on her mother.

Two weeks later, Jessica's section leader told her the manager of their area wanted to see her.

'What about?'

He hesitated. 'Your future.'

'Oh.' She'd been half-expecting this. The company made a big thing of 'developing' staff and promoting internally. Only she wasn't seeking a promotion. All she wanted was to tick along in her job and carry on writing as much as she could.

He made a shooing motion so she went along the corridor and knocked on Fran's door.

'Ah, Jessica. Come and sit down. I'd like to discuss your future in the company.'

She could guess what was coming.

'It's about time we gave you some overseas experience. How do you fancy a stay in New York?'

'I'd hate it.' She spoke without thinking, blurting out the truth, something she couldn't seem to train herself out of. She could have kicked herself when she saw Fran's disapproving expression.

'Oh? Why is that?'

'I'm not fond of big cities.'

'New York is where our head office is. We only send our most promising people there. You're one of the quickest learners we've ever employed.'

'Thank you. But there's something else: my mother has just been diagnosed with breast cancer.' She hated using her mother as an excuse, but consoled her conscience with the thought that her mother would benefit from more visits if Jessica managed to stay in England.

'Oh dear! I'm sorry to hear that. Of course this isn't the time to send you overseas. Do you mind me asking? How bad is it?'

'She's just started treatment, so we're not sure what's going to be happening.' Tears came into her eyes and she fumbled for a tissue.

'We won't send you away yet, then. Where do your parents live?'

'Rochdale, to the north of Greater Manchester, only we still think of it as Lancashire.'

'Would it help to get a posting to our Leeds office for a while?'

'Yes. I think it would.'

'It'll mean a sideways step, less keeping up with the pointed end of new developments.'

'It'd be worth it.'

'I'll see what I can arrange.'

Jessica went back to her section and reported the conversation, not expecting anything much to happen for a while.

But she hadn't counted on Fran's famous efficiency. Within the week, her manager had arranged to shuffle some staff round and post Jessica to Leeds.

That meant she needed a car and had to find herself somewhere else to live, not to mention packing up her possessions.

Inevitably her writing suffered, but her mother's delight at having her living closer made up for that, and her father was very happy to be able to help her find a car, for which he paid.

She was shocked. 'You shouldn't have done that, Dad. You must let me pay you back.'

'Our Peter gets a car from the business, and it's about time you had some benefit from my success, too. We're a registered company now, with two shops, and both are doing well. Our Peter's got plans for another one. Eh, he's a go-getter, that one is.'

Her brother wouldn't be happy about her getting one, she was sure. She and Peter weren't close and all he seemed to care about was making money. 'But I don't work in the shop, so why would I be entitled to a car?'

'Because you're our daughter and we'd love to help you. Why did we go to Australia for a few years and work so hard, if not to be able to give you and your brother better chances in life? You can't both inherit the shops, and the way you two have always fought and quarrelled, you couldn't run the company together, either. But you'll still get your share one day. You must let me slip you something every now and then. Family comes first with us Lords.'

That had been dinned into her since childhood. She gave him a big hug. 'Thank you, Dad.'

Her father's casual reference to Australia made her dream of it again that night. She'd been seven when the family came back to England. Her mother hadn't been able to settle abroad, so far away from their family, but Jessica had been born there and knew nothing else. She'd been deeply upset at being brought to a strange, cold country, where she was the youngest in her generation, an outlier age-wise, and had no real friends among the Lord clan, not even her older brother.

One day she would go back to Australia to see if it was as wonderful as she remembered: the sunshine, the wide blue sky, the beaches and, above all, the more relaxed feel to the place. One of the first things she'd do was visit the Swan Valley, near Perth. Her parents had taken her and her brother there a couple of times. Jessica hadn't been old enough to taste the wine, of course, but she'd loved seeing the vineyards, with their rows of dark green vines, and had enjoyed picking her own bunch of grapes. But she couldn't go yet, not till her mother was better.

She settled down easily into the small branch in Leeds, making friends with Lisa, and going out with Thomas a few times. She was quite prepared to go to bed with him, but as they agreed after a preliminary and unsatisfying fumble that ended with them both feeling vaguely embarrassed, they made better friends than lovers.

She was beginning to worry that she hadn't met any guy she wanted to sleep with, was beginning to think there was something wrong with her.

In the meantime, she was still obsessed by her writing and it saved her sanity while travelling to and from Lancashire.

To everyone's relief, little by little her mother made progress.

Jessica wondered what had happened to the writing competition and had mentally dismissed it, deciding she'd not got anywhere. Then one day she received a letter saying that due to there being 1,200 entries, the verdict would be delayed, but that she had got through to the last thirty.

That made her day.

At twenty-seven, Jessica told herself, she had plenty of time to achieve her ambition of getting her novels published.

But she missed having solid writing time, missed it so much.

Two

Jivan ignored the people who tried to speak to him as he left the studio. He walked outside, relishing the cool, fresh air after the overheated studio. Getting into his car, he pulled out a fistful of tissues to wipe off the TV makeup, but didn't set off immediately.

He shouldn't have agreed to do the interview. He'd butted heads with Sally Mennon before at a writers' festival, and he didn't like her or her interviewing style. Well, she was famous for making people angry enough to reveal more than they'd intended. But his publicist had been very persuasive and it was only a half-hour segment after all.

He'd thought he could stay calm, but 'cuckoo in the nest' had riled him. It was so accurate a description of his place in his mother's aristocratic family – the half-Indian bastard son of their rebellious daughter. He let out an angry huff of air at the memory of his childhood.

Taking his time, he drove home to Richmond. He wasn't in a hurry to confront his wife, who would be furious about his behaviour on TV tonight. Well, Louisa would be even more upset by the end of the evening because he'd decided it was time to have things out with her about their unsatisfactory marriage.

He was dreading the confrontation, though. She could be . . . vicious, had shocked him a few times during their three years of marriage with sudden quarrels. He detested quarrels, craved a quiet, peaceful home and life. Strange that, when he wrote thrillers for a living.

Louisa greeted him by bouncing out of her chair and yelling, 'Are you out of your mind, Jivan Childering, antagonising a woman like Sally Mennon?'

'I must have been out of my mind to have agreed to go on her show.'

'It was brilliant exposure. But no, you had to waste your opportunity, didn't you? You're getting a reputation for being rude and arrogant, did you know that?'

'And your point is?'

'If you want to climb to the very top of the bestseller lists and stay there, you need good publicity, not bad.'

'My books seem to be selling very nicely, Louisa, without me kow-towing to people like that horrible woman.'

'Your books could sell a good many more copies if you would only put more effort into the publicity. I'm going to practise interview techniques with you tomorrow and I'm not taking no for an answer. After all, I used to be a publicist, and a damned good one too. You don't have to *care* about the questions, you idiot, just give suitable responses.'

His stomach lurched and he felt faintly nauseous. Time to do it. 'I'm not going to practise anything. Least of all with *you*.'

'What the hell do you mean by that?'

'I want a divorce, Louisa.'

There was utter silence as she gaped at him.

'Why?' She threw the word at him like a bullet.

'Because I don't appreciate a wife who shares her favours around as freely as you do.'

'Then you ought to bloody well pay me more attention your-self. What am I expected to do? Stay at home all day and twiddle my thumbs? Give up sex entirely?'

'You could have got another job, kept up your skills and had something to do all day apart from going to bed with any Tom, Dick or Harry.'

'I didn't marry you to keep slaving away for idiot PR companies.'

'Why did you marry me?'

'Because we fell in love.'

'No. I fell in love but you didn't. I don't think you're capable of loving anyone except yourself.' He'd come to the conclusion that Louisa had married him for his money and fame – and possibly because she thought his mother's connections would help them get into the top social sets.

But she'd fooled him for a time and he'd believed she loved him. He'd been really sucked in, so happy . . . for a while. Then so hurt and disappointed.

'You knew I'd have books to write, PR tours to undertake. The writing is what earns the money you've been spending so freely. Which reminds me, I cancelled your credit card today.'

The first vase narrowly missed his head. The second one didn't.

It knocked him out for a short time and he bled so freely, even Louisa was frightened of what she'd done and drove him to the nearest hospital A&E department. There, after hanging around for a couple of hours, he had the cut on his forehead stitched carefully by a plastic surgeon.

As soon as she was sure he was all right, Louisa let her anger off the rein and for once forgot to be careful what she said in public.

'I should have thrown the whole cupboard full of china at you!' she shrieked when he told her to go home on her own and leave him in peace.

He saw two nurses at the nearby central desk exchange glances.

Later, as they were waiting in a cubicle, he tried again to send her home, because his head was thumping. Louisa told him he was ungrateful and worked herself up into another bout of yelling. Everyone nearby heard her telling Jivan that her affairs meant nothing and *he* was nothing but an old-fashioned fool.

She was wrong. They had meant something to him and had hurt him badly. He'd believed he'd found someone who would love him for himself, unlike his mother or father.

Yet again, he'd been let down. Well, it wouldn't happen again.

He could live a full life on his own, what with his writing and keeping fit, not to mention the gun club he'd joined for research purposes, to make sure his hero did the right thing. He'd stayed in the club because he'd found he had an aptitude for shooting, a good eye and a very steady hand.

He moved his things out lock, stock and barrel, and found a quiet flat in another suburb.

Louisa's ranting at the hospital was helpful when it came to the divorce, but even so, the dissolution of their marriage didn't happen easily. She contested every stage, insisting she didn't want a divorce, begging him to go with her for counselling.

He refused to do that, so she refused to negotiate a financial settlement, as required by law. When the legal system forced her into it, she and her lawyer tried to take everything she could from him, including future earnings from his writing.

He'd rather have given up writing than work to pay her. He could have lived, if he was careful, on the small income his father had settled on him. And she knew it.

But he found good lawyers as well, and in the end the legal boffins reached some sort of agreement on behalf of their clients and persuaded both clients to accept it.

In order to get her off his back, Jivan gave Louisa the Richmond house as a final and absolute financial settlement.

Believing she'd got as much as she could out of him, and that he wasn't good enough with the press to climb to the top of the literary tree, she signed on the dotted line and immediately put the house she'd claimed to love up for sale.

Louisa went back at work as a publicist and Jivan thought that would be the end of it. Another big mistake.

She'd whispered to him when the divorce went through that she'd make him sorry, though he couldn't understand why she was so angry with him. *She* had been the unfaithful one, after all.

As the months passed, he found himself being repeatedly harassed, in big ways and small. Not only were hostile articles published, supposedly based on interviews he hadn't given, but Louisa – it must have been her – played other dirty tricks on him.

A caterer turned up at the house he'd rented one weekend with party food costing a fortune. He hadn't ordered it and got into a legal row when he refused to pay for it.

Subscriptions to pornographic magazines were taken out in his name and the filthy things came through the post for months before he could stop them.

Several times windows were smashed in his new flat in the middle of the night. He had CCTV fitted but that didn't help much, because the perpetrators wore hoodies and balaclavas and kept their faces away from the cameras.

People complained that he'd not turned up for events he'd been booked for. Only he hadn't even heard of half the events, let alone agreed to appear there.

He couldn't believe it when the harassment continued into the following year. Some of the news articles came from a journalist called Frenton, who was a friend and occasional lover of Louisa.

As soon as the negative fallout from one article died down, another would appear. The lawyer he consulted said it wasn't worth trying to prosecute those publications, who were known for making up stories about the rich and famous. Most of the time they got away with it, so they didn't mind paying a fine occasionally and it didn't stop them.

'Fact of life in your position, my dear chap,' the lawyer said, and sent him a massive bill for this unwelcome opinion.

But the harassment was slowing down his writing, making him reluctant to go out in case they followed him and snapped photos to which they could pin misleading labels.

Women! You were better off without them . . . however much your body protested its celibacy.

To his relief, his editor, Anna Stephens, knew him well enough to ignore the rumours, and proved to be a rock in the storms that swept his life.

She was old enough to be his mother and was not only a good editor, but had a sane view of the world. He found it comforting to talk over a few problems with her, something he could never have done with his own mother, who was in America at the moment living it up with her latest husband. She hadn't been in touch since sending him a message after his divorce: 'Better luck next time.'

Next time! As if he'd put his head on the chopping block a second time.

That comment was typical of his mother. Amanda had been born a Childering and reverted to the name between marriages. She'd been drifting in and out of his life when convenient since he'd been a small child. She was now on her fourth husband.

'You're well out of that toxic marriage,' Anna told him gently one day. 'Try not to dwell on it, Jivan. These things happen.'

'Louisa was right about one thing: I did leave her alone a lot. My lifestyle simply isn't compatible with wedded bliss.'

'She knew what she was getting into when she married you. She'd been around the tracks.'

'Did you know what she was like?'

'I'd heard rumours, but you were so happy, I didn't like to tell you about her reputation. I hoped she'd settled down and really did love you. She put on a good pretence for a while, even fooled me, and I'm not easily fooled.'

'What she loved was my bank account and the fact that I was a famous novelist, related to some of the top families. But she gets bored easily if she's on her own and then she's unpredictable. I'm beginning to think, no, I'm sure that she's got mental health problems.'

'Well, leave that mess behind you and let's concentrate on the manuscript you've just turned in. It was worth waiting for. It's brilliant, far more powerful than *Swift Justice*. We're going to push it hard.'

'That's nice,' he said absent-mindedly. But he was already thinking about a sequel. And how to find a peaceful place in which to live and write. So he didn't realise the implications of her words until later.

When the telephone at work rang, Jessica picked it up, while clicking 'Save' on the computer with her other hand. 'Jessica Lord.'

'My name's Anna Stephens. I'm the Publishing Director at Meridian Books and I'm phoning to tell you that you're one of the three finalists in our *Write a Bestseller* competition.'

Jessica gasped and the fingers of her left hand jerked on the keyboard, sending random letters flickering across the screen.

'Hello! Are you still there, Jessica?'

'Yes. But – I can't believe it.'

The voice had a tone of gentle amusement. 'Well, it's true, I promise you. I'm sorry it took so long to judge the entries, but we had almost twelve hundred of them. Your novel was excellent and we'll be happy to publish it.'

Jessica couldn't string any words together. Her wildest dreams had just come true. There should have been bands playing and fireworks exploding around her. Instead she felt spaced out and had to keep gulping for oxygen.

'We're having the presentations next week in London. You won't know which of the three prizes you've won until then, I'm afraid. Will you be able to come, Jessica? Meridian will pay your fare from Leeds and your hotel bill for that night, of course.'

Tears started trickling down her cheeks. 'I still can't believe it,' she confessed to the voice on the other end. 'I'm not – thinking straight.' She pulled off her glasses and brushed away the tears impatiently. 'Yes, I think I can attend. I mean, I'm sure I can.' She would go to the presentations if she had to *crawl* all the way there.

'Good. I'll ask my assistant to book you into the hotel we're all using and she'll get back to you with the details. I'll see you next week in London.'

When Jessica put the phone down, the air seemed to roar around her and she couldn't move.

'Jess, are you all right? Jess?'

She blinked hard and looked up to see her workmate, Lisa, standing beside her, looking concerned.

'What?'

'You're crying. Was it bad news?'

'Oh. Am I? Er – no. No, it wasn't.' She managed to force some words out, though what she really wanted was to go and sit quietly on her own until she could come to terms with what had happened. But her friend was waiting for details.

'It was good news, actually, Lisa. Very good. Um – my novel's won a prize in a big national competition. And – oh, goodness, I haven't taken it in properly myself yet – they're going to publish it!'

Lisa shrieked loudly and did a war-dance round the office, which of course made everyone else rush over to find out what had happened.

They all knew about Jessica's hobby – or rather, obsession – but no one had taken her efforts all that seriously until now. Suddenly her fellow workers were crowding round, congratulating her, patting her on the back, all trying to ask questions at once.

In the end, she cut things short. 'I need to see Eileen to ask for time off.'

On the way to the assistant manager's office, she made a detour to stand in front of the mirrors in the women's cloakroom, staring blindly at her reflection, wondering if she was dreaming.

But even when she splashed cold water on her face, she didn't wake up. The tiled walls remained firm and substantial around her and in the end she dared admit to her reflection, 'I've done it! I'm going to have a book published.'

At that moment, she believed in Santa Claus and the tooth fairy, and was utterly certain there was a pot of gold at the end of every rainbow.

The next day was Saturday, so Jessica went across to Rochdale in the afternoon to see her parents. She wanted to tell them in person about her prize.

Her father insisted on studying the entry form. 'It sounds to be quite a big competition. Well done, love.'

'What's the book about?' her mother asked.

'It's another fantasy story. About some aliens on an imaginary planet.'

'Don't you ever write about real people?'

'My characters are very real to me, Mum.'

Her father went to get a bottle of champagne out of the chiller cabinet in the off-licence, which he'd added to the original shop and which was very profitable. He brought Peter back with him and poured out four glasses. 'Here's to you, love. Congratulations. I hope you've won the first prize.'

Peter raised his glass. 'I'm glad you've been lucky.'

Lucky! Trust her brother to put it down to luck. It was hard work that had got her there, not luck. But she'd long ago learned not to get into arguments with Peter, because there was no way you could ever convince him of anything he didn't want to believe, especially where his little sister was concerned.

Her father took another mouthful of champagne. 'Ten thousand pounds would be a tidy sum to have behind you. If you win that first prize, you should put a deposit down on a flat or a terraced house and get your foot on the property ladder. Prices are much lower in Rochdale than Leeds. You could rent a place till you find a job nearby.'

'Let's wait and see which prize I get.' Much as she loved him, she knew her father wouldn't understand that it was having the book published she cared about, not the money. And she didn't intend to tell her parents yet that once her mother was out of danger, she was going to resurrect her dream of returning to Australia.

She'd heard a rumour that the company was opening another branch there. If that was true, she'd apply for a transfer.

She still had to go out to work, but one day, if her novels sold reasonably well, she hoped to be able to earn her living as a writer. Oh, that would be such bliss! She was so tired of working in noisy, open-plan offices.

Her life would be even more blissful if she lived somewhere sunny. She had never got used to cold winters and grey, lowering skies. Strange how her childhood memories of sunshine and wide blue skies hadn't faded, still filled her dreams.

It was hard going into work after the weekend. When you'd just had your biggest dream come true, who wanted to concentrate on modifying and creating software programmes to suit specific business needs?

'Here comes the lucky lady!' Guy called out as she walked into the office on Monday.

'*Lucky*?' That was what her brother had said and Guy's remark made her furious all over again. She went across and barred his way. 'Where's the luck? Winning that prize was the result of several years' hard work. I get up at four o'clock most mornings to write. I put in nearly as many hours in front of a computer at home writing stories as I put in at work. So what the hell has my winning a prize got to do with *luck*?'

And although she loved writing, there had been times when

she'd despaired of ever making it into print. She was twenty-eight now. Four full novels she'd written, including the prize-winning one. She'd wept over each rejection.

Guy held both arms wide in a gesture of surrender. 'Hey, sorry!'

She forced herself to smile and stood aside. 'No, it's me who should be sorry, biting your nose off like that.'

'Well, however you did it, I'm glad you made it.' He patted her arm before walking away, but she could see him roll his eyes at Ron on the other side of the room.

Two macho idiots, those, who treated women like dirt. They still expected their female colleagues to be grateful for an invitation to the pub 'with the lads' after work. They couldn't even say 'with the team'.

She sat down in front of her computer and tried to concentrate, but her productivity had never been so low.

Three

Jivan's new book soared to the top of the bestseller lists and a film option was taken out on it almost immediately.

Money poured in and he had to take time away from writing to do even more publicity.

To his surprise, Louisa phoned him one evening and asked if they could meet and talk, though how she'd got his personal phone number, he couldn't understand.

'Why?'

'We were good together. I really regret our break-up.'

'We were never really *together*. You made sure of that. After all your harassment, I have no intention of even meeting you, let alone getting back together.' He put the phone down. Did she expect him to forget the nasty tricks she'd been playing on him?

During the next few weeks, however, she accosted him several times in public places and pleaded loudly with him to take her back. The press always seemed to be on hand.

What had he ever seen in her?

And what was she after now?

More money probably. She must realise he'd never take her back, so it must be the money.

The dirty tricks started up again. In the end he had to hire a detective to trace a couple of them to her and take out a restraining order before she would leave him alone.

His mother got in touch with him too. She was delighted about his fame and fortune, but at least she didn't need his money, because she'd done well out of her marriages.

After her wild fling with Jivan's father, a rich Indian businessman, Amanda had returned to her old social circles, angry because Ranjit refused to marry her.

When Jivan was three, she'd married a man she'd grown up with and had settled down to run a large country house.

Ranjit remained in England and Jivan went to stay with his father every now and then. As he grew old enough to understand, he realised that his mother wouldn't let him see his father more often, and he heard them quarrel about it.

Amanda's marriage only lasted a few years, long enough for her to produce twins. But Jivan was at boarding school and didn't see much of them, and anyway, his half-brothers were several years younger than him so they had little in common.

The twins and their father were pleasant enough when he bumped into them at their mutual grandparents' gatherings, to which Jivan was still invited, give the Childerings their due. But they weren't close.

He went to the gatherings because he loved the big old house, had learned about every corner of it on his visits. In fact, he probably knew it better than his mother did, for all she'd grown up there.

He realised she was still speaking on the phone and tried to pay attention.

'Darling, I'm so proud of you. Just let my relatives try to put you down now! Oh, and your brothers send their congratulations. They're very good about ringing me up once a month, better than you.'

'Sorry. I'll try to remember. I get lost in my writing.'

'Well, when Chuck and I come over to England you must come out of seclusion and let me give a party for you, to celebrate your success.'

'We'll talk about it when you next come over.' She rarely did. For some reason America seemed to suit her better than England, and Chuck was her richest prize as a husband, happy to load her with presents and take her on luxury holidays.

Jivan wondered occasionally what his biological father thought of his success. He remembered spending time with Ranjit when he was little, had enjoyed listening to stories about Indian gods and goddesses. But he hadn't seen or heard from his father since he was nine, at which point his father had given in to his family's pleas and gone back to live in India. Like Amanda, he had married suitably, a bride chosen by his family, but he had stayed married to her. Presumably they now had children.

Ranjit hadn't got in touch with his son once since he left England. If he couldn't be bothered to keep in touch, then Jivan wasn't going to keep track of what his father was doing.

It was hard enough keeping track of his mother.

When the day came for Jessica to attend the presentations in London, it was a relief to get away from all the fuss and teasing at work, not to mention the congratulatory phone calls from her extended family.

Sitting on the train heading south, she picked up her book. Jivan Childering's latest thriller *Shere Magic* had come out a month ago and had hit the bestseller charts immediately. She hadn't been able to resist buying it now that she had actually argued with the author.

It was another gripping tale, but like his last two books, it was very masculine in orientation, with only a few stereotyped female characters: two well-behaved and one very evil. Even more than last time, they seemed to be there to decorate the scenery rather than truly participate in the action.

She frowned and wondered if his personal life was still being reflected in his books. She'd heard about his divorce problems. Hadn't everyone? The paparazzi had been all over him for a while and his wife had wept publicly about it, blaming him.

Since then, Childering had kept his personal life remarkably quiet, though she'd seen some rather nasty articles about him in magazines.

After a few minutes, Jessica closed the book and sat holding it, thinking in wonderment that one day she too would have her name on the cover of a novel.

When she arrived in London, the late afternoon sun was shining, making everything look its best. She took a taxi to the hotel, enjoying revisiting the capital.

The interior of The Royal Aztec came as a shock, so discreet and tasteful was the foyer. It absolutely shrieked of money, with its pinky-beige marble floors, massive arrangements of flowers and bowls of pot pourri as large as baby baths.

The receptionist welcomed her with as much warmth as if she were a long-lost cousin and Jessica relaxed into the luxury of it all with a sigh of pure happiness. She had never, in all her life, stayed in a hotel where a polite young man in a smart black suit escorted her upstairs, carrying her battered suitcase as if it were made of gold and ushering her into her room with what could only be described as a flourish.

When he had left, she found she had a whole suite to herself. Goodness! The Meridian people were doing things in real style! Beaming, she explored the small kitchen, lounge, bedroom and the huge bathroom with spa tub. She sniffed the complimentary bottles of hand cream and bath bubbles and turned taps on and off for the sheer hell of it.

When the room phone rang, she jumped in shock, then rushed across to grab it, recognising Anna Stephens' warm, friendly voice at once.

'Welcome to London, Jessica. We're all meeting in the lobby at quarter to seven and then going on to the restaurant together for the presentations.'

Jessica looked at her watch. It was already twenty past six. 'Oh, goodness, and I haven't even started to unpack!'

'Don't worry! We won't go without you.'

Jessica changed her clothes quickly and pinned her hair back with hands that were trembling. She was sure her eyeliner was crooked and hoped she'd got her lipstick on correctly. She didn't usually bother with makeup because she'd been gifted with a naturally good complexion.

When she looked at herself in the full-length mirror, she sighed. A heroine would have blonde or auburn hair and would be sylph-like, not a full-bosomed size 14 – and a heroine would definitely not wear glasses. A real heroine would also have a gorgeous designer dress to show off her elegant figure on an occasion like this, not a simple blue sheath and jacket from a small boutique near the office.

Her eyes seemed larger than usual tonight, though, the blue more vivid. Perhaps it was the excitement. She took a deep breath and wondered for the hundredth time which of the three prizes she had won. Whichever it was, her book was going to be published, and that was what mattered most.

At the mere thought of that she did a little dance round the room, stopping to stand in front of the mirror again.

'Jessica Lord, the famous writer!' she said aloud, gesturing with her hand to an imaginary audience.

She spoiled the effect by chuckling at herself, then glanced at her wristwatch. 'Whoops!' After squirting on some of the perfume her mother had bought her for Christmas, she inclined her head to the woman in the mirror and marched off to meet her fate.

In the lobby several people were standing around near the entrance, chatting quietly to each other in the polite, restrained way strangers do. As Jessica stood hesitating near the lifts, an elegant grey-haired woman left the group and walked towards her. 'Jessica?'

'Yes.'

'I thought you must be. I'm Anna. I'm so pleased to meet you at last. How was your journey?'

'All right – I think. I was too excited to notice.'

Anna smiled, then looked at her watch and frowned. 'We're just waiting for Jivan Childering, then we'll leave for the restaurant.'

'*Jivan Childering*!'

'Yes. He's going to present the prizes tonight.'

Jessica swallowed hard and tried to smile. 'Oh! That's – um, that's marvellous.'

'Yes, you'll be able to chat to him about your writing. He's one of Meridian's bestselling authors.'

Somehow, Jessica managed to keep the smile pinned to her

face. Childering wouldn't remember that TV programme, surely? He'd forgotten her name even during the show. And she hadn't really been rude to him – well, perhaps just a little. Who was she kidding? One newspaper had mentioned her comments and his arrogant reaction to them.

Her stomach felt as if it were full of demented butterflies struggling to get out. Realising Anna was speaking to her again, she forced herself to pay attention.

'Have you read any of Jivan's books?'

'Oh, yes. All of them. He's one of my favourite authors.'

'Oh, good! You'll be able to say something sensible about them, then. He hates people trying to pretend they've read his stuff when they haven't.'

The group around them suddenly fell silent and when Jessica turned to see what had caught their attention, her heart started beating faster.

There he was. Tall, elegant and somehow twice as vivid as the other men. He still seemed like a prince from a fairytale to her, or a hero from a romance novel. In appearance, anyway.

He hesitated for a few seconds by the lifts, then squared his shoulders and began to walk across the foyer.

Jessica was puzzled. For a moment he'd looked nervous, or perhaps anxious was a better word. No, she must have been mistaken. Someone who had been famous for several years couldn't possibly be nervous about appearing in public.

He came to a halt next to her and Anna, giving the group a vague half-smile. It was her companion whom he addressed. 'As you can see, Anna, I'm on time tonight.'

His voice was warm, his expression friendly and he bore little resemblance to the arrogant individual with whom she'd argued on television. Jessica felt herself relaxing. Perhaps the evening wouldn't be too bad, after all. He might be an innately shy person underneath that gorgeous exterior, or he might have quarrelled with his wife the night he had appeared on Sally Mennon's programme. Everyone had their off days, but of course people noticed it more if you were a celebrity.

Anna smiled and allowed him to kiss her cheek. 'I was determined you wouldn't be late, Jivan.'

One of his hands remained on her shoulder for a moment as

if the two of them knew each other well, and he chuckled, a rich, deep sound. 'Yes, but *three* reminder calls were a bit excessive, don't you think?' His eyes were alight with laughter and his teeth shone white and even in a generous mouth.

Jessica's breath caught in her throat. This was the real Childering, surely?

'Nothing is excessive when it comes to getting you to a function on time!' Anna retorted. 'I learned the hard way that when you're engrossed in a story, you can forget the real world completely. Now, let me introduce you to our clever winners.'

He turned round to be introduced to her and Jessica watched in amazement as his expression changed. The warmth vanished and the cool mask fell back into place. He looked slightly menacing now, his hair shorter than it had been on the show, emphasising the lean planes of his face. He was wearing evening dress and one narrow gold ring gleamed on the third finger of his right hand.

Sam Shere! she thought suddenly. That's what Sam Shere would look like if he were a real person. Childering has exactly the same impact as his hero does. I wonder if he knows it?

Anna gestured towards her, 'Jivan, this is Jessica Lord, one of our finalists. She's just been telling me that she's read all your books.'

He nodded and paused, frowning. 'Jessica Lord? The name sounds familiar.'

'We've never met before,' she said hastily. Well, it was true, even if misleading.

He shook her hand and murmured something which could have been, 'Pleased to meet you.' He was already turning away as she started to reply.

'I'm pleased to meet you, too, Mr Ch—' The words faded on her lips and disappointment surged through her in a bitter tide. Well, this only confirmed her first impression that he was an ego-head. She mustn't be important enough for him to bother with.

'Call him Jivan!' said Anna firmly. 'We're not standing on ceremony tonight.' She gave him no chance to hang back, but took him round the group, introducing him to each person in turn, moving along quickly.

With them all he was cool and polite. There was not the slightest trace of the warmth he had shown to Anna.

Jessica realised that she was still staring across the foyer at him and forced herself to turn away. 'Are you one of the finalists, too?' she asked the man next to her. He was plump and middle-aged, with a cheerful expression.

'Yes. Isn't it exciting?'

'I'm still tap-dancing on the ceiling,' she confessed, warming instantly to him. 'I can't believe it's real!'

He nodded. 'It's taken weeks for it to sink in that I'm really going to get a book published.'

A short time later, Anna marshalled them outside and into four taxis. Jessica was trying so hard to avoid sitting with Jivan that she didn't watch where she was stepping and tripped up, dropping her handbag. 'Damn!'

Its contents rolled everywhere. Why had she been born so clumsy? By the time she'd picked everything up, the first three taxis had left and she found herself being ushered into the back of the final taxi.

She bent to get in and froze. The very man she had been trying to avoid was already sitting in the back. And there was no one else with them except the driver. She could hardly refuse to get in, so took a deep breath and sat in the corner, keeping as far away from Childering as she could.

As the taxi drove off, she realised he had said something. 'Oh! I'm sorry. I was miles away. What did you say?'

'I asked if you'd been writing for long.' His tone was completely disinterested and he wasn't even looking at her.

She usually kept her temper under firm control, having had that lesson dinned into her from early childhood by her mother, but tonight her anger spilled over. 'You needn't make polite conversation with me if you'd rather be quiet.'

His indrawn breath was as sharp as her words had been. She sneaked a quick glance sideways, but his face was in shadow and she couldn't see the expression on it. However, she did notice that he clenched his hands into fists in his lap, then uncurled them slowly.

She turned away, ignoring her supercilious companion. At the thought of the presentations, she couldn't help wishing again she were not so ordinary. How wonderful it would be to be ravishingly beautiful, the sort of woman who looked like a famous author, someone the press would fall over themselves to photograph. Without realising it, she started smiling at the mere idea.

'May I share the joke?'

'What? Oh.' She looked at him doubtfully, but there was genuine interest in his face and tone this time. 'It's nothing, really. I was just smiling at myself. This presentation night is the sort of situation one reads about in a novel, only I'm not beautiful enough to be the heroine.'

She spoke matter-of-factly. She had no hang-ups about her appearance, didn't usually give it much thought.

'Don't be so sure. Heroines come in all shapes and sizes.'

'Mostly model-sized and blonde! And they definitely don't wear glasses, only I can't get on with contact lenses.' Jessica smiled, unable to stay annoyed tonight, whatever the provocation. 'Please don't think I'm fishing for compliments. I do have a mirror and I try to be realistic. Anyway, I'm a writer, not a heroine.' She forgot him completely for a moment as the joy of having her novel accepted for publication surged up yet again. 'This is all so *exciting*!'

Then she realised how naive that must have sounded and flushed, clamping her lips tight on any more childish comments. But she could feel his eyes upon her and she was surprised to see a more gentle expression on his face.

'Don't be ashamed of being excited, Jessica. Joy itself is very attractive and you should share that and your enthusiasm for writing when you give talks, which every writer seems to get asked to do.'

'Do you still feel enthusiastic about writing?'

'I love the act of telling a story, not so much the other jobs, like publicising a book.'

The taxi drew up outside a large brightly lit restaurant, where the rest of the group were standing in the lobby. The spell was broken and perhaps it was just as well.

When they got out, Jivan was ushered inside as if he were royalty and Jessica was swept across by someone from Meridian to join the other winners.

Jivan was surrounded by an animated group, but his expression had grown cool again and he looked to Jessica as if he would have preferred to be left alone.

Watching one or two of the women pestering him, trying to catch his attention, Jessica remembered that Sally Mennon had tried to talk about the way women threw themselves at him. He had changed the subject firmly. She grimaced. It must be dreadful to be the target of such behaviour.

Oh, no! When she dropped her bag, he must have thought—

From now on she wouldn't speak to him, wouldn't even look at him, unless he addressed her first – and even then she would answer him coolly and move away from him as soon as she could.

Well, thank goodness he hadn't remembered her from the talk show. That would have been the final straw.

She must stop behaving like a child at a birthday party. She would be calm and sophisticated.

A few minutes later she realised that she'd completely forgotten her resolution, the excitement of the other two finalists re-igniting her own joy. She smiled as she carried on chatting to them. This was not a night to stay calm.

At the table, Jessica surreptitiously slipped the name card from her place into her handbag. It said *FINALIST* after her name, and she knew she would long treasure it. When the meal was over, she would ask the waiter if she could take tonight's special menu away with her as well.

Across the room Anna nudged Jivan and whispered, 'Did you ever see anyone look as radiant as our Jessica does tonight?'

'No. She seems to be overflowing with happiness. That's not surprising. We all feel like that when we get our first novel accepted.'

'Even the great Jivan Childering?'

'Oh, yes. Even the not-so-great Jivan Childering.' Surprise echoed in his voice. 'You know, I'd almost forgotten how I felt then, Anna. It all seems a long time ago now.' And it felt as though it had happened to another person, one not as battered by life.

'Tell me about it. You can't have totally forgotten.'

He fumbled through his memories. 'I felt wildly excited when I read your acceptance letter. I must have re-read it about twenty times before it really sank in. My flatmate wanted to go out to the pub and celebrate, but I wasn't interested in drinking. I didn't need booze because I was high on sheer excitement.'

He smiled. 'I didn't sleep at all that night, just lay there, lost in the wonder of it.'

'And then your book sold very nicely and we had to reprint. You were quite young for such success.'

'Twenty-four.' He sometimes felt like ninety now, not thirty-two. He changed the subject to avoid further confidences. 'Do you know anything about Jessica Lord's background?'

'Nothing much beyond the fact that she works in computing.'

He studied her across the room. 'She's quite lovely, though *she* doesn't think so.' The quizzical look in Anna's eyes made him frown. 'Don't look at me like that, Anna. The last thing I need at the moment is involvement with a woman. My ex is still stalking me.'

'Louisa doesn't let go easily, does she?'

'No. She's pestering for a reconciliation, but still playing nasty tricks on me.'

'We need to find some way to protect you.'

He leaned closer. 'I need to discuss this with you privately. Would you be free tomorrow afternoon?'

'For you, I'm free any time.'

'I'm thinking of moving overseas and becoming truly reclusive. If I stay out of sight for a few years, she'll stop. I could reappear in short bursts to do PR stuff.'

She looked at him, head on one side. 'I suppose we could make it work. You shouldn't have to turn into a hermit, though.'

He shrugged. 'If I'm to finish the next book on time, I need some quiet time anyway. And you've done it again, got me talking about myself. Let's talk about Jessica Lord instead. Tell me what her book is about.'

'It's a fantasy tale. Mostly about some rather engaging aliens, who prove more than a match for groups who want to take over their planet. It's very original and witty.'

As he glanced across at Jessica, she looked up, catching his eyes on her. For a moment she stared across the room, then her face lost its joy and she nodded to him coolly before turning back to the man sitting next to her.

Anna let out a long, low whistle. '*What* did you say to her in the taxi to provoke that reaction?'

'I suppose I was a bit – well . . .'

She finished for him. 'Stand-offish, if not downright cutting. You're getting paranoid about women throwing themselves at you, Jivan.'

'She dropped her handbag, spilled everything. I thought she'd done it on purpose to get into the last taxi with me. If you'd seen some of the tricks women have used, you'd understand why I thought that.'

'I have seen them. But she's an invited guest not a gate-crasher. Excuse me a moment. I just have to check that things are ready for the big event.'

Anna was clearly annoyed with him but Jivan didn't need that to make him feel guilty that he should in any way have tarnished Jessica Lord's joy in this very special occasion. Guilt continued to nag at him throughout the meal as he surreptitiously watched her. She had an open, friendly expression and the spectacles didn't detract from her looks in the slightest; in fact, they suited her, drawing attention to her eyes, which were so vividly blue and sparkling with intelligence.

In fact, he really liked her face. She looked like a real person, as unlike his skeletally thin ex, with her cool, lacquered sophistication, as you could get.

Once, when she thought no one was looking, he saw Jessica press her hands to her flushed cheeks as if to cool them down. Nerves, he decided, mixed with excitement. Been there.

No, she wasn't one of those aggressive women who seemed to keep popping up at him from nowhere. In fact, it wasn't often that he got the chance to meet someone as unspoiled as she was.

He hadn't needed to trample on her joy and he would try to make that up to her later on . . . if he could find a way.

Four

The speeches began and Jessica sat entranced, listening to the CEO of Meridian speak about the rapidly changing publishing industry. She still felt as if she were dreaming.

For a moment she let herself consider what she might do if she won the first prize. Maybe she could use the money to take a few months' leave and work on her next novel without the need to work elsewhere most of the week. It was so hard to find the time to write. A couple of Sundays ago, one of her cousins had turned up at her flat and insisted on taking her out to a gastro-pub for lunch. Why hadn't she just dug her heels in and kept to her original refusal?

She was too weak-willed, that was the trouble, especially with her family. She didn't like to upset them. From now on, she was going to put a huge effort into her writing, every spare minute. No wasting time on drinking in pubs.

'. . . and I call upon our main speaker of the evening, Jivan Childering, to take the podium.'

Jessica snapped back to attention.

He walked out with a lithe, graceful stride to face his audience and spoke briefly, but very tellingly, about a writer's self-imposed loneliness. He gradually brought his talk round to this evening and three people's reward for all the solitary effort it took to write a book.

As the audience applauded, Anna Stephens stepped forwards. 'And now, Jivan, we'll ask you to present the prizes.'

He looked at a piece of paper and read out, 'Third prize goes to Bob Danzer, for his book, *Dangerous Package*.'

Jessica sat up in shock. She'd told herself to expect only the third prize. This meant— Oh, it meant she'd done better than that!

The woman next to her nudged her. 'Not you!'

'Second prize: Kath Grayley, for her book, *Lady in the Shadows*.'

Jessica gasped. The people on her table were all nodding and smiling at her.

'First prize goes to Jessica Lord, for her book, *One Small Planet*.'

Her neighbour had to poke her in the ribs to get her to stand up. She made her way towards the front of the room and on to the small dais, feeling as if everything was happening in slow motion.

Jivan greeted her with 'Well done!' His smile was warm and friendly.

She nodded, swallowing hard and trying to breathe normally. A million faces were turned her way. Noise roared around her like waves upon a shore, lights spiked into her eyes and her throat was a dusty desert.

Jivan seemed to guess how she was feeling. He squeezed her arm briefly, smiled encouragement and began to speak, 'I'm delighted to present the first prize to you, Jessica.'

He offered her a sealed envelope and she took it in nerveless fingers, almost dropping it, so that he had to clasp her hand around it.

'Thank you,' she managed.

'I'd like to offer you my personal congratulations. To come first out of twelve hundred entries in this biennial competition is quite exceptional.'

The room exploded into applause.

He gestured towards the microphone with an encouraging smile. Suddenly her mind cleared and she knew what to say.

'I'd like to thank everyone in Meridian Publishing for giving me this chance. It's the most wonderful thing that's ever happened to me. But my winning does have its amusing side. I'd like to share with you the reaction of one of my colleagues to my success. He asked what I'd written. I told him – a fantasy novel. He looked disappointed for a minute, before he said, "Oh! I thought it was a literary prize!"'

People started chuckling quietly.

'Then,' Jessica continued, still amused by this memory, 'he seemed to realise that he was being a bit tactless and he said encouragingly, "Still, never mind, it's a start!"'

She waited while the audience laughed, sharing her delight at the ridiculousness of such intellectual snobbery.

Jivan was chuckling by her side. Jessica's breath caught in her throat. How gorgeous he looked when he relaxed! No, she mustn't stare at him. Instead she looked towards the front row, where Anna Stephens was beaming at her.

For the first time Jessica wished she had someone of her own to share this moment with, but she hadn't invited any of her family to fill the one guest place she'd been allowed. They were so used to considering her odd that they'd be bound to share that with others, and they might even tell people about some of the sillier things she'd done as a child, because half the time she had been so lost in her imagination, she hadn't realised what was going on around her.

To her astonishment, Jivan kissed her cheek before handing her down from the podium. 'You've done remarkably well,' he said softly. 'I'm looking forward to reading your book. And I'm sorry I was a bit tetchy earlier.'

She felt as if she floated back to her seat. Opening the envelope, she stared entranced at the cheque for ten thousand pounds. Someone touched her arm and she blinked up at them.

'I wonder if you'd mind coming along for some photographs.' The man gestured to the side of the room. She saw the other prize winners gathering there and put the cheque carefully into her handbag before following them out into the lobby.

She moved as the photographer directed, twisting and turning her head on command. She still felt as if she was in a dream, the most marvellous dream of her whole life.

Anna and Jivan, sitting at one of the front tables, were discussing the main prize winner.

'I hope that photographer has caught Jessica's joy,' Anna said. 'It'll make a great cover photo. She's pretty, too, which never hurts when we're publicising a book. More importantly, if she continues to write as well as this she could go far. I do hope she won't waste her talent.'

He looked at her in surprise. 'Is that likely?'

'Who knows? Marriage might stop her writing. I've seen it happen. And even with a supportive husband, child-rearing might intervene. That book of hers was highly original. Even I enjoyed reading it and I don't normally like fantasy. She manages to make her characters and situations seem absolutely real, and the alien culture is thought-provoking as well as credible. We're very hopeful for her.'

He nodded, his eyes still on the lovely woman in blue. Suddenly he envied Jessica Lord, envied the freshness in her, the joy and naivety that life had started beating out of him while he was still a child. Louisa had only added to his sadness.

'You look tired, Jivan.'

'Jetlag.'

'Or worry about Louisa. Is she still causing trouble?'

'She tried to accuse me of raping her a couple of months ago, but luckily there was a reader who'd followed me outside to get my autograph and he saw exactly what happened.'

'Didn't you press charges?'

'I couldn't face it.'

'Pity. Anyway, let's talk about something more cheerful.' Anna took hold of his hand for a moment.

He nodded, gave her hand a quick squeeze and managed to smile and nod as the others chatted.

But strangely enough, what cheered him up most was the radiant face at the other side of the room. Could Jessica Lord really be as nice as she seemed? He'd like to get to know her better, but of course that was impossible, given his problems and where he was going to live for the foreseeable future.

Anyway, he'd promised himself he wouldn't get involved with any other woman, however nice she seemed at first.

At the end of the evening, one of the Meridian people came over to Jessica's table. 'We're going back for drinks in the bar of the hotel. Would you all like to join us?'

To Jessica's delight, everyone accepted. She didn't want this evening to end. She had never realised before what fun Cinderella must have had before the clock chimed twelve, or how abrupt the transition into loneliness must have been afterwards.

They piled into more taxis and she hung back to let Jivan go first. She nipped into the ladies when she got to the hotel, so was the last into the bar. A dozen lively people were crammed round two tables pushed together. The group included Anna and Jivan – and, oh dear, the only empty chair was next to him.

She sat down warily, and to her relief the person on her other side asked her something. When the guy turned to speak to someone else, she sat back, enjoying watching the group, listening to what they were saying.

She glanced to her left and saw that Jivan was looking at her.

'It's a novelist's weakness,' he murmured.

'I beg your pardon?'

'Watching people. I was watching you and you were watching them.' He gestured to the group around them, his smile warm. Everyone was chatting noisily, and with Anna away at the ladies', the two of them seemed to be alone at their end of the table.

'They seem to be a nice crowd.'

'They are. Meridian have a good reputation as a publisher and I know from experience that they treat their authors well. Have you recovered from the euphoria of the presentations yet?'

'Not really. I'm still high on happiness.'

Anna came back and they all chatted for a while, then someone came up to say goodnight.

One after another, people excused themselves. Jessica, deep in conversation with one of the publicists, didn't notice that there were only three people left until her companion yawned and excused herself.

Jessica sighed. She still didn't want the evening to end, but was very conscious that she was alone with Jivan and mustn't make him think she was pursuing him. 'I'd better get to bed, too.'

His voice was gentle and understanding. 'You don't really want to leave, though, do you?'

She glanced at him uncertainly. 'Well, no. I know I won't be able to sleep. Euphoria still rules!'

'Have another drink with me, then, or a coffee. We can have decaf.' He smiled at her astonishment. 'I'm a poor sleeper and I'm not ready for bed yet, either.'

Did he really mean that, or was he just being polite?

He seemed to read her thoughts. 'I meant it.'

'Well – all right, I will. If you're sure you don't mind. I know I couldn't sleep.' She was mad to risk another rebuff, but she couldn't resist the temptation. 'I'll have a coffee. Decaf.'

She looked round. They were the only people left in the bar. A tired-looking man was clearing the other tables, but he smiled and told them to stay as long as they wanted.

'I think I'll have a cognac.' Jivan gave their order, tipped the waiter generously, then leaned back in his chair. 'Tell me about yourself, Jessica.' He frowned. 'I still keep thinking I know that name.'

Her heart missed a beat. 'There's nothing much to tell. I've led a very ordinary life.'

'There must be something special, for you to write prize-winning books.'

'Not really. At one stage my parents emigrated, so I was born in Western Australia, but when I was seven, we came back to live in Lancashire. It was a very big shock to me and I felt out of place in England.'

'Maybe that's why you understand what it's like to be an alien.'

'Perhaps. It's not that my family aren't loving – well, not my brother, but the rest of them. It's just that I've never felt totally at home in England, especially during the winters.'

'Why haven't you gone back to live in Australia, then?'

'My mother had breast cancer. I couldn't leave. But she's recovering now and the prognosis is good, so I'm starting to make plans.' She could feel herself flushing. 'I don't usually tell people that.'

'I'm honoured. Go on.'

'My father owns two newsagents' shops and off-licences, but my brother runs things now. When my mother was ill, Dad wanted to spend more time with her. I went to the local high school and although I did well in my studies, I was hopeless at sport. You can't get a much more uninteresting background than that.'

'How did you come by that vivid imagination, then?'

'My mother says I was born fanciful and she still worries that she failed to train me out of it.'

He chuckled. 'Do you still live near your family?'

'Quite close, in Leeds. Sometimes I think I'm too close to them. Who knows where the company will transfer me to next, though? What about you and your family? Are you close.'

'Not really. I moved away from home a long time ago, and I'm about to move to some isolated place and get on with writing my next book. I don't know where I'm going yet.'

He looked tense and distant as he said that, so she spoke hurriedly, not wanting him to withdraw from her. 'If the company doesn't transfer me soon, I shall have to move away from the north. I can't write as often as I'd like when my family live nearby. They're always expecting me to go and see them, or else they hold big parties for all the relatives, or they turn up to visit me without warning at weekends, just when I'm settled at my computer. And I have *dozens* of cousins who like to go for a drive and drop in to see me.'

He chuckled, his expression softening again. 'That's not so terrible.' He began fiddling with his brandy glass. 'You came to London on your own tonight. No man in your life?'

'No. I don't have time.'

'I thought most women wanted to find a husband and settle down.' There was an acid undertone to that statement.

'Not me. Oh, I'd like to find a husband – I'm not that different – but I don't want to *settle down*. And I don't have a maternal bone in my body. I can't even imagine having a child.'

'One day, Cinderella, you'll find your Prince Charming, and then you'll want it all. But be very careful. Don't ever rush into marriage; try living together first. We writers are strange animals and we don't take easily to being harnessed.'

She eyed him sideways. 'Running an agony column now? Lovelorn writers, bring your problems to Uncle Jivan!'

He laughed. 'No. Just offering you the benefit of my own experience. If you want to write, Jessica, then focus on that till you're established. Anna says you have considerable potential.'

'Did she really?'

He chuckled. 'Would Uncle Jivan lie to you?'

The coffee arrived and he changed the subject firmly to a discussion about computers.

Half an hour later, the conversation died a natural death when they both started yawning at the same time.

As they separated to go to their rooms, Jessica thought: this is a turning point in my life. I wonder where this new path will lead me.

All she knew at the moment was that she didn't intend to waste this opportunity. And if she got what she wanted, tomorrow's path would be very different from today's.

Five

Before Jivan could put his plans to move away from England into operation, Louisa began to pop up at his public functions or sit at the next table in a restaurant. This time she didn't do anything to disrupt the events, but her mere presence was enough to spoil his enjoyment.

The other petty harassment escalated, however. He once again found himself subscribed to magazines he detested, was billed for holidays he was supposed to have booked but hadn't, and found himself dealing with all sorts of minor irritations.

Then there was a major disturbance when people he was slightly acquainted with began turning up at his flat one evening for a party he was supposed to have invited them to. There were no caterers this time, no preparations, just the embarrassment of explaining to these people that it was some sort of sick practical joke.

He had no doubt who had organised it. What the hell would she do next?

He stopped trying to write and put his luxury flat on the market. More money than he'd expected was pouring in from things like foreign sales of his novels or audio rights, and he made arrangements to rent a house in Australia, remembering how vividly Jessica Lord had described it. If he didn't enjoy life there he could always move again.

He made the various arrangements through his new agent. Anna had recommended Emil Halford, who was very experienced in the publishing industry and was, she said, utterly trustworthy. Even the landlord of his new house didn't know who Emil's 'cousin' John Simpkins really was.

Jivan chose an isolated house in the Blue Mountains inland from Sydney, with stunning views and no close neighbours. He took care to go to Australia by a roundabout route, leaving the airport in Singapore. He even changed hire cars twice once he got to Australia, to prevent anyone from following him.

If that was paranoid, too bad. He was desperate to get away from Louisa and finish his current story.

It was quite a large house, but they'd needed to find a big place in order to get total privacy and good security systems.

Thank goodness for the Internet because he could stay in contact with his agent and publisher online.

He now had no idea what Louisa was doing and wondered vaguely whether he should pay someone to keep an eye on her for him, then dismissed the idea. She wouldn't be able to find him now, he was sure, and would eventually grow tired of hunting, so that was an end to it.

Maybe the book he was writing was influencing his plans, but he decided to live in a different Australian state each year and use different airlines and plane routes whenever he had to go back to the UK, to make it even harder for anyone to follow him. Actually, it would be interesting to get to know the different parts of this huge country. He was looking forward to that.

But after a few weeks the loneliness began to get him down. He didn't speak to anyone from one day to the next, except the lady who cleaned the house for him. She had been employed by the owner for a while to look after it and she understood that the people who lived here wanted peace and privacy.

He wondered if she recognised him. She didn't seem to but she did tell him a little about herself and the small town nearby when she saw that he really wanted to chat.

Each week she shouted her usual, 'Goodbye, sir!' as she left and then the silence came back.

He hadn't realised how very alone he'd feel, how depressing it would become.

Damn Louisa for doing this to him!

When Jessica got back to Leeds, her colleagues at work were excited about her winning the first prize, her manager less so.

'I suppose this means you'll be resigning?' he asked sourly.

'Goodness, no. I couldn't afford to.'

'But you'll want to write from now on, won't you?'

'It's hard to earn a living writing.'

'Yes, so I've heard.'

'Anyway, I've been writing all the time I've been with you and you've never complained about my work.'

The frown vanished. 'So it's just a hobby, then?'

She didn't contradict him but it wasn't 'just' anything, let alone a hobby; it was her passion. If she'd been able to earn a living, even a modest one, she'd have quit this job in a flash. She wasn't going to tell him that, of course.

'That's good, because I was going to ask you whether you'd like to transfer to New York. It was mentioned to you before, apparently, and you didn't like the idea.'

'To be truthful, no. And I still don't.' What's more, she'd resign and find another job if they insisted on sending her there.

He studied her thoughtfully. 'You do need broader international experience, though. If you're not interested in New York, I was told to ask you about Australia. We're opening a new branch there, as you may know.' He raised one eyebrow, waiting for a comment.

She stared at him as this sank in. 'Wow! I'm definitely interested in that. Whereabouts in Australia? Doing what exactly?'

'It's in Perth, Western Australia. We already have branches in the eastern states, in Sydney and Melbourne. You'd be helping the manager set the new branch up from scratch, then acting as team leader – which would mean more money. As it'll be a smallish branch, you'd also have to do anything and everything necessary.'

'I'd really like that, James. I was born in Western Australia and I've still got Australian citizenship as well as British. I've always wanted to go back there to see if it's as good as I remember.'

He nodded, looking smug and pleased with himself. 'We did notice that Aussie element in your personal records, but New York would have been a better experience to add to your CV. Anyway, it'll save us a lot of trouble with the Australian immigration people if you take the job down under.'

He studied her face. 'You know what, that's the happiest I've seen you look all year.'

'It's solved a dilemma for me. I didn't want to hurt my parents, and as I told you my mother is recovering from cancer. She's a lot better now, thank goodness. If I've been transferred to Australia, they won't like it, but they won't feel I'm trying to get away from the family.'

She knew her parents would urge her to get another job and stay in England. Only she wasn't going to.

'How soon can you leave?'

'How soon do you want me there?'

'Within the month.'

'That's fine by me.'

'Good. I shall miss you, though. You're a very reliable worker.'

What he meant was she didn't leapfrog from one company to another like some of the guys did, just got on with her job.

Jessica found it hard to get to sleep that night. What an incredible year! She'd had her first book accepted for publication, and now another ambition was about to be achieved.

Was she doing the right thing? How could you know for sure? Well, you couldn't. But she had to try or she'd always wonder.

It had been just over twenty-one years since she'd been brought back to England. How unhappy she'd been!

She hoped Australia would live up to her memories. This was such big step to take.

Jessica packed up her flat quickly, and luckily, the guy replacing her at the Leeds branch was coming up from London and was happy to take it over.

Though she was thrilled to be going, she was absolutely dreading telling her parents. She decided it'd be best to do that in person once she'd packed up. She'd ask her father to sell her car, because she'd be going back to the London office for a couple of weeks for some further briefing and training, and she didn't enjoy driving in London. She'd be flying straight to Australia from there.

She went home on the Friday evening of that week. After the first flurry of greetings and hugs, she sat down with her parents over a cup of tea and made her announcement.

'You're going where?' Her mother's mouth fell open in shock. 'Richard, did you hear that?'

Her father looked at her grimly. 'Why are you doing this to us, Jessica?'

'I'm not doing it to you. I've been transferred. I'll be helping to open a new branch out there.'

Her mother burst into tears.

'I forbid it!' shouted her father, banging his fist on the table and turning an unhealthy shade of red. 'Do you want to break your mother's heart?'

'It's my job,' Jessica repeated. 'I couldn't have stayed where I was. They're insisting on me broadening my experience. It was either go to New York or to Australia and I chose Australia.'

'Why? New York is closer.'

'I've always wanted to go back for a holiday, you know I have. I should have done an overseas stint earlier, but they let me wait till you were all right, Mum.'

'But it's so far away!' her mother sobbed. 'You'll be all on your own there and you won't like it. That's why we came back to England, you know it is, because we wanted to be near our families. You wait. You'll be so lonely and you won't have a husband to comfort you, as I did.'

She tried to be patient with them. 'I don't have any choice.'

'Get another job, then,' her father said.

'They're a decent company to work for. I'd rather stay with them.'

There was a pause, then, 'You promise you're not emigrating.'

'I'm being transferred, Dad. Look, I'm hoping you'll have room to store my things. There are some bits and pieces I don't want to get rid of. Does that sound like emigrating?'

Her parents let the matter drop then, but from the glances they exchanged, she knew they would try again to persuade her not to go to Australia.

Fortunately, that evening, Peter and Kerry came round and announced that they were expecting a baby. Maureen's attention was diverted from Jessica; she had been longing to be a grandmother.

From then on her mum was radiant, boasting to customers and friends alike about the coming event. She came home from the shopping centre on the Saturday afternoon with what seemed like the entire stock of the local wool shop, with which to knit some little garments.

Jessica left them on the Sunday morning with relief that she had got it over with. Thank goodness for Peter's baby.

* * *

Jessica thought she'd said goodbye to her family, but her parents turned up unexpectedly at the hotel where she was staying in London so that they could be with her for her last evening.

She was exhausted by some intensive training in a package of new software developments and the briefings about what the company wanted in the new branch. She'd planned to wash her hair and get an early night, but had to go out for a meal with them instead.

Her mother wept several times during the course of the evening, which made Jessica feel terrible.

When they got back, she said firmly, 'My flight leaves at six in the morning. Please don't get up to see me off. I'll have to leave for the airport at three thirty and anyway, I don't want to get on the plane with a tear-stained face.'

'I agree. I think your mother has had enough stress,' her father said. 'We'll say goodbye to her now, Maureen.'

Jessica saw that his eyes were suspiciously bright, too, and gave them both another hug.

Her childhood memories were of a flight that went on for ever, so she wasn't looking forward to spending about twenty hours in transit. But in fact the air time passed quickly because she slept for a large part of it.

And then the plane was preparing to land and people were gathering their belongings and peering out of the cabin windows to catch glimpses of the city below.

Her spirits lifted. The first stage of her odyssey was nearly over.

On the way from Perth airport into the city, Jessica stared out of the windows of the taxi in delight. One thing was just as she'd remembered: clear, bright sunlight and cloudless blue skies. But there were more tall buildings in the city centre now and the traffic seemed far busier.

The company had found her some temporary serviced accommodation in a block of flats. It was twelve storeys high and very noisy, with people coming in and out at all times of the day or night, presumably on temporary visits to Western Australia's capital.

The flat was supplied with tea and coffee-making facilities, a packet of two plain biscuits and nothing else, but the information sheet in the folder said there was a café, a small shop and some automatic dispensers of various foodstuffs on the ground floor. She dumped her luggage and went down, venturing outside and standing on the pavement in the sunshine, revelling in it.

She didn't want to go indoors again, but forced herself to be practical and bought some food from the shop before going back to unpack her things.

When the phone rang, she jumped in shock.

'Paul Harrop here.'

Her new boss. 'Oh, hi!'

'Just checking that you got here OK. How's the flat?'

'It's fine to start me off.'

'We've leased a car for you. When you come into the office tomorrow, I'll sort out all the paperwork. See you then.'

She found out later that this was typical of Paul's thoughtless attitude. Hadn't it occurred to him that she needed a day or two to settle in before she started work? He was more interested in computing than in looking after his staff.

She'd have liked a few days to recover from the flight and the inevitable jetlag. She also needed to find herself somewhere quieter to live. As the nearby lift pinged again, she grimaced. She was already finding that sharp sound very irritating.

She didn't sleep well, because people were constantly on the move, their voices echoing down the corridor. And when the lifts weren't pinging, they were whining their way up and down the building.

Her first morning at work was crazy. Paul had only moved into the office a couple of days ago, and hadn't even got himself a secretary yet. Nothing had been sorted out and she found herself acting as a supplies officer and human resources manager till someone called Janice came on board.

If she hadn't stood up for herself, Paul would have dumped the contents of his desk on her as well.

'That's not in my remit – and I don't know enough yet about the local scene to attend to it anyway.' She plonked the pile of papers back on his desk.

He grinned. 'Worth a try. You might actually like paperwork.'

'And pigs might fly. You need to get yourself a secretary. Now, I shall be out this afternoon. I have no food in the flat and I need to sort out some permanent accommodation. It was unreasonable to ask me to come to work today.'

One of the other guys came across to join them. 'My cousin Amy does house rentals. Do you want me to phone her?'

'Yes, please.'

He came back a few minutes later. 'She says she has three furnished places vacant and can show you round them this afternoon, if you like.'

'That'd be great.'

He jangled a bunch of keys. 'For your temporary car. Let me show you the staff parking.'

'I hope the car's got a satnav in it. I don't know Perth.'

'I thought you were born here?'

'I was seven when I left and I haven't been back since.'

'Ah. Well, luckily, the car does have a satnav.'

She felt nervous when she took it out that afternoon, but she had to get used to driving in Perth. With the satnav's help and some very cautious driving, she made it to the estate agent's to see what was for rent.

To her relief Amy drove her round after that. The second place they looked at was a furnished villa unit at the end of a row, with carports between each dwelling. She wouldn't have any noise from shared walls, thank goodness, and she could use one of the two large bedrooms as an office. She took it and arranged to move in the next morning. Just let Paul complain!

Her immediate neighbours introduced themselves as she was moving her pitifully few bits and pieces in. They were an old couple, who said they liked a quiet life. 'So do I,' she assured them.

They gave her directions to the nearest shopping centre and she rang work to say she wouldn't be in that day. She stocked up on all sorts of items, including bedding. Her car was full of parcels by the time she got back and her bank account was considerably lighter.

Now she felt ready to settle into her job.

Unfortunately, as the days passed, she found it hard going. She'd never worked anywhere as badly organised. Paul didn't know how to delegate or even how to assign jobs, let alone share necessary information.

He was definitely struggling in his new role. Who on earth had appointed him? She could have done better than him standing on her head. Only she didn't want to be in charge of anything. Like her new neighbours, she wanted a peaceful life.

Over 2,000 miles away on the eastern side of Australia, the loneliness was starting to get to Jivan. He didn't want to be with people all the time, but he didn't want to be a recluse, either.

Though he met local people when he shopped in the small town, he had been so wary of revealing his identity when he first got here that it was now they who kept their distance.

He had tried to change his looks as much as possible, even adopting the unshaven look that was fashionable, but which he didn't like the feel of. He sometimes shook his head at himself in the mirror, because he looked downright scruffy.

He wasn't using his real name and had set up a credit card under the name John Simpkins, by special agreement with his bank.

He had to hire a part-time secretary and found one locally. She wasn't a reader, so didn't care about his books, didn't even seem aware of how well known he was. Since she was also a volunteer with the local ambulance service, with special training to act as a paramedic, she led a very busy life.

There was still no sign of Louisa and he prayed she was moving on to something else.

During the long, quiet evenings, he mulled over his situation and felt annoyed – no, make that downright *furious* with himself for letting her do this to him. He should have fought back instead of running away.

As a result, he asked Anna if she could find him a private investigator in the UK to keep an eye on his ex, someone with above average skills, if possible, and never mind the cost.

'About time,' she said. 'If you hadn't done this, I'd have suggested it. We want you to do more PR than you have been doing. Your film will be coming out soon and you have to be at the premiere of that, preferably with a partner.'

'Yes, Mama,' he teased.

Anna emailed a couple of days later and asked him to phone when he had a moment.

He knew her work habits well enough to catch her in the quiet hour she tried to start her day with, which was teatime in Australia.

'Ah, Jivan. Good.' She hesitated, then said, 'Bad news, I'm afraid. There have been more articles blackening your name. Do you want copies?'

'No. They sicken me. But when I get someone lined up to keep an eye on her, perhaps you'd pass them on to the private investigator.'

'Of course. I've heard of a rather special company which deals in protection for celebrities. I'm checking them out now. And Jivan . . . if there's anything I can do to help, on a personal or professional level, don't hesitate to ask.'

'Thank you, Anna. I know that.'

He sat for a long time staring at the computer, his thoughts bouncing round his skull like angry wasps. Any normal person would have let the matter of a marriage break-up drop by now. He felt pretty sure Louisa had gone beyond stalking into what was to him unknown territory – some form of mental illness, perhaps.

On that thought, he got online to research stalking. Why hadn't he done that sooner? What he found confirmed his suspicions that she was acting abnormally and made him feel more worried than he had before about his personal safety.

According to one site's classifications, Louisa fitted into the category of either a 'resentful' stalker or a 'rejected' stalker.

He definitely needed professional help to deal with this.

The following day Anna got back to him with the name of a company that dealt with big-time stalkers for the stars and he contacted them at once, asking if he could speak to someone about a problem he was experiencing.

They replied by suggesting he Skype, so that they could see one another and speak at length if necessary.

So that they could see whether *he* looked to be a lunatic, he guessed, feeling resentful himself about that. Could you see such a thing in a person?

He shrugged and emailed straight back to agree.

They replied to ask how urgent the matter was, and when he said not immediately urgent, they suggested a time the following week, when an operative who specialised in cases like his would be free to take on another client. In the meantime he should be very careful about his personal safety.

Well, at least he had done one thing right in getting away from his ex; he had protected himself.

He felt better about himself when he switched his computer off.

Six

Jessica's job wasn't as demanding as she'd thought it would be, which was good in one sense. But when the work failed to build up as rapidly as her former boss had told her was expected, she began to wonder if the company would change its corporate mind about the viability of a West Australian branch.

She hoped they'd give it a little longer. She was enjoying being here in the west and didn't want another major upheaval in her life.

During the Christmas break, she decided to visit a few places she'd known as a child. The first one was Mandurah, which she checked up online first. To her astonishment the town had more than doubled in size and it now had several man-made canal developments lined by huge waterside homes. She went for a boat ride round the canals, thinking how wonderful it would be to live on the water. Afterwards she strolled along the foreshore, enjoying the hot summer weather, even though other people complained about it being too hot.

Apart from opening her present from her parents and going out for a meal with her work colleagues, she didn't pay much attention to the seasonal jollities.

She had made friends with Janice, who was in charge of human resources, and they went out together for a celebratory meal just before the holiday, but Janice had a brother living in a country town and would be spending Christmas with him and his family.

Her mother had written long letters, worrying about Jessica being lonely or, in the last letter, being in danger in a land with so many poisonous spiders. Apparently her parents had watched a programme about Australian spiders on television. Why they were getting so het up when they hadn't seen many during their time here, she couldn't work out. Like other children, she'd quickly learned not to poke her fingers into holes where spiders might be lurking. And she wasn't going to start doing it now.

When her brother found out that he and Kerry were expecting a boy, her mother's letters alternated between worrying about Jessica and telling her about the family discussions re names for the baby. In the end they chose John Richard, but the child was already known as 'our Johnny'.

Keeping in touch would have been easier if her mother had used a computer, but Maureen didn't like them, even though she used one in the shop. She said they were a cop out and people ought to take the trouble to personalise things when keeping in touch with one another. She therefore wrote her letters by hand and sent hard copies of photos, a lot of photos, as if she was determined to keep her distant daughter fully involved in family affairs.

Jessica had wondered about going home for the christening when the time came, and certainly her mother was urging her to book her flight and even offering to pay the fare.

Before she could make a plane reservation, however, and well before the baby was due, she began to suspect that something was going on behind the scenes at work.

In February it was leaked that the company had been taken over by one of the big multi-nationals. The staff worried to one another that the new owners might close down the West Australian branch, since they already had a branch in Perth.

They were right. The closure happened almost immediately and with no warning. One evening things seemed perfectly normal as they closed up the office and went home. The next morning, when the staff got to work, they found the premises occupied by a close-down team and security officers.

They were escorted to the conference room where a hard-faced woman addressed them, making no attempt to soften the blow.

'I'm in charge of the closure of this branch. You will have one hour to clear your personal possessions from your work stations. You are not to use your computers during that time.'

She waited till the muttering had subsided, then went on, 'Boxes have been provided for any personal papers and effects. You'll leave them here and they'll be checked carefully to make sure there's nothing going out that shouldn't, after which they'll be delivered to any address in Perth you specify. Your salaries and accrued leave will be paid out within the week. References have been provided and will be sent to your home addresses by your former employer.'

'Can you just tell us—' someone began.

'No other questions will be answered, but you may have a copy of the prepared media statement if you wish.'

And that was that.

Jessica left her former colleagues in a café arguing furiously about their rights to clear their personal stuff off their computers and went home. It felt strange to have nothing to do on a weekday. She made herself a cup of tea and sat outside in her small courtyard, trying to decide what to do next. She had the money for her fare and a little left over, if she wanted to go back to England, but once she got there she'd have to find a new job quickly and her former employer no longer existed.

It had cost a lot to set herself up in Perth, because she'd needed a car as well as a new desktop computer, printer and things for her little home. She hadn't touched the money from her writing prize, which was in a long-term savings account at the bank, but maybe she should use it now to buy some writing time.

In the end, she could come to no decision and decided to take a week or two to think about the future while she studied the job market here in Perth. She could get on with some writing, too. That would be no hardship.

The following weekend, a friendly new neighbour from the villa three doors away popped in to see her. When Jessica explained what had happened, Deb insisted on taking her to a party to cheer her up.

'Come on! You can't stay indoors moping. You're bound to find another job soon in the IT industry.'

'I don't think I—'

'I'll pick you up at eight. Wear something smart. They're nice people, but yuppies. They want me to do them a mural.' Deb had already talked about her work and the high prices her paintings were starting to command.

Oh, why not? Jessica thought. It was lonely being at home all day on your own.

The party was in a private house in City Beach. Around it were parked late-model cars. Inside, the decor was elegant, the music soft and the people well-dressed. A security guard was on duty at the front door, caterers occupied the kitchen and a bar had been set up in the games room overlooking a huge swimming pool.

Most of the people seemed to be in couples and within a few minutes, Jessica was wishing she hadn't come. Deb had gone into a huddle in a corner with a tall man whose expression said he was much taken by her. She seemed equally taken by him and he was making her laugh.

'All alone?'

Jessica turned round. 'Yes.'

A man was smiling at her. His eyes flickered briefly to her left hand. 'I'm Mike Larreter.'

'Jessica Lord.' She studied him in turn, quite liking what she saw. Tall, older than her, skin rather weathered, as if he'd spent a lot of time outdoors. He wasn't fat, but he was certainly well-built, looking as if he worked out regularly.

'You must be English.' He stretched out one fingertip to stroke her cheek. 'The beautiful skin gives you away. You can't have been here long.'

She shook her head. 'Not long, no. And you?'

'Aussie born and bred, and proud of it.'

'Actually, I was born here, too, but my parents returned to England. I never forgot Australia, though, and when I got a chance to work here, I snapped it up.' And might regret that now. Her mother was right about one thing. She felt very vulnerable without any family nearby to help her in this time of crisis.

As they chatted, she found that he was recently divorced and braced herself for the usual bad-mouthing of his ex-wife. But he barely mentioned her. In fact, he talked mostly about his job.

He was a human resources manager in the public sector, and he was having enormous difficulty in getting people who understood computer systems to set up a new database they needed.

Jessica spoke without thinking. 'I could do that standing on my head.'

He broke off in mid-sentence and stared at her. 'You could?'

'Of course I could. That's what my job is – was – adapting software programs to companies' needs and setting up specialised computer systems.'

'You look too young and pretty to be doing that sort of thing.'

She sighed and raised her eyebrows.

He threw up his hands. 'Sorry. Didn't mean to be sexist, but I'm older than you, so I'm allowed to slip up occasionally. Tell you what, let's not talk business tonight.' He grimaced at the noise around them. 'Why don't I take you out to lunch tomorrow and we'll discuss things then? If you really are looking for a job—'

'I am. My company just got taken over and our branch was closed down.'

'Then we may be able to help one another.'

She had no hesitation in accepting his offer.

He stayed beside her for a while and then introduced her to some other people before he left to go on to another party.

She was sorry to see him leave. Mike was good company, a bit sharp in his views of the world, but interesting to chat to.

Since Deb seemed to have hooked up with the tall guy, Jessica excused herself just before midnight and called a taxi.

One week later, she had a three-month temporary contract and a demanding new job. Her mother was upset that she was unable to make it to the christening, but you couldn't ask for leave when you'd just started work on a project.

Mike's deputy, Barbara Ross, helped her to settle into the new job, which was fiddly but not difficult.

Within the week, Mike went off on a secondment to another government department, leaving Barbara in charge. Immediately people seemed to relax and smile more.

They didn't see him again for six months. By then, a full-time computing job had been created and advertised, and Jessica had applied for it, gone through a gruelling interview and been appointed. She was now a permanent public servant, or as her colleagues joked, she had donned the golden handcuffs of job security – well, as near to security as you could get these days.

After the shock of her sudden unemployment, Jessica rather liked the thought of a permanent job.

She also liked the way most people came to the office, got on with their work and then went home at weekends to enjoy themselves. There was little or no overtime, which suited her just fine.

In fact, Australians seemed to enjoy their leisure time far more than the people she had worked with in England. In her opinion, that gave a better balance in their daily lives.

She slid gradually into a regular routine. Do your job in working hours, then do your own thing at weekends and some evenings, which for her meant writing. And the more she wrote, the more she wanted to write.

Her novel had been published and was selling well and the sequel was nearly finished. Because of all the changes in her life, she hadn't been able to write it as quickly as she'd hoped, but she was pleased with the basic story.

Her mother worried that she was working too hard at her writing and not having a good social life. She even phoned up to talk about it.

'How are you going to meet men, Jessica love, if you stay at home all weekend?'

She tried to be patient, but it was the same old tale. Her mother wanted her to get married.

'I do go out, Mum. And I have made friends, Janice and Deb. But no, not a steady guy.'

'Why not? What are you doing wrong?'

'Who says I'm doing something wrong. Maybe fate just hasn't pushed anyone suitable into my path. I won't go into a permanent relationship until I'm sure of the guy. And I've told you before, I don't intend to marry unless I can find someone I love as much as you love Dad.'

That shut her mother up till next time, but actually Jessica didn't want a steady boyfriend at this stage in her life. She wanted to get established as a novelist and earn her living from writing. That wasn't going to be easy, but some writers managed it.

In her letters home during the following year, Jessica talked about the lovely sunny weather, even in winter, and the people she worked with. She didn't mention her writing, except when her second novel was accepted.

As usual, her mother didn't ask her what the novel was about, just congratulated her, then devoted the rest of the letter to little Johnny.

'Can't you come home for a visit, at least? You've never even seen your nephew. If it's the money for the fare, we'll buy your ticket . . .'

She wrote back, 'I'm waiting till I can come for a month, and I'm too new here to have accrued so much leave.'

She posted some presents to her family in England early in October and a parcel from her parents arrived for her at the end of November. It sat by her television set waiting to be opened, alongside a miniature Christmas tree thirty centimetres high.

There was just the one present and she felt rather sad that this would be her second Christmas on her own. Next year she would definitely go back for a visit. Or even perhaps find a job in England.

And devoted as she was to writing, she knew she had to find something more in life. But what?

She hadn't met a guy she *could* fall in love with. Perhaps she never would. She was too picky. An image of Jivan Childering flashed into her mind, but she banished it sternly. No use wishing for the moon. She might find him more attractive than other men, but why should he even remember her in his busy life? He must know dozens of gorgeous women.

And she missed her family quite badly at times.

Were all immigrants like her, torn every which way between the old and the new?

She loved Western Australia and its warm climate. But would it be enough for more than a few years? She was beginning to doubt it.

Things changed drastically at work when Mike Larreter returned from his secondment just after Christmas.

'Have you seen him yet?' Barbara asked, as they ate lunch together.

'I'm booked in for a session with him this afternoon.' Jessica grimaced. '*Getting to know one another*, he calls it. Why do you ask?'

'Our Mike's changed. He's come back a bitter man. He expected to get the job he was seconded to. He's hell-bent on climbing the corporate ladder, you know. So now he seems determined to make a name for himself here and show the other department what they've missed out on. Or that's my analysis, anyway.'

'You're a very wise woman, Barbara, so you're probably right.' The older woman had become a sort of honorary aunt to Jessica.

'Thank you, dear. And don't forget to bring your bathers on Sunday. My Don has got our pool just right and there's a hot day forecast.'

Jessica was feeling lonely enough at the moment to break her vow to write every weekend, so she went to Barbara's social gathering. But they were all married couples and she felt out of place.

The pace of work hotted up, but Jessica didn't find Mike bitter. In fact, she found him quite attractive. She hadn't had a date for a while, so when he invited her out to dinner, she thought why not? It was a bit risky, dating your boss, but she didn't answer directly to him in her daily work and she definitely didn't feel like spending another Saturday evening on her own.

It was good to dress up and go out. She enjoyed the meal and Mike's company, too, but suspected he'd set out to charm her.

After they'd eaten, they walked through Northbridge and sat drinking a cappuccino outside a café. The summer nights were balmy.

When Mike dropped her off at her villa, he tried to coax his way into her bed. She told him bluntly, 'I'm not into casual sex, Mike.'

'You said you didn't have a current partner. Don't you miss the sex?'

'No.' She wasn't going to tell him she was still a virgin, that her one attempt to remedy that had ended in laughter and a good but platonic friendship. She didn't know Mike well enough, and anyway, it seemed almost shameful in this day and age to have reached the advanced age of thirty without indulging in sex. 'Let's just say that I'm not into risk-taking.'

He started to say something, stopped, then shrugged. 'Oh, well. One can but try. Blame it all on my crude masculine hormones.'

A couple of weeks later he asked her out again, this time to a cocktail party.

She looked him straight in the eyes. 'I shan't change my mind about having sex.'

'I guessed that. But at least you won't bore me.' His lips curved into a smile. 'The lady who favoured me with her attentions last weekend should have been born in the sixties. She's certainly into making love not war, so my hormones enjoyed the outing. But she had a minimalist brain and the rest of me got bored.'

She didn't like the cynical way he talked about women, but in the end she accepted the invitation out of sheer loneliness, and even asked him in for coffee when they got back. 'One coffee, no sex, just a little conversation,' she warned, before he could accept. 'As you see, I believe in laying my cards on the table.'

'Point taken. Tell me about your writing instead.'

But when she started trying to tell him about her planet, she could see that he had no real interest and they ended up talking about computers and work, as they often did. Barbara was right: Mike was ferociously ambitious.

When she mentioned to Barbara that she and Mike had been out a few times, she thought she saw a strange expression on her colleague's face for a moment. But she might have been mistaken because Barbara didn't make any derogatory comment about him.

Going out with Mike occasionally was pleasant, but Jessica knew she wasn't in love with him, and she was quite sure he wasn't in love with her, either. She doubted he would really love anyone but himself, and she could guess why his wife had left him.

She told herself she shouldn't go on accepting his invitations because their relationship was leading nowhere, but he always behaved well, and it was good to get out occasionally.

Seven

At the end of March, which was early autumn down under but still warm, Jessica received a phone call from her editor. It came at eleven o'clock at night, just after she'd fallen asleep. She fumbled for the phone without switching the light on.

'Jessica? Anna Stephens here.'

'Oh, hi!' She couldn't prevent herself from yawning.

'Did I wake you up?'

'It's eleven o'clock and I'm an early bird.'

'Sorry. I never go to bed till after midnight myself, so I assumed you'd still be up. Anyway, this is worth being woken up for.'

'Oh?'

'It's my great pleasure to inform you that you're a finalist in this year's Australasian Star-Writer Awards. You're up for the best new fantasy series. Now that you're living down under, you were eligible so our Australian branch entered your books.'

Jessica gasped, tried to find words and failed utterly. This was a well-respected fantasy award.

'I thought that'd stun you.' Anna chuckled.

'I . . . how . . . what . . .'

'The award is being presented in Melbourne this year and we hope you'll be able to attend. We think you stand a good chance of winning, but even if you don't, being shortlisted will help us publicise your books down under.'

'Melbourne!'

'You've only to hop on a plane and you'll be at the other side of Australia in a few hours.'

'I— Anna, I can't take it in.'

'You should be getting used to your books winning awards by now. This is your second time, after all.'

'I don't think I could ever get blasé about that. Anyway, when are the presentations?'

'In two weeks' time. Are you still working in that government department?'

'Yes.'

'When are you going to stop doing that and devote yourself to writing full time? We'd take two books a year from you if you could produce them.'

'Unfortunately my books don't earn me enough to live on yet.' But it was tiring trying to juggle her writing with a job that was growing more demanding and a boss who had tunnel vision about the project and wanted it finished yesterday, but who refused to assign any additional staff to the job.

'Congratulations from everyone at Meridian. I'll email you all the details and look forward to seeing you in Melbourne. I have to go over to San Francisco, so I'm travelling via Australia and attending.'

'That's rather a long way round.'

'Well, I have some other business down under and it's not every day that one of our authors gets shortlisted for a Star-Writer award. We're all thrilled to pieces.'

When Jessica put the phone down, she lay smiling in the darkness for a long time. Then she sighed. If only she could stop work and write full-time! But though she was always very economical and had some savings now, there was no way she could afford it for more than a few months. The ideal solution would be to find part-time work, but then she'd lose her permanent job.

She suddenly wondered if she'd even get the time off to pick up the award. With Mike in slave-driving mode, it was a struggle to get any leave at all in their area.

Well, from now on she wouldn't agree to any overtime, even if Mike didn't like that. She'd been feeling a bit under the weather lately. Nothing she could put a finger on, but definitely not her usual self.

Barbara had noticed, of course, and asked if she was all right.

What Jessica needed was a rest.

When she went into Mike's office the next day and told him her news, she expected congratulations, but he sat for a moment, frowning at her, then asked, 'Are you going to resign now?'

'No. I can't afford to.'

'But you've just been shortlisted for a big award.'

'Yes. It's very prestigious.'

'How much money is the prize?'

'Five thousand dollars if I win first prize.' She waited, but he didn't answer her original question about taking leave. 'So can I take a few days off to attend the ceremony?'

The frown was back. 'It's very inconvenient.'

He was enjoying this, she realised suddenly, enjoying the power he had over her.

She wasn't going to put up with that, so looked him straight in the eyes and said, 'If you don't give me the time off, Mike, I'll resign.' And to her own surprise, she meant it.

He held up one hand. 'Hey, I didn't say I wouldn't, only that it's inconvenient. You can have a couple of days off. Of course you can.'

'Three days. The presentations are on a Wednesday night. Even if I fly back the next day, I'll only be here for the Friday and I'll be too tired to be much good to you. I might as well take the Friday off and have a bit of a break. I'm getting very tired with all the overtime.'

'You don't work for whole weekends, just later in the evening and the occasional Saturday morning.'

'Most Saturdays, lately.' She wouldn't tell him till she got back about her decision to do no more overtime. 'So, do I get my three days?'

He sighed, the very picture of the aggrieved executive. 'Oh, very well. Put your leave form in. But no more than three. I want you back here on the Monday, raring to go.'

The phone on his desk rang and he picked it up, not even apologising to her as he did so. 'Hello. Mike Larreter.' He covered the mouthpiece and whispered, 'I'll take you out for a drink after work to celebrate, Jessica.'

She shook her head. 'Thanks, but I can't. I've got something on.' She had nothing arranged, actually, but she no longer enjoyed Mike's company. It was difficult to end things completely, however, when he was her boss as well. What had she ever seen in him? He was another person who hadn't asked about her book, only the money.

And he'd recently pressured her again for sex, even tried to physically feel her up against her wishes.

She smiled wryly. Having waited so long, she might as well

ensure that her initiation was more than just for sexual relief. She wanted it to be an act of love.

As she got ready for the presentations in her Melbourne hotel, she smiled into the mirror. This time she had a very elegant outfit, the nicest formal wear she had ever owned. The material was a mist of subtly blended shades of green, with an ankle-length skirt and a silk jacket in the dominant green. It had cost her an arm and a leg, but she had given in to the temptation, for once.

She was, Jessica realised, as she went down to meet Anna in the foyer, far more confident than she had been last time she won a prize, and whether she won the award or not, she intended to enjoy the evening.

'I have a surprise for you,' Anna said, clasping Jessica's hand and beaming at her.

'Another surprise?'

'A different sort of surprise.' She beckoned to someone behind Jessica. '*Voilà!*'

Jivan Childering walked across the foyer to join them. He shook Jessica's hand and held it for a moment in his. 'I was passing through Melbourne on my way home, and Anna invited me to come tonight. I was in on your first prize and I'd love to be here for your second. Do you mind?'

He had a genuine smile on his face tonight.

'No, of course not. I'm delighted. Though I can't guarantee to win the award.'

'It's a great series. It deserves to.'

'You've read the books?'

'Of course I have. They're excellent stories.'

A shiver of delight ran through her and she couldn't help beaming at him.

Anna's voice interrupted them, bringing Jessica back to earth. 'I have a taxi waiting. Shall we go, Cinderella?'

'I don't feel like Cinderella this time.'

'What do you feel like?' Jivan asked.

Jessica shrugged. 'I don't know. But not Cinderella. That was last time.'

'You don't look like her tonight, either.' He swept his eyes admiringly across her body, not lingering, not harassing, but in an age-old salute from a single male to an attractive female.

She smiled back at him. As usual he was looking very elegant.

Whoa! she told her body. He's not for you.

But she could look, couldn't she? And dream.

Because she was sitting at a table with Jivan and Anna, Jessica found herself a major focus of interest from the press.

'Give us a smile, love,' one journalist called.

Jessica could feel herself blushing.

Jivan chuckled. 'I'd forgotten how easily you blush.'

'It's the bane of my life,' she muttered.

'It's charming.'

As the dinner ended, the MC stood up to bring them all to the main point of the evening.

When her name was called out as the winner in her category, Jessica had her speech prepared, just a short one, and thought she delivered it quite well; she ought to – she'd practised it in front of the mirror several times.

She returned to the table, cradling the delicate silver figurine holding up an arch of stars. Cameras started flashing, again focusing on her and Jivan.

'Are you two an item?' one journo called. 'What will your ex-wife say? She's been hinting at a reconciliation.'

Jivan lost his smile at once.

It was Anna who saved the day. 'You're off track there, on both issues. Jessica and Jivan are both Meridian authors. I'm the one who invited him here tonight for the presentations, not only because he happened to be in Melbourne but because he was the one who presented the other prize to Jessica in England.'

'What other prize?'

'She won our *Write A Bestseller* award with the first book in the same series. Have you read them? You should. Give me your card and I'll send you some copies. You'll see why the books have made such an impact.'

Anna made sure that she and Jessica walked out together at the end of the evening, with Jivan on his own behind them. 'Poor man. He has only to look at a female for the journos to start making innuendos. They won't leave him in peace.'

As the taxi arrived to take them back to the hotel, Jivan spotted someone he knew and called out that he would grab another taxi and follow them shortly.

Jessica guessed he was doing this because of the journos. She didn't blame him for travelling back separately, but felt disappointed, because she'd hoped to chat to him tonight, as they had before. Sometimes, she felt absolutely starved of another person to discuss her craft with.

She'd met a few other writers in Perth, but they were mostly unpublished and the majority didn't have the fire in their bellies to succeed. One of them had had a rather intense and distinctly miserable novel published by a small press publisher no one had ever heard of and gave himself airs about that, sneering at her for writing 'rubbish'.

She declined Anna's invitation to share a nightcap. 'I'm quite an early bird, really, and with the time differences between Melbourne and Perth, I'm more than ready for bed.'

'Then let me just congratulate you once again. I'm afraid I'm flying out at some unearthly hour of the morning, so I won't even be able to have breakfast with you.'

Jessica had expected to have trouble sleeping after the excitement of the evening, but she was so exhausted after the months of gruelling work that she fell fathoms deep into a dark well and didn't emerge until eight o'clock the next morning.

She felt ravenously hungry so got straight out of bed and into the shower, slinging on some casual clothes. She could have had room service, but didn't feel like eating on her own after such a lovely evening, so went down to the hotel's coffee shop for breakfast.

The first person she saw was Jivan, his back half-turned towards her, a newspaper in his hands.

She hesitated, not knowing whether to join him, then he looked up and smiled as he caught sight of her, gesturing to the chair next to him. She sat down, gave the waitress her room number and ordered a cooked breakfast.

'Tired?' he asked.

'No. I slept like the proverbial log. Best night's sleep I've had in ages.'

'You were looking tired behind the joy yesterday.'

'Yes, well, I've been working hard.'

'On your next book?'

'I should be so lucky. Earning my daily bread, actually. Big project, lots of overtime.' She grimaced.

His voice was sympathetic. 'It's hard being a part-time writer.'

'But better than not being a writer.'

'What time does your plane leave today?'

She smiled. 'I'm not leaving till Sunday. I couldn't get back to Western Australia in time for work today, so I thought I'd enjoy the weekend. I've never visited Melbourne before.'

'You'll be staying on at the hotel, then?'

'Yes, I'm indulging myself a little.' It wasn't something she often did. Her parents' stringent training in not being extravagant made it hard for her to indulge in luxuries.

She wondered what her family would say about this win. They'd be pleased, but her mother would rather hear that she was getting married. She pushed that thought away. 'I thought you'd have flown out with Anna.'

'No. I've some personal business to attend to here. I'm leaving on Sunday, too, but I'll be flying home to Queensland, not going back to Britain.'

'You live in Australia now, Jivan?'

'Yes, but I'd be grateful if you'd not tell anyone.'

She must have looked puzzled, because he added, 'My ex-wife is stalking me.'

Jivan was surprised that he'd mentioned the stalking. He usually kept the information to himself.

When Jessica didn't pursue the matter, he added, 'You may have gathered from newspaper articles that I had rather an acrimonious divorce. Since then I've been having trouble with my ex, who won't leave me alone when I'm in England.'

'She's stalking you?'

'Yes. And blackening my name. She's very inventive about it, too.'

'I'm sorry.'

'So am I. She's become obsessive. That's why I moved to Australia.' He changed the subject firmly. 'Never mind her. What are you going to do with yourself today?'

She shrugged. 'Just go walkabout, I think. Amble round the city centre. The concierge gave me a map and pointed out a few places I might enjoy. I thought I'd book a coach tour for tomorrow. I want to see as much as possible while I'm over in the east.'

'The city centre's easy enough to navigate. It's all built on a square grid. Very unimaginative, but you can't lose your way, at least. We're near the river and station here, so make sure you're going downhill when you want to come back to the hotel and you won't go far wrong. And tomorrow you might enjoy a coach trip to Sovereign Hill and Bendigo. That's a whole day affair. You're a bit late for it today.'

'What's there to see?'

Jivan loved the way her eyes were sparkling with interest, her whole face alight with it. And best of all, Jessica Lord wasn't making any attempt to flirt with him.

He realised she was still waiting for him to answer her question. 'Sorry. I was just remembering it. Sovereign Hill is a re-creation of an old gold-mining town of the 1850s. You can ride on stage-coaches, pan for gold, view underground mines from a tram or on foot. In fact, do all sorts of fun, touristy things. The staff dress in period costume.'

'That sounds fascinating.'

'Some people don't like history being commercialised, but I do. It brings the era to life for me when I walk into an old chemist's shop, full of coloured bottles and mysterious potions. It's not at all the same to read about it.'

Eight

Breakfast was over all too soon and Jessica said goodbye to Jivan with regret. He was such an interesting person to talk to.

She went up to fetch her things and walked out alone to explore.

After a while, she stopped at a café and wrote a postcard to her family, giving them her news, then concentrated on enjoying herself.

In spite of a couple of breaks for coffee and lunch, by

mid-afternoon her feet were aching and she was feeling tired, so she visited a bookshop and treated herself to a couple of nice, thick paperbacks.

She sighed at the prospect of another early night with a book, even if it was a book she'd been dying to read. Story of my life, she muttered.

Of course the first person she saw as she entered the hotel restaurant that evening was Jivan. As he looked across at her, his expression wasn't at all welcoming and there was a visible hesitation before he nodded a greeting.

She gave him a quick smile and made her way across to an empty table at the opposite side of the room, choosing to sit with her back to him. She concentrated on the menu, feeling a little hurt by his attitude, but determined not to give him any reason to think she was pursuing him.

Before she could order, a shadow fell across the menu. She looked up and there he was.

'Sorry. I was miles away when you walked in, thinking about something. As we both seem to be on our own, maybe you'd like to join me for dinner, Jessica?'

She kept her expression as cool as possible. 'Thank you for the offer, but you mustn't feel obliged to entertain me, Jivan. I'm perfectly capable of looking after myself and I don't want to impose on you. Nor do I want to give the gutter press false ideas about us and set them baying after you again.'

'If you're willing to risk them telling lies about us, so am I.'

'Oh. OK, then. I don't mind.'

He looked down at her, his expression thoughtful. 'I can't guarantee to be entertaining, but I really would welcome some company tonight, though I didn't realise that until you came in. One grows tired of dining alone in strange cities. Being a best-selling novelist is supposed to be a glamorous life, but mostly it isn't.'

'Well . . .' She still hesitated, not wishing to be rude, but unable to forget his cold expression when he had first seen her.

'Please come and join me.' He gave her another of those genuine smiles which warmed his whole face. 'I'd join you here, but I think I have the better table by far.'

She moved across the room and allowed a waiter to fuss around them, setting her a place. When the man had gone, she looked at Jivan. 'Have you ordered yet?'

'No. Not yet. Are you hungry?'

'Absolutely ravenous! I did a lot of walking today.'

'What did you see?'

She enumerated on her fingers, 'St Paul's Cathedral, Princes Bridge, the Botanic Gardens and the Yarra River. Then shops, shops and more shops.'

'Did you buy any clothes?'

'No, books. Much more fun.'

When their hors d'oeuvres arrived, she bit into a juicy prawn and made a satisfied noise in her throat. 'Australian seafood is the best in the world.' She selected another and couldn't help noticing that he was spearing his food lethargically, as if he had no real appetite.

None of her business. She concentrated on her own meal, letting him pace the conversation.

'Did you arrange a trip for tomorrow, then?'

'Oh yes. I took your advice and booked a coach tour to Sovereign Hill, or rather got the concierge to book for me. I especially fancy riding on a stagecoach. I've never ridden on one and I'd like to, in case I ever write a historical novel.'

'Are you likely to do that?'

'Maybe one day. It's my second interest. I wrote one once, when I was much younger, but it was pretty awful. It was a good plot idea, though, and I'd like to rework it when I have more time. Do you always write thrillers?'

She realised with a jerk of embarrassment that this might be tactless, but it was too late to change the subject now. Would she never learn to watch her tongue? 'Sorry. I didn't mean to sound nosey.' She blushed and speared another prawn to hide her confusion.

'I, too, wrote other things in my salad days. The publishers weren't interested, so I continued to experiment and found they were very interested in my thrillers. So I kept on doing it, because I enjoy the challenge of fitting the pieces of a puzzle together, and thinking out shocks and turn-arounds. I also enjoy the financial fruits of my labours. Money can be a useful commodity.'

'Tell me about it.'

'What would you do if you had one wish granted, Jessica, and money no expense?'

'Give up my day job to write.'

'Don't you enjoy your work at all?'

She shrugged. 'It's all right. But my boss is out to make a name for himself before he hits forty and that's only a couple of years away so he's pushing us hard.' She sighed. 'He might be a nice guy if he weren't so ambitious. We've been out together once or twice. I haven't told him yet but that's over now.'

'Because of the prize?'

'No. Because of the sort of man he is and how he's treating his staff.'

'How will he take his dismissal?'

'Not well. Mike's a good hater. Boasts that he never lets anyone get away with messing him around.' She sighed, shaking her head vigorously. 'Why am I talking about him, for heaven's sake?'

'It's Uncle Jivan's Problem Page again.'

They both chuckled, remembering their conversation in London.

For the rest of the meal they chatted comfortably, but he made no effort to prolong matters beyond a glass of port in the bar, nor did he escort her up to her room.

A coolness and distance came over him towards the end of the evening, as if he were warning her off. *Come no further! Here be dragons!*

That was fine, she told herself firmly, as she walked across the foyer. If he didn't fancy her, that was his privilege.

The trouble was, she found him very attractive indeed.

Tonight she had felt alive again, she thought, as the lift started moving. Fully alive, interested in a man.

But would she still feel good when she got back to Perth?

The following morning she breakfasted in her room, determined not to force a situation where Jivan would feel compelled to invite her to share his table again.

She walked quickly out of the hotel afterwards, both relieved and disappointed not to have bumped into him.

The coach firm's departure point was just a couple of blocks away. She strode along, taking everything in, avid for the new experiences the day would bring. The sky was cloudy and there were very few people around. At eight fifteen in the morning the shops weren't open yet and the streets were quiet – perhaps people didn't start work as early here as they did in Perth? Or perhaps it was just in this district?

The alleys between the tall buildings seemed slightly sinister without people bustling around. Maybe that solitary van was carrying stolen merchandise . . . She chuckled as a plump older man got out of the van with a parcel, complaining to someone inside it that his damned knee was playing up again today.

She boarded the coach, the first passenger to arrive, smiled at the driver and settled into the front seat behind him. The other passengers started to trickle on board and she pulled out her brochure to study the route they were to take.

'Mind if I join you?' a voice said above her head, and she jumped in shock, dropping the leaflet.

'Jivan! I thought you had some appointments today?'

'Last-minute rescheduling. *Do* you mind if I join you?'

'No, of course not. I was miles away when you spoke. You startled me.'

'I noticed.' He picked up her brochure from the floor, his warm hands touching hers briefly and sending a shiver along her arm. His smile was relaxed this morning. *She* was feeling anything but relaxed.

As he slid into the seat next to her, he smiled. 'Telling you about Sovereign Hill made me feel nostalgic to see it again. I haven't done anything frivolous for months. Like you, I've been working too hard.'

'Well, it's great to have company.' She stopped trying to remain calm and detached, and settled down to enjoy the day. This time he was the one who had sought her company.

And they did enjoy themselves! Sovereign Hill was a place of utter magic from start to finish, or perhaps they were both in the mood to create their own magic.

All the shopkeepers in the 'town' wore period costume, which meant long skirts for the women, with a few of them wearing crinolines. The men had side whiskers, and brightly coloured waistcoats with heavy gold watch chains draped across them.

Here and there actors were playing the parts of citizens, even a wedding group with a drunken bridegroom, who came staggering along the street behind his bride and had to be coaxed into the stagecoach with her.

Jivan signed them up to pan for gold in a stream, and it was much harder than it looked. Jessica spluttered with laughter as he spilled the wet grit all over his expensive trainers.

'Let's see you do better!' he challenged.

She took a lot more care when swilling the water around her own flat pan, crowing triumphantly when she found some minute specks of gold left in the edges of the central hollow. The attendant put these into a tiny box lined with cotton wool for her to take home.

Afterwards they visited the gold mine, opting to walk through it rather than take the tram. Inside, it felt chill and damp almost immediately, as if they really were deep underground. Scattered around in alcoves branching off the main walkway were tableaux with realistic life-sized models of miners at work. They looked like people suddenly frozen into position. Some were kneeling in cramped tunnels, others wielding pickaxes or pushing trolleys.

Partway through the mine, Jessica was separated from Jivan and deliberately allowed the other group members to get ahead of her so that she could feel the atmosphere better. It was unnerving to stand there on her own with the water dripping down somewhere close by and the flickering candles blowing to and fro in a draught. After a few moments she decided with a shiver that the tableaux were altogether too convincing and hurried to join the rest of the group in case one of the fibreglass miners suddenly came to life and reached out to grab her.

Sometimes a vivid imagination could be a disadvantage.

It was part of the pleasure of the day that no one recognised Jivan behind his dark glasses and that he entered into the fun of everything, including a stagecoach ride. The coach rocked about so much she had to clutch his arm to steady herself, but he didn't seem to mind.

To her surprise the horses were lathered with sweat after only ten minutes, and Jivan teased her for feeling guilty.

'They are pulling other people, too, you know. It's not your fault alone.'

'Yes, but so many people. There must be – what? – twenty people on this heavy coach, and only five horses. It doesn't seem fair.'

He shook his head at her and chuckled. 'You're too soft-hearted, but it's a good fault.'

After that, they went to have their photo taken in period costume, a crinoline for her, and false side whiskers and bowler hat for Jivan.

Across the road was an emporium which stocked crinolines and miners' gear for the tourists. She was very tempted to buy herself a crinoline as a souvenir, even going so far as to try one on. Jivan, with a stockman's hat perched on his sleek dark head, encouraged her to do so, but in the end she refused. Better to save her money at this stage.

'Let me buy it for you, as a memento of the day,' he suggested when she turned away.

'Oh, no! Really, I couldn't! Besides, I wouldn't have anywhere to store it. I live in a very small unit.' To her relief he didn't press the point.

They came out on to the main street again and bought ice creams, a treat she rather doubted would have been found in an original gold-mining town, but who cared? They were delicious.

After that, they stood side by side to watch a blacksmith at work. Jivan's shoulder was pressed against hers. If it had been any other man, she would have linked her arm in his, but she wasn't going to risk doing anything that might spoil the outing.

It was growing harder to remember to be careful how she reacted to him.

It wasn't a busy day at Sovereign Hill, so there were almost as many actors and shopkeepers as tourists. Jessica stopped at the top of the street to take a photo and look back. 'You were right about it bringing history to life. You can imagine what it would really have been like, can't you? The mud and the horses and the chaos.'

'Yes.' But his eyes were on her, not the street, and his expression was thoughtful.

By then it was time for them to return to the coach.

'I don't want to go back to reality,' Jessica mourned.

'We all have to do that.' His voice was flat, with an echo of bitterness.

She was prepared to bid him farewell at the hotel, but it was he who detained her. 'Would you like to eat out somewhere with me tonight? In Chinatown, perhaps?'

'Er – well, if you haven't anything better to do, that'd be lovely.'

'I haven't.'

'Are you sure? You mustn't feel obligated to entertain me.'

'You said that before, but I asked you of my own accord because I'm enjoying your company.'

She stared at herself in the mirror as she was getting ready. 'You're attracted to him, Jessica Lord, you silly fool!' She spoke it aloud, to remind herself not to hope. 'And he doesn't fancy you in the slightest. Not even enough to kiss you goodnight or hold your hand.'

She grimaced at her reflection. 'Well, make the most of what you have got, kiddo. It's better than nothing. At least now you can say you know the great Jivan Childering. And you'll have a photograph to remember this day by.'

The evening was low-key but enjoyable until one of Jivan's fans recognised him. Jessica stepped back to let him deal with it. As the woman fawned all over him, she saw that rigid look come into his face, stripping it of all warmth, though he answered the fan's silly questions patiently enough.

When the woman started making veiled suggestions that she was free to show him the sights of Melbourne the next day, with a little extra personal attention thrown in, he grew visibly angry and Jessica was afraid he was going to say something rude.

She decided to intervene, so stepped forward and took his arm. 'Jivan, darling, isn't it time to go now? You know we have a heavy schedule tomorrow.'

Once they were out of the bar, she let go of his arm and moved away from him. 'I hope you didn't mind. I thought you needed help.'

'I did need it. Thank you.' The words were clipped and sharp.

She giggled suddenly as something occurred to her. 'I was trying to act like a *femme fatale*. How did I go?'

His smile softened and she could see the tension leave his shoulders. 'You were perfect. An absolute charmer. I'm really grateful for your quick thinking and help in getting rid of her, Jessica.'

'Does that sort of thing happen often?'

'Yes. Far too often for my liking. Thanks to certain members of the press, some of my female readers think I'm a playboy and treat me accordingly. I could be knee deep in such women if I wanted to!'

His voice was burred with scorn and disgust. 'I usually keep out of public view in Australia. Thank goodness I don't live in Melbourne, or the paparazzi might find out and start chasing me.'

'Well, I promise not to treat you as anything but good old Uncle Jivan for the rest of the evening,' she said lightly, and felt his tension ebb still further.

'How about tomorrow?' he asked at the lift. 'I'm free again if you are.'

She abandoned caution. 'Sounds lovely. What shall we do?'

'Leave that to me.'

He took her to the art gallery, which he said was not to be missed, and they spent an enthralling couple of hours looking at paintings by most of the famous Australian greats she'd ever heard of, and a good few European artists, too.

'What's Perth's art gallery like?' he asked as they left the building.

'I don't know. I haven't visited it yet. I keep meaning to, but, well, Mike is keeping me too busy. And when he's not cracking the whip at his staff, he's socialising with people who might be useful to him one day, for which he sometimes needs a respectable woman by his side.'

'But why—' He broke off abruptly. 'I beg your pardon. I have no right to ask that.'

She shrugged. 'Why did I go out with him? I was in a new country and I was lonely.' And, she couldn't help thinking, I shall be even lonelier when I get back, after this golden interlude.

His hand rested on hers for a moment. 'Don't sell yourself short when you get back to Perth, Jessica. You can do better than this Mike fellow. You're excellent company, intelligent and lively.' He hesitated, then added, 'Just because I'm not interested in forming relationships at the moment doesn't mean that I don't find you attractive.' He ran a fingertip down her cheek and then leaned forward to press a very gentle kiss on her lips.

She could smell that faint spicy tang of his cologne. A strand of his hair had fallen forward and it tickled her face as he kissed her.

As he moved away, she swallowed to drive away the tears his kindness had brought to her eyes. Damn it, she would not cry for what she couldn't have! To her relief, her voice wobbled only slightly as she said, 'Well, thank you for that vote of confidence, Uncle Jivan!'

'You're welcome. Now, about this afternoon?'

'I've heard they have good river cruises. Do you want to come on one? Don't feel you have to.'

'I'd love to come. I was reading the tourist brochures last night as well. There's one where they give you a lesson in boomerang throwing. Bet I can throw mine further than you can!'

She chuckled, on safe ground again. 'I don't need to bet on it. You will. I'm the worst thrower and catcher in the whole world. Always have been. You'll probably pretend you're not with me when you see how bad I am.'

'No one is that bad.'

Later on Jessica tried her hardest to throw the boomerang correctly, but both her shots ploughed it into the ground a short distance away from her feet, making everyone else on the tour laugh good-naturedly.

She watched enviously as their Aboriginal guide helped Jivan to hold the boomerang correctly. It spun right across the field. It had amazed her that you held it vertically to throw it. Her instinct would have been to hold it parallel to the ground.

'See what I mean, Jivan?' she said as they were walking back to the boat. 'I'm the worst shot in the world.'

'The very worst.' He was still chuckling. Even the smallest child on the tour had thrown the boomerang further than she had.

All too soon their final evening together ended. This time, he did escort her up to her room. He looked into her eyes for a minute, then bent his head and kissed her gently on the cheek.

'I've enjoyed your company very much, Jessica. If a promotion tour brings me to Perth, may I take you out to dinner again?'

'That would be delightful.' She was very proud that she had

kept a smile on her face. She started to turn away. She would not cling to him!

'You'll need to give me your address, then.'

She swung back, startled. 'You really meant it?'

'Of course I did! I wouldn't have asked otherwise.'

She could feel her face flaming. 'Oh. Well, if you'll come in for a minute, I'll write my address down.'

He stayed near the doorway, making no attempt to come further inside or to touch her again, so she didn't offer him a coffee.

'Here. I've written down my work phone number as well.'

'I live somewhere for a while, then move on, and I'll be moving soon, so I won't give you an address. But email me here and it'll always get to me.' He handed her a business card containing only an email address made up of numbers. He didn't even write his name next to it.

That brought home to her how careful he always was not to leave traces of himself anywhere. It must be his ex-wife who had done this to him. How sad! He should be out in the world, enjoying the fruits of his success.

At the door he turned. 'Keep up your writing, Jessica. You've deserved both prizes, you know.'

She forgot her personal worries for a moment. 'It seems impossible that all this is happening to me. I still keep thinking I'm dreaming.'

'This is the second time in five minutes you've not believed me,' he said with mock severity.

'Sorry. I'm not used to it all yet.'

'Then get used to it. You're going to be a very famous writer one day. And I *will* catch up with you when I visit Perth, truly I will. Goodnight, Jessica.'

This time she allowed herself to watch him walk away, but was relieved that he didn't turn as he got into the lift and catch her standing in her doorway staring longingly after him.

He haunted her dreams that night, of course.

He was in them for many nights afterwards, too. And for weeks she had only to see a tall man with blue-black hair in a crowd for her heart to start beating faster.

Oh, she was a fool!

Nine

In March an email arrived for Jessica with a brief note from Jivan and a digital copy of the photograph taken of them in period costume at Sovereign Hill attached.

She printed it out on photographic paper, bought a frame and put it on top of her television set. How happy the two of them looked!

And how unhappy she'd been since she returned. Work was a constant battle not to let Mike overload her, not to work weekends.

One evening she saw Jivan in a television interview from England on an arts programme. He was talking about his new book and this time, with a sympathetic interviewer, he came across well.

Her birthday came and went, unheralded except for a few cards and a present from her parents. Two days later, she attended an office party given to promote good corporate feeling – not that Mike really cared about such things, as they all knew, but he liked to go through the motions.

It was suggested very strongly that they all attend or she'd not have gone. During the evening, Jessica fended Mike off when he tried to suggest they get together again. As if she would ever consider it! She spent the rest of the evening sticking close to Barbara.

'Very wise to detach from him,' her friend and mentor said. 'He's a bad man.'

'You should have warned me before.'

'Yes, I should. Sorry.'

A week later Jessica came down with the 'flu, and although Mike shouted angrily at her down the phone when she rang to say she couldn't get into work, she felt so ill she dragged herself to the doctor.

'You look dreadful, Jessica. Take the whole week off and see me on Monday before you even think of going back.' He leaned back in his chair and studied her. 'I'd say you're also suffering from stress. Am I right?'

She nodded.

'Do you want this to turn into post-viral syndrome, which can debilitate a person for years?' When she looked puzzled, he added, 'Sometimes known as chronic fatigue syndrome or ME.'

She was aghast. 'Have I got that?'

'Not yet – well, I don't think so.' He frowned at her like a severe schoolmaster. 'You might come down with it, though, if you don't look after yourself better.'

'I'll take as much time off as you feel I should.'

'Good.'

She felt only relief as she left his surgery. It was almost worth having 'flu to get a week away from the office.

But when she felt no better at the end of that week, she went back to see the doctor feeling seriously worried.

'It gives me no satisfaction to say I told you so,' he commented.

He signed her off for a further seven days, but refused to do it for longer. 'I'm glad to hear that you're resting. It's the only thing to do with viruses. But I want to keep my eye on you. Is there something worrying you? Money? Boyfriend?'

She shook her head. It seemed ungrateful to complain about your job when so many people hadn't got one. 'Just been working too hard, I think.'

It was all she could do to stagger back to her car and drive home, and as she sagged against her front door, she was thankful she hadn't had an accident while driving, so light-headed did she feel.

She knew it was cowardly, but she rang Barbara's direct line at work and asked her to give Mike a message.

'You must be really ill. I'm coming round to see you at lunch-time and no arguments about that, please.'

Her kindness reduced Jessica to tears, but she did need help, understood better now what her mother had told her about having family close to you.

About eleven in the morning the doorbell rang. Jessica, who had been dozing on the bed, stumbled along to answer it. Afraid it might be Mike, come to harass her, she peered out through the security peephole before she opened the door, gasping when she saw who it was.

Jivan!

Oh no! She'd forgotten he was coming to Perth. Why did he have to arrive when she was looking and feeling so awful?

She opened the door and stood blinking at the painful brightness of the autumn sunlight on her watery eyes. She tried to summon a smile, but it was a non-starter. 'Hi, Jivan! I'm afraid I've got the 'flu.'

'Yes, your friend Barbara told me when I rang your work number.'

A wave of dizziness made everything swim round her and she had to clutch the doorframe to steady herself.

'She also told me that you were run down. She's really worried about you. Look, can I come in?'

She felt deeply embarrassed. Fancy leaving him standing on the doorstep! 'Sorry. I'm not – not thinking very clearly at the moment. Aren't you afraid of catching something?' The room was still lurching round her and she put her hand on the wall to hold herself steady.

'I rarely get ill.' He pulled a bunch of flowers from behind his back. 'I thought these might cheer you up.'

'Oh, Jivan, thank you!' Tears filled her eyes. She held the bunch awkwardly, wishing she could smell the flowers, but her nose was too stuffed up.

As she turned, she staggered and Jivan's arm was suddenly there, supporting her.

'Sit down and tell me where your vase is. I'll put these in water for you, then perhaps I could get you something to drink.'

She leaned against him for a moment. His kindness was the final straw. She'd felt so alone and helpless lately, had wept several times. She couldn't stop the tears now.

'What's wrong?'

'It's just you being kind. Oh, damn! I can't s-stop crying.'

He guided her to the couch and she sank down on it, closing her eyes. 'I'm sorry. I can't think properly.'

His voice was coming and going in the distance, and the words weren't making sense. She realised he was kneeling beside her and made a huge effort to understand what he was saying.

'Would you like me to make you a cup of coffee or something, Jessica?'

'I don't think I have any coffee left, or milk. I haven't been able to get out to the shops for a few days.'

She gave in to temptation and let herself lie down, sighing with relief as he pushed a cushion under her aching head.

Jivan's voice cut sharply through the grey mist. 'Jessica, have you been to see a doctor?'

She blinked up at him. 'What? Oh, yes. This morning. He said rest – said I was suffering from stress as well as a virus.'

'And are you? Last time I saw you, you were hoping to take some leave without pay.'

'Mike wouldn't let me. And I don't want to lose my job.'

She heard sounds of water running and opened her eyes to see a vase of flowers standing on the small table near her head. 'Lovely,' she said faintly, then let her eyes close again.

She heard the fridge door open and shut. Footsteps came closer. She felt Jivan's presence beside her.

'Jessica, there's nothing in the fridge. Have you been eating?'

'Not hungry.'

'That's no way to get better! Look, I'll go to the shops and buy you a few things, light invalid food. Will you be all right till I return?'

She thought about sitting up but couldn't be bothered to make the effort. 'There's no need to do that. I've got some stuff in the cupboard.'

'Not much. I looked in there, too.'

'I can't ask you to – to—'

'Who else is there to help you?'

She sniffed and swiped at her sore red nose. 'Barbara would come if I asked.'

'Why haven't you asked, then?'

'She's got her own family to look after. And I don't want to give her this 'flu. I don't want to give you the 'flu, either.'

'I'm staying, so you'll have to put up with me. I'm going to call a taxi and go out to buy you some groceries. We'll talk again when I come back.'

'I haven't got any money. I haven't been able to get to a cash machine.'

'You can pay me back another time. I know you're not going to run away.'

She opened her mouth to protest, but couldn't summon up the energy. 'Thanks.'

He spoke again, his voice echoing somewhere a million miles away from where she was lying. 'Can you let me have a door key, Jessica, then I won't have to wake you up if you're asleep? I'll just call for a taxi first.'

'Key's on the hook near the front door. Car key, too. Car's parked outside. White Honda. Take that.'

'OK. Where's the nearest shopping centre?'

She felt as if she had a head full of grey wool, as if she had to poke each word through it. 'End of street. Turn left. Can't miss it.'

Before he set off, he put a pillow under her throbbing head instead of the cushion. She felt much more comfortable with the cool cotton pillowcase beneath her and let herself drift into sleep – just for a few minutes, just till he came back . . .

When she awoke, it was dusk. A lamp was glowing in the corner of the room and there was a savoury smell wafting across from the kitchen, which was in the short side of the L-shaped living area. She pushed herself up on one elbow and stared round. 'Hello!'

Jivan appeared from the rear of the kitchen and she smiled at the sight of her frilly yellow apron tied round his middle.

'How do you feel, Jessica?'

She considered this for a moment as she yawned. 'A little better, I think. I'm sorry I crashed on you. I've been sleeping badly for the past week. Going out to see the doctor this morning exhausted me.' She yawned again, a huge yawn that nearly cracked her face in two.

His voice was soft. 'Go and have a quick wash, then I'll bring you something to eat. Your friend Barbara phoned, but I told her I was looking after you, so she said she'd come round another day.'

'Nice of her. Nice of you, too.' Jessica couldn't stop yawning. All she really wanted to do was go back to sleep.

It wasn't until she was in the bathroom, staring at her flushed face and sore nose in the mirror that she realised how awful she looked. She cleaned her teeth and tied back her hair, but that was as much as she could manage. By the time she went back into the living room, she was feeling dizzy and distant again.

'Table or a tray?' he called from the kitchen area.

She stood there, swaying. 'I . . .' She couldn't seem to make the decision.

Suddenly he was there beside her, guiding her back to the couch. 'I'll bring you a tray. Sit down, but don't go back to sleep yet. Not till you've had a bowl of my nanny's best broth.'

'Your nanny?'

'Her recipe. She always made it when I was ill.'

'Your grandmother?'

'No. Nanny. As in hired help to bring up the child. My mother led a busy social life. I saw more of Nanny.'

'Oh.' Jessica allowed him to tuck a sheet around her legs, because although the weather was warm, she was feeling shivery now.

A tray appeared on her lap as if by magic and she sat staring at it, finding it hard to summon up the energy even to pick up the spoon.

'If you don't eat it all up, I'll spoon it into your mouth myself,' he threatened.

That made her smile. She took a taste, then another. 'This is good!'

She finished the whole bowlful and let him take the tray away.

This time, she knew she'd said thank you, so she was quite pleased with herself. But she had to lie down, just had to.

Jessica felt totally disoriented when she awoke in the morning and couldn't at first work out why she was on the couch. Then she remembered Jivan helping her.

She got up to go to the bathroom and looked into the kitchen as she passed. Everything was immaculate. How kind of him to tidy up before he left!

But as she passed the spare bedroom, she stopped dead in shock. There he was, sprawled on the narrow single bed next to her computer desk, one foot dangling off the edge. She leaned against the doorway for a moment. He looked younger when he was asleep.

As if he could feel her staring at him, his eyes flickered open and he sat up.

'Jessica! How are you feeling?'

'I'm a bit dopey, but not as dizzy as I was. I'm on my way to the bathroom. You – er – go back to sleep.'

He stretched and smiled lazily at her. 'I'll not need any more sleep. I went to bed early. I haven't had such a long, unbroken sleep in ages. I'll go and put the kettle on, shall I?'

She nodded and went into the bathroom. She felt tears rising in her eyes again at the mere thought of him staying to look after her. 'You're a stupid idiot!' she told the pale face with its red nose that stared back at her from the mirror. 'What the hell is there to cry about?'

She pulled off her smeary glasses and washed them, then managed a quick shower. Afterwards, she realised that she hadn't brought a dressing gown in with her. Her nightdress was a sweaty tangle of cotton on the damp floor and she couldn't bear to put it on again. Wrapped in her towel, she tiptoed out towards her bedroom, hoping to get there without him noticing.

Jivan immediately poked his head out of the kitchen. 'Are you all right?'

'Yes.'

He grinned. 'Very fetching outfit.'

She could feel herself blushing, knowing she was showing a lot of leg. 'I forgot my dressing gown.'

'Do you want breakfast in bed?'

'No, thank you. I'd rather eat at the table with you.' It would be lovely to have company for the meal. She had spent so much time alone here in the last few months.

By the time she got to the table, she was tiring fast and wishing she had gone back to bed.

He pulled a chair out, pushing her firmly into it. 'No, you can't help, and after this, you'll go and lie down again, young lady. Uncle Jivan's orders.'

As he served breakfast, he said, 'I have to go out for some publicity sessions today, but I'll be back later to see to your evening meal. You're not to do a thing while I'm gone, do you hear?

Except stagger to the kitchen around noon for another bowl of my broth.'

'But I can't – you can't— You must have other things to do than look after me!'

'Refusing my help?'

'No, of course not. I just – well, I feel guilty. I mean, I'm not your responsibility.'

'If that's all, you needn't worry. Looking after you is making me feel virtuous. It's a rather unusual feeling for me so I beg you not to deprive me of the experience. I might want to put it in a book one day.'

She chuckled but it was a rusty sound and the effort made her cough.

He waited till she'd finished coughing then asked quietly, 'I'm assuming you want me to stay? Do you? Or would you rather I left you in peace?'

She couldn't lie to him. 'It's lovely to have you here. I don't know how I'd have managed without you.'

'Good. I'll go and get the rest of my things from the hotel while I'm out.'

She was surprised when her spoon clinked against an empty dish. The porridge with dried fruit and nuts in it had been delicious.

'Bed, now!' he said firmly as soon as she had finished, and she couldn't find the strength to argue with him. She had grey clouds inside her head and she ached all over.

She woke briefly around lunchtime, surprised to find she was hungry. In the kitchen she found a note propped against the kettle. 'Soup in fridge. Don't forget! I'm bringing something back for tea.'

This time she was less dizzy, and managed to prepare and eat the food without any problems.

She had intended to stay awake afterwards, but once again her body had its own agenda and she slept the afternoon away, waking only when she heard the front door open.

Jivan appeared in her bedroom doorway. 'Sorry if I woke you.'

She smiled and stretched. 'I was just coming to the surface anyway. Goodness, I can't remember ever sleeping so much.'

He came to sit on the end of her bed. 'You're looking a bit better. There's a faint touch of colour in your cheeks today.'

'And in my nose,' she quipped.

He smiled. 'There, too.' Then he stood up. 'No peace for the wicked. I have some cooking to do.'

'Jivan, you shouldn't be doing this! I—'

'I thought we'd already settled this argument, Jessica. The hotel is taking all my messages, but it's a lot quieter living here so I'm getting a benefit from it, too. Or were you just being polite earlier when you said you'd like me to stay?'

'Of course I like having you here.'

'Then I'll not need to move back to that impersonal hotel room. It's a relief to come back here after a day of meeting strangers, and not to have to dine in the public eye and have people come up to me. Or even worse, dine alone in my room. Those Meridian publicists are slave-drivers, you know. They set up such hectic schedules, I sometimes feel like a mouse on a running wheel.'

'Are you just saying that to reassure me?'

'No. I'm relieved this tour is almost over. Perth is the last stop and things are winding down now, thank goodness, though they added one or two small events which meant I had to stay longer than expected.'

And he was gone, humming to himself as he clattered about in the kitchen.

She lay back and listened to the busy noises and the happy humming, which made her feel less guilty about him staying. You didn't sing if you were unhappy. And he had a nice tuneful voice.

She decided to get up to eat. She still felt weak, but not as bad as she had been. Making a big effort, she got out her best dressing gown, a drifting flowery thing she only wore to cheer herself up when she was feeling down. She felt shy as she went into the kitchen wearing it.

His eyes were searching, but he seemed satisfied with what he saw. 'I like your robe. Very glamorous.'

'It was a present to myself last year. I fell in love with it and I didn't need it, so I made Christmas the excuse to buy it.'

★ ★ ★

Jivan didn't comment on the sadness of a lovely young woman having to buy herself a present. He hadn't even bothered to do anything special at Christmas. His mother had invited him to visit her, but he hadn't felt like making the long flight to the UK.

And anyway, she only wanted to show off her famous son at her parties. She never had been a loving mother. He'd had more love from his father . . . until Ranjit went back to India and started another family.

He had come to realise that Jessica was as lonely as he was. It was the writer's curse, as he knew only too well. You didn't get books written by partying. But if he hadn't been in hiding, he would have spent more time doing things like going to the theatre or seeing the few people he considered true friends.

Unfortunately, whenever he went to the UK Louisa always found out where he was within a day or two, and then the rumours about his lifestyle started again and she played nasty tricks on him, or paparazzi followed him, hoping to get a scoop on a scandal.

What scandal? He was living as celibate a life as any monk at the moment.

'What the hell do you want from me?' he'd asked Louisa the last time she'd caught him on his own in a hotel bar during an unavoidable visit to the UK.

'I want us to get back together.'

'Get together? You must be joking! After all the trouble you've caused me? No way. And how would you benefit from having a husband who hated you?'

'I'd benefit because I'd not have to work. I'm well over running around pushing idiots into the limelight. I *deserve* to enjoy the benefits of your success, have servants and a big house, buy what I want.'

'I don't live like that.' Though he could afford to, he supposed.

'You forget how I helped you when we were first married, when you were starting off as a writer. You *owe* me a share of your success, dammit, and I won't leave you alone until I get it. We could have a marriage in name only, except I'd go to big functions with you.'

Where she had got those ideas from, he didn't know. Sure, she had given him some hints about dealing with the press and presenting himself on TV when they were first married, but that would have meant nothing if his books hadn't taken off. She really had gone beyond reason this time.

He realised he'd been standing lost in thought and looked across at Jessica.

'Are you all right, Jivan?'

'Yes. I was just remembering something.'

'Something unpleasant, from your expression.'

'Yes.'

He banished the thought of Louisa and gave his attention to his sick friend. And yes, he realised, Jessica had become one of his true friends now.

He nodded towards the table. 'If madame would be seated, I'll serve the meal.'

'Thank you, kind sir.'

Jessica had seen that Jivan was deeply upset by his thoughts, but if he'd wanted her to know the details, he'd have told her. She didn't like people prying into her affairs and he was probably the same.

She sat down and watched him serve a chicken casserole, with fluffy mashed potatoes and broccoli. 'I'm feeling hungry again. I haven't felt hungry for ages.' Weeks, actually.

The food tasted as good as it looked and her plate was empty before she knew it. 'You're a very good cook. However did you whip this up so quickly?'

'I'm delighted you approve. But I can't claim all the credit. I bought a cooked chicken, some mushrooms, a packet of mashed potatoes and a jar of my favourite ready-made sauce. But I did open the jar all by myself.'

She laughed. 'Then you're a connoisseur of sauce mixes.'

He inclined his head. 'Why, thank you, ma'am.'

She couldn't quite fathom the look in his eyes tonight. He seemed different from the man in Melbourne in a way she couldn't understand. He's enigmatic, she thought. That's the word. 'There's a cask of white wine in the fridge. Why don't you have a glass with your meal?'

'And you?'

'No, thanks. I'm only just getting my head back together. I don't want to risk losing it again.'

'You sure you don't mind if I have one?'

'Not at all. You've more than earned it.'

He served himself and raised the glass to her before drinking. 'To your recovery, gracious hostess, your complete and lasting recovery.'

She felt shy and breathless. 'Th-thank you.' She couldn't help wondering why he had stayed to look after her. But she was enjoying his company so much she wasn't going to quibble about it.

In fact, just having him there made her feel better. Much better.

Ten

Jivan stayed with Jessica for a week, vanishing during the first couple of days to attend signing sessions and a TV interview. He also attended one evening function.

In between engagements, he shopped for her, cooked for her, washed for them both and cleaned the house, all with practised efficiency. Clearly he was used to living alone and doing for himself.

Best of all, he talked to her. In fact, they talked for hours. About writing, about their views of the world, about books they'd read. Not about his personal problems, though. Or about hers, either.

On the third evening he asked if she would sign his copy of her award-winning novel. 'I like to have author-signed copies of my friends' books.'

She stood frozen for a moment. 'I can't imagine signing a book for you. I have all your books, you know.'

'I'll sign those, if you like. It's a fair return.'

'I'd love it.' Before he could change his mind, she went and got his books from the shelf near her bed. 'Here.' She held out a pen.

He looked at the pile of rather battered volumes. 'You've either lent them to all your friends or you've read them more than once.'

'I haven't lent them to anyone. I've re-read them several times. I love the complexity and cleverness of your stories.'

He stared at her, then started signing, but she rather thought she'd seen a look of pleasure replace the sadness in his eyes.

'You'd make some woman a wonderful housekeeper,' she joked the next evening as she sat down to yet another delicious meal. 'How did you learn to do all this?'

'From books or online. A man has to eat, after all, and in the early days I couldn't afford to eat out all the time.' He stared into space, then added, 'I cooked for my wife too, though she doesn't eat much. She's skeletally thin.'

'It must have been hard to see your love fade.'

'Louisa was never in love. She was interested in being the wife of a famous person and didn't care at all about my books, as long as I was successful. She found it very boring that I had to spend so much time working, though she hid that well at first.'

'Didn't she have any interests of her own?'

'Oh, yes. Herself. After she gave up her work in PR, she began working out at the gym daily to make her body perfect. She loved buying clothes and, as I found out later, enjoyed a little variety in her men. I think she must have been unfaithful almost from the start, but it was three years before I found out. And yet, she didn't want us to divorce.'

'But you did.'

'To me, it's not a marriage if you're unfaithful. The one and only thing we did agree on was that we didn't want any children.'

She looked at him in surprise. 'You sound very vehement about that.'

His expression was sombre. 'The world I was born into wasn't easy for children of mixed race, though it's better now.'

'The world you were born into?'

'My mother's family is very upper crust. I think her affair with my Indian father was her one and only act of defiance – and his. They're both back in their respective folds again, though she changes husbands rather more often than others do. But as

I've found, being a writer doesn't fit with family life and children need parents who are *there*.'

'I'd like to have children one day – if I ever meet anyone suitable.' When he didn't respond, she sneaked a glance sideways and saw that his mouth was a grim straight line, so waited quietly for him to speak.

After a while, he went on, 'I might as well finish the tale, if we're going to stay friends, which I hope we shall do, but after this I don't want to talk about my marriage again. I was the one who insisted on the divorce, and then had to fight to retain even my future income from writing. In the end, I offered Louisa the house and all it contained in return for a final settlement, and threatened to stop writing completely if she asked for more. I have a small private income from a godmother, and she knew I could survive without my writing money.'

Taking a deep breath he added, 'But since I became successful, she's begun stalking me. I love the warmer climate here, but she's the main reason I moved to Australia. I thought she'd gradually turn to other things. Only she hasn't.'

'She must be crazy.'

'Yes. I think she is. I intend to move every year or so, renting a house through my agent under an assumed name.'

'Wow! That's terrible. You shouldn't have to live like that.'

'I think she's mentally ill, but it'd be hard to prove it.'

He sat twisting the empty wine glass between his fingers for a minute or two longer, then looked up. 'That's enough about me.'

She dared to lay her hand briefly on his arm and clasp it for a moment.

'Let's talk about your future now, Jessica. What are you going to do with yourself?'

'What do you mean?'

'Are you really going back to your job? From what you've told me, it sounds as if that man's trying to make your life as miserable as he can.'

'Oh, he's doing more than try. He's succeeding.' Her voice broke on the last syllable and she had to take a deep breath before she could continue without breaking down.

'There's nothing else I can do but soldier on, Jivan. If I could get six months of leave without pay, I might just about manage to live on my savings for that long. But Mike won't allow me any leave at all, not even one lousy week.'

'Why not?'

'Since he missed out on a promotion, he's out to prove he gets results that don't cost the earth, so he's overworking us.'

'Can't you find another job?'

'I'm thinking about it.' She yawned and smiled at him. 'I'm tired now. I think I'll go to bed. I've enjoyed our talk.'

'So have I. Friends now, eh?' Once again he planted a chaste kiss on her cheek.

Once again she wanted more.

She heard him power up his computer and started falling asleep to the faint rattle of his fingers on the keyboard.

She'd never expected to feel sorry for him, but she did.

The next day, while Jivan was out, she sat at the computer for the first time since her illness and spent an hour reading through and revising the last chapter she had written. She felt alive and happy for the first time in weeks, though still rather shaky physically.

She couldn't even think about going back to work yet, and she was sure the doctor would agree.

When the doorbell rang, she exclaimed in annoyance, then automatically saved the file she was working on before going to look out of the peephole. Oh, no! Mike Larreter.

For a moment she thought of not answering, but she knew he would have seen her outline through the frosted glass panels. She opened the door but made no attempt to open the steel mesh security door. 'What do you want, Mike?'

'To see you.'

'Why?'

'To see if you're all right.'

'I'm OK. Getting better slowly. You know what 'flu's like.'

'Open the door and let me in, Jessica. We can't talk like this.'

'We have nothing to talk about that can't be said when I get back to the office.'

He folded his arms and leaned against the wall. 'I'm not going away till I've talked to you properly.'

'Then you'll have to stay there. This is the only way you're going to see me.' She could hear how sharp her voice was and felt the tension rising inside her. The fear, too. She wasn't inviting him into her home, didn't feel safe with him since his attempt to force her into love-making.

Then Jivan appeared, striding along the path towards her unit. Jessica closed her eyes in gratitude to whatever fate had sent him back at that precise moment.

He stopped and stared at Mike, then at her. 'Is everything all right, Jessica?'

'It is now you're back.' With him there, she was no longer afraid to open the door. 'This is Mike Larreter. From work. Mike, this is Jivan Childering.'

The two men nodded, making no attempt to shake hands.

'You're supposed to be ill, not entertaining guests!' Mike's expression was tight and suspicious. 'I really do need to talk to you.'

Reluctantly she let him inside.

Mike scowled at Jivan. 'I need to see Jessica alone. About work.'

Jivan's face was expressionless as he looked at her. She nodded reluctantly, in response to his unspoken question.

'I'll be in my room. You've only to call out if you need help.'

When he'd gone, Mike turned to her, his expression furious. 'What the hell have you been saying to him about me?'

'I haven't told him anything but the truth.'

'Is that writer fellow staying with you?' His eyes narrowed and he studied her blushing face. 'He is.'

'None of your business.'

'I think it is. You can't be all that ill if you're entertaining a lover.'

'For heaven's sake! Jivan's a friend and fellow writer, not a lover.'

'What's he doing here, then? He doesn't live in Perth. I've seen articles on him. He's stinking rich and never settles anywhere for long. And he treated his wife really badly.'

He gestured around him. 'You must be really good in bed if he's putting up with a hovel like this!'

She would not be goaded. 'Jivan's in Perth for publicity sessions. Where he stays has nothing to do with you!'

'No, but what *you* are doing has. I need you back at work ASAP, Jessica. The whole project's stalled without you running it. No one else has your skills. You look well enough to come in, so I'll expect you back tomorrow.'

She let go of her anger and shouted, 'Well, you won't get me back tomorrow! The doctor's signed me off for the whole week and I have to see him again before I can return to work.'

'That's just crap and you know it!'

'I know nothing of the sort!' She fought against an urge to weep, but tears welled in her eyes involuntarily.

He took a deep breath and said through gritted teeth, as if he was having trouble controlling his temper, 'Look, you're putting the whole schedule out. Where's your professional pride?'

'I've been ill, Mike, really ill. Not just 'flu, but stress, if you must know – stress caused by work pressures. Senior management shouldn't be so mean with staffing if they want this project finished quickly. I told you when we started that we'd be lucky to finish by the target date. I even put it in writing! And you agreed with me then, promised you'd try to get someone else to work with me. But you didn't.'

Jivan appeared in the doorway. 'Look, darling, I know you don't like me to interfere, but I promised the doctor I'd see you took it easy.' He came across and put his arm around her possessively.

Surprise kept her silent. Luckily, Mike was staring at Jivan, not at her, with a vicious look on his face. She decided to play along with Jivan, so leaned against him. 'There's no need for you to stay any longer, Mike. I shan't change my mind. I doubt I'll be back at work until the week after next.'

'At the soonest,' Jivan said.

'I'll bring disciplinary charges against you for this, you lazy bitch!'

Jivan let go of her and stepped forward. 'I don't like your language, Mr Larreter. Nor do I understand how someone can be disciplined for being ill.'

'They can be disciplined for *feigning* illness and then using their sick leave for other things, like entertaining their latest lover!'

Jivan's expression was a masterpiece of scorn. 'I don't exactly call it "entertaining" when someone lives here.'

Mike's face turned an unpleasant purple-red. 'You didn't wait long to change lovers, did you?' he threw at Jessica.

'You and I were never lovers and you know it, Mike. I don't think you know what l-love is.' Her voice was shaking and she felt as if her legs wouldn't hold her up for much longer.

Jivan muttered something under his breath, drew her over to the couch and sat her down gently. 'Just when we were beginning to make some progress. Stay there.' He stood up. 'I think your unwelcome visitor is having trouble finding the door. Shall I help you out, Mr Larreter, or can you remember the way?'

The two men were roughly the same height, but suddenly the gentle friend who had looked after her for the past few days had turned into a menacing stranger. It was a side of him Jessica had only seen once before, on the Sally Mennon Show.

'Don't you threaten me!' Mike blustered, but he started edging towards the door.

'Why should I need to threaten you, Mr Larreter? I'm merely suggesting that you leave. Jessica's ill. She can't even cope with one visit from you, let alone come back to work.'

Mike glared at him for a moment longer, then turned abruptly and left. But the look he threw over his shoulder did not bode well for Jessica when she returned to her job.

Jivan was still frowning as he shut the door. 'You can't go back to work with that fellow, Jessica, but I don't see why he should get away with his blackmail. Are you a member of a trade union?'

'Well, yes. Barbara suggested I join. Why?'

'I'll call them for you. He's harassing you. They'll probably have an officer out here within the hour to check things out.'

'Is that really necessary, Jivan? Look, I'll just resign and – and then . . .' Her voice wobbled and she couldn't finish the sentence.

'No, you won't resign! Not yet, anyway. That way Larreter wins. And afterwards he'll treat other people in the same way. Bullies need pulling up short. I learned that when I was very young.'

With bewildering speed, a union official, Linda, turned up to see her. Jessica tried to explain what had happened, dissolved into tears and Linda made an emergency appointment with her doctor.

'I'll leave you in Linda's care,' Jivan said. 'I have another appointment. You have my contact number if you need me. Don't hesitate to use it.'

'I'm sorry.'

'What for?'

'Giving you all this trouble.'

'You didn't make the trouble, Mike did, and it's my own choice to help a friend.' He kissed her cheek, an impersonal brush of the lips, then left.

'Is that *the* Jivan Childering?' Linda asked in awed tones.

'Yes.'

'The writer?' Still there was an echo of disbelief in her voice.

'Yes.'

'And he's a friend of yours?'

'Mmm.' Jessica realised suddenly that Jivan really did feel like a friend now – a good friend. 'I'm a writer, too, in my spare time.'

'Wow!'

Later that day, after the doctor had confirmed that she was still unfit for work, the union contacted her department, and Bob Courcey, the Director responsible for their area, turned up to see her. He questioned her closely but gently about what had happened.

Linda stayed with them, interjecting quietly, but not displaying any aggression. Well, it would be hard to be aggressive with Bob. He was a large, gentle rock of a man, famous for never raising his voice, whatever the provocation.

Later, he phoned Jivan on his mobile to ask for details of Larreter's threatening behaviour today. 'It's not that I disbelieve you, but it's better to obtain all the facts first hand.'

Bob left shortly afterwards, assuring them both that the harassment would stop immediately. At the door, he clasped Jessica's hand for a moment. 'Why didn't you come to me for help before? This overworking you has obviously been going on for some time.'

'I . . . don't like making a fuss.'

He pressed her hand then let it go. 'You won't be bothered by that man again, I promise you. In fact, you won't have to work with him at all after you come back. I'll make sure of that.'

He saw how troubled she was looking and added, 'This isn't a complete surprise to me, you know. Larreter's always been rather cavalier in the way he uses staff. That's why he didn't get the promotion when he was on secondment. And why he will be sidelined with us from now on.'

When Bob had gone, Linda coaxed Jessica to lie down then left her to rest. The sickness certificate from the doctor now read two more weeks and Jessica supposed Mike would be reprimanded for being over-officious.

She lay, feeling exhausted, and began mentally drafting her resignation. If she had to wash dishes or work as a waitress to support herself, she would, but she wasn't willing even to work in the same department as Mike Larreter.

She had never been this ill before in her whole life and it terrified her how long it was taking to recover.

What would she have done without Jivan?

She had a much better understanding now of her mother's desperation to return to England. It was terrifying to be completely on your own, with no one to turn to, and because of her writing she hadn't made strong networks of friends.

Should she go back to live in England?

No, she couldn't bear that either. Her family wouldn't say 'told you so' but they'd think it.

But what was she going to do?

She was still trying to work it out as she drifted off into a troubled doze.

Eleven

The next morning, Jessica woke up early. She felt a little lethargic, but her head was clear and she was ravenous. Jivan's bedroom door was closed, so she tiptoed into the kitchen, quietly put on the kettle and some bread in the toaster. He must have got back late last night. She hadn't heard him come in, though she'd tried to stay awake.

When the toast was ready, she turned round to get the butter and found him leaning against the doorframe, watching her with a strange expression on his face. 'Oh, Jivan! You made me jump! Did I wake you?'

'No. How are you feeling today?'

She smiled. 'Hungry, as you can see.'

'Not dizzy?'

'A bit weak still, but my head's clear.'

'Good. Your eyes look brighter, too.'

'Jivan, I—'

'Jessica, I—'

They both broke off and then smiled at each other. The kettle came to the boil and bubbled on until it switched itself off.

When Jessica still didn't move, Jivan reached across her towards the jar of tea bags. 'Why don't you go and sit down? I'll make the tea. There's something I'd like to discuss with you after breakfast.'

'All right.' They were both in their night clothes, and she felt suddenly shy. She concentrated on spreading jam carefully into every corner of the golden toast, then was suddenly unable to resist taking a huge bite, and another.

'You seem hungry. That's a good sign.'

She paused with the toast halfway to her mouth. 'Aren't you going to eat anything, Jivan?'

'Later.' He stared into his cup, frowning as if something was worrying him.

She wondered if he had to leave and was trying to tell her so gently. He did, after all, have his own life to think about, and another book to write. 'Is something wrong?'

'Not wrong, exactly, but I do have one or two concerns I'd like to share with you.' He took a deep breath. 'My mother is one of my concerns. She's pressing hard for me to visit her in America.'

'Oh?' Jessica tried to keep her tone non-committal.

He swirled the tea round in his mug. 'I can't do that just now. Anyway, I'm not close to her, though I get on all right with my half-brothers. Well, who wouldn't? They're pleasant guys who've had everything easy. They found nice women to marry and have charming children. Thomas, the older one, will inherit the family estate and currently manages it for his father, who's had a minor stroke. Lucas, the younger one, is a lawyer, a partner in a nearby practice. They're inseparable, as you'd expect from twins.'

'Why is your mother so eager for you to visit her?'

'She's what you'd call a socialite and desperately wants to be seen with her famous son – even though that son doesn't enjoy her sort of social life. If she knew where I was living, she'd have descended on me here, I'm sure.'

'Your family don't know where you live?'

'No one does, except my agent and editor. Emil manages my interface with the world and has kept it hidden, and Anna . . . Well, you've met her. She's been more like an aunt than an editor to me.'

'It sounds like the material for a novel to me, a story at the glitz end of the spectrum.'

'You could write a very long novel about my life, but I doubt people would enjoy it.' His voice was so low she had to strain to hear it as he added, 'I don't enjoy the recent complications, that's for sure.'

'Your wife?'

He nodded.

She couldn't resist laying her hand on his. 'I'm sorry.'

He took her hand, holding it in both of his, and looked her straight in the eyes. 'I'm not asking for pity, Jessica. I know I've got problems now, but there were benefits to my upbringing as well, and in many ways, it's made me what I am, a successful author.'

'What about your biological father? Is he still alive?'

'Oh, yes. He lives in India, where I'm sure he's surrounded by luxury and servants. After he went back, he made a good marriage and had three children. It's ironic, really. In England I was considered by some members of the family as too Indian to fit in, yet my *Indian* father hasn't once tried to get in touch with me since he left England when I was nine. Perhaps I'm too English for him and his new family. My mother made sure I had a thoroughly English upbringing, but even she can't change the colour of my skin and how I look.'

Clearly he found this painful. 'Perhaps you should try to find out how he really feels? If you haven't been in touch, you're only guessing. Why don't you go and see him?'

'No way. I don't even know his address.' He tried to laugh, but it was a failure, a sad little sound.

Jessica still had no idea of what Jivan wanted, but if he was going to ask a favour of her, any favour, she'd be more than happy to oblige. She owed him so much, didn't know how she'd have managed without him this past week.

The doorbell went. 'Damn!' He stood up. 'I'll go.'

It was a courier with a letter, for which Jessica had to sign. When he'd gone, she came back to the table and sat looking at the departmental logo on the envelope. 'I don't want to open it, Jivan.'

'Shall I open it for you?'

'Would you? I know I'm being a coward, but I can't help thinking that it might be from Mike and . . .' Her voice trailed away.

He scanned the single page and then passed it to her. 'Nothing to worry you. It's not from him, but the CEO of your department, and a copy has gone to your union.'

She took the letter from him. It expressed regret that she had been upset in any way, due to an unfortunate misunderstanding (unspecified). The Director urged her to take as long as she needed to recover fully from her illness.

She looked up and smiled. 'It's from the Big Panjandrum – that's what us lesser mortals call him, anyway. It's an apology. He won't be happy with Mike about this – and that'll make Mike even angrier with me. Anyway, that won't matter because I came to a decision last night. I'm going to resign and concentrate on my writing, for a few months at least. I'll make do with the computer I've got, live very frugally and—'

He touched her lips very gently with the tip of one forefinger. 'Let me say my piece first, then. I have a better suggestion – well, I think it's better – and it may help you decide what to do.'

'You won't persuade me to stay on at work, whatever my rights are,' she warned. Although his hands were now lying on the table again, she could still feel the soft, warm touch of his finger on her lips.

'I won't try to. Jessica, look, I don't know how to put this tactfully, but— Well, I think we can help each other. I have a few friends in the UK, all the money I need, but at the moment

I'm better staying out of the country most of the time. It's been lonely in Australia and I'm still pestered by female fans when I go out and about. You saw how it happened in the restaurant in Melbourne and you defused it nicely. I find it both distasteful and embarrassing and I admit I don't handle it well sometimes.'

'I can imagine.'

'And then there's my ex, as I've explained.' He pushed his chair back abruptly and began to pace the room, three steps to the window, three steps back, words coming in short bursts.

Her heart ached for his stiff anguish but he still hadn't said what he was proposing.

He came to a halt beside her. 'You're very easy to be with, Jessica. You don't fuss. You're not trying to throw yourself at me.'

He paused for so long she asked, 'I'm not quite sure where this is leading.'

'I'm trying to ask you to come and live with me.'

'What?' Hope flared, dying almost immediately as she looked at his face. This wasn't an amorous proposition – unfortunately.

'And I'm asking a little more than that. Would you also pretend to be my – er – my live-in girlfriend? In public, that is. I can assure you that I'll not annoy you with my attentions when we're alone together.'

'That seems rather an extreme solution. Why don't you just buy a flat in a security block?'

'I'd hate to live in a flat. I think this idea would be a good solution for me and my mother won't butt in if she thinks I'm with someone. And if Louisa hears about us, she may accept that I've found someone else and I'm never having her back.'

Jessica could only stare at him, not knowing what to say.

'I need time to write my next book, Jessica – time and peace. And so do you. You'd have no expenses, since I have a spare bedroom and, well, what do you think?'

'I don't know.' She'd give anything to be his live-in girlfriend if he loved her, but she wasn't sure she could pretend affection in public and then switch it off when they were alone. She'd be bound to give herself away. At least as things stood now, they were friends.

He took a deep breath and said in a rush, 'As I said, it would be necessary to act in a loving manner in public. That's why it's such an imposition, why I've hesitated to ask you, but having seen what you've been going through, I think it would be a good solution for you as well. I can promise I won't intrude on your writing time very often.'

It was her turn to struggle for words. 'I'm not good at telling lies, Jivan.'

'I know. Your honesty is one of the things I like about you. No pretence. No posturing. No complaining and bitching, either.'

Goodness, she thought, what on earth had his marriage been like?

He still kept his distance physically, using only words to bridge the gap between them. 'You've become a very special friend, Jessica.'

She had to ask. 'And what if one of us falls in love with someone else? What happens then?'

He shrugged. 'You might fall in love. I definitely shan't. I have no belief whatsoever in romantic love. It's an illusion. I don't deny that attractions occur – physical attractions, anyway – but I don't believe that romantic relationships can last in real life, and I don't intend to chase any more mirages.'

'That's why your hero always walks away at the end of the book.' She spoke without thinking.

'Perhaps. But I like to write stories about Sam Shere, so I need to keep him unattached romantically. It's strange, how real he seems to me now.' He took another deep breath. 'I'm not asking this lightly, Jessica. I've thought it over very carefully. If you had no living expenses, you could concentrate on your writing. And I'd enjoy your company when we're not writing. I, um, get a bit lonely at times.'

She didn't know how to answer, but that last admission made her heart break for him. She sat tracing the pattern of the tablecloth with one fingertip. 'It still seems a strange solution, more like something out of a gothic romance.'

'Perhaps I'm a strange sort of man. I sometimes think so. Will you at least think it over? Or are you turning it down straight away? If you are, I won't pester you, but—'

'I'm not turning it down, but I do need to think about it, Jivan.'

'Yes, of course. Now, I must get ready. I'll be out all day. I'm doing research, seeing a guy about some gadgets he's invented, which might fit into my next story.'

'Will you be back for tea?'

'Yes, but don't try to cook anything. We can get some Chinese takeaway.'

After he'd left, she sat for a while, staring blankly into space, then went to switch on her computer. She had a sudden idea and decided to make notes about it. As usual, she forgot everything when she started writing, not even bothering to get washed and dressed.

She spent over an hour revising the last couple of chapters and adding a new scene. She hadn't felt so happy in a long time. If she had uninterrupted time every day . . . Oh, Jivan's offer was so very tempting.

When she grew tired, she lay down on the bed to read and didn't wake up until nearly noon and even then she certainly wasn't full of energy. In fact, her recovery hadn't been nearly as quick as she'd hoped. She'd researched chronic fatigue syndrome online and was desperate to avoid that complication.

She really did need rest and somewhere peaceful to live.

But Jivan didn't want a relationship, just a calm, friendly arrangement, and she wanted more. She had been half in love with him from the first time they met, when he presented her prize. The past few days, the way he'd looked after her had only made her fall more deeply in love with him.

Could she hide her own feelings if she lived with him? She could try . . . would try. Oh, face it, Jessica, she told herself. You'd live with him on any terms. Some liberated woman you are! she mocked herself.

It was a relief when the phone rang. 'Jivan Childering, please!' said a man's voice before she could speak.

'I'm sorry. He's not here at the moment. Can I take a message?'

'It's the *Southern Herald* newspaper. We'd like to arrange an interview with Mr Childering.'

'You'll have to ask him about that.'

'Aren't you his secretary?'

'No. I'm just a friend. I believe you should ring him at the Hyatt.'

'Thank you. We'll do that. Miss Lord, isn't it? Are you a close friend of Mr Childering?'

She put the receiver down abruptly, realising that the reporter had been stringing her along in order to pump her for information. As she started to walk towards the kitchen, the phone rang again. She let it ring through to the answering system and heard the same voice, so didn't try to pick up.

Within seconds the phone rang a third time. She took an uncertain step away from it and stood hesitating, not knowing what to do. How on earth had they found out he was here?

No one had known except a few people at work and why would they— And then she realised. Mike Larreter must have done this. As payback. Who else could it be?

After a while, the phone stopped ringing. She waited, nerves on edge, but nothing happened.

This sort of thing would happen regularly if she lived with Jivan. How did he stand it?

Could *she* bear it?

Twelve

Later, Jessica went across to the window and stared out. No one was in sight.

Jivan wasn't the only one who got lonely.

She put the kettle on. 'Well, at least someone is coming home at teatime,' she said aloud.

'They say it's the first sign of madness, talking to yourself,' someone said from outside the open window, and chuckled.

Jessica stared at the figure framed in the window. 'Barbara! What are you doing here in the middle of a working day?' She rushed to open the door.

Barbara dumped a massive bouquet of flowers on top of the table and flung her arms round Jessica. 'We've all been so *worried* about you! If your Jivan hadn't phoned me a couple of times to say he was still looking after you, I'd have been round before this.'

Another hug, then Barbara held her at arm's length to scrutinise her face closely. 'You look as if you've lost weight and you're paler than usual. Shouldn't you be sitting down?' Not waiting for an answer to any of her questions, she guided Jessica across the living area and plumped down beside her on the couch, talking all the time, as usual.

'Oh, it's sheer heaven to be out of the office on a sunny day! I'm here on the Big Panjandrum's orders, no less. Flowers, courtesy of the department. And I'm to make sure that you're all right – do your shopping, if needed, whatever!'

'Goodness! That's star treatment!'

'Mike's going round looking like a thundercloud. Our eager beaver manager has got himself in everyone's black books. And that couldn't have happened to a more deserving person.'

'He'll worm his way out of it again.'

'Not in our department, he won't. The union's been in and has demanded a written apology from him.' She fumbled in her handbag and held out a slightly crumpled envelope. 'This is it.'

'File it where it belongs, in the rubbish bin. The mere sight of his handwriting makes me feel dizzy again.'

Barbara chuckled. 'No sooner said than done. He didn't mean a word of the apology, anyway, so who cares what he wrote?'

She came back and sat down, her voice gentler. 'How are you coping, though? Who's doing your shopping?'

Jessica flushed. 'Jivan is. He's been staying with me. He's—'

Barbara grabbed her arm, bouncing up and down on the couch in her excitement. 'Oh, wow! Tell all! Did Mike run into him when he came round to harass you?'

'Well, yes. He did.'

'No wonder he was so furious. Oh, if only I'd been a fly on the wall! Wait till I tell the girls about this.'

'Barbara, you mustn't!'

'I'd find it hard to stop myself, dear! Our pet rat needs taking down a few hundred pegs.' She saw Jessica's expression and grimaced. 'But it would make things worse for you when you came back to work, wouldn't it, if I spread the good news? What a pity!'

And that reminder of what it was like at work was the final straw. 'I'm not coming back. Don't say anything because I haven't resigned yet, but I shall do. I mean it about wanting to write,

Barbara. I asked for some leave without pay, but Mike refused, so . . .' she shrugged.

'They might allow you to take leave now.'

'No. I've made my mind up. I couldn't return to that sort of institutional life. It's less real in there than on my imaginary planet. No, I'm leaving.' She felt as if a huge burden had been lifted at the thought of never having to work with Mike Larreter again, preferably never even seeing him again. And also of not spending her days in offices that didn't even have windows, just blank walls and partitions, with every noise echoing around you.

'Would you like a cup of coffee, Barbara?'

'I'd love one. But I'll make it. I've brought us a quiche for lunch and a salad platter. You haven't eaten yet, have you? Are you hungry?'

'Very hungry.'

The phone rang.

'Leave it!'

Barbara gave her a puzzled look. 'Is Mike still pestering you? Because if so—'

'No. It's probably the press. They've found out Jivan's staying with me. Someone rang from the *Southern Herald*. I didn't twig straight away that they were trying to dig up information. They had my name already, though, goodness knows how.'

'Does it matter so much?'

Jessica nodded. 'Yes, it does. Jivan has a stalker and he needs to keep where he's living secret!'

'It's just like a soapie! Wait for the next exciting instalment . . .' She saw the frown on Jessica's face and said softly, 'I won't say a word to anyone, love – not till your romance hits the headlines, at least, then I'll look unbearably smug and say I knew about it all along.'

'It's not a romance.' She only wished it were.

'Oh, come on. Who are you kidding? Your whole face softens when you say his name.' She held up one hand. 'I won't tease you. Sit down at the table and Madame Barbara, famous chef de takeaway, will dish up the quiche.'

Once the meal was over, they drew up a shopping list together, then Barbara went out to stock up the larder. While she was away, Jessica arranged the flowers, then had another little rest which turned into a nap.

She woke when Barbara returned and they unpacked together, giggling over the latest departmental rumours and gossip. Eventually Barbara sighed. 'I suppose I'd better get back on the treadmill for the last hour. Can I just ask? How serious is this Jivan thing?'

Jessica flushed. 'We're only good friends. Unfortunately.'

'But *you* wish it were more?'

'Yes. But it isn't. And don't – don't believe anything you see about us in the papers or online. Don't believe we're together in that way unless I tell you. I'll keep in touch, but I think I'll be moving away from here soon.'

'Make sure you do keep in touch.'

'I will. I'm not so over-supplied with friends that I can abandon one as good as you.'

Which won her another of Barbara's hugs.

'People are asking about you. They like you, you know. You could have had more friends if you'd gone out with the others more often.'

'And then I'd not have had time for my writing. It's a catch twenty-two situation, isn't it?'

As she stood at the door waving, there was a flash. It took a moment for it to register that someone had taken a photo of her.

She darted back inside and slammed the door. She'd have to get used to this sort of thing now, because she was going to accept Jivan's offer.

Happiness filled her. She was going to write full-time *and* spend her days with Jivan.

For a time, at least.

She would make the most of it.

Jivan came home just after six o'clock, by which time Jessica had a simple beef casserole simmering in the oven and had set the table. He stopped in the doorway to sniff appreciatively and say, 'Mmm. Delicious!'

'You haven't tasted it yet.'

'How did you get the ingredients? I had the car.'

'Barbara came to see me and did some shopping.'

'I think her visit must have done you good. You're looking more cheerful.' He stretched, rolling his shoulders about as if he was very stiff. 'I tried to call you at lunchtime, but the phone was engaged.'

She took a deep breath. 'I wasn't answering it anyway.' There was no easy way to break the news. 'Jivan, the press seem to have found out that you're staying with me. And they knew my name as well as the phone number.'

His lips became a thin bloodless line and his hands clenched into tight fists. '*You* didn't say anything to anyone, so who can have done this?'

'Not Barbara. I trust her absolutely.'

'That only really leaves one person at your department, doesn't it?'

'Yes. It's exactly the sort of thing Mike would do. Besides, who else could have given them my home phone number? It's ex-directory.'

'What did you say to the press?'

'More than I should have done. I'm so sorry. It took me a while to realise what was happening. By then I'd said enough to confirm my name and give away the fact that I'm not your secretary.'

She was frightened by the depth of anger on his face and said quickly, 'I'm not used to dealing with them, Jivan. And – and I'll perfectly understand if you want to move out of here and take back your offer.'

'Do *you* want me to move out?'

'No, of course I don't!'

He merely raised an eyebrow at her, his expression chill and supercilious. 'Does that mean that you've decided to accept my offer?'

'Yes. If . . . well, can we discuss what the arrangements would be after dinner?' She didn't want to discuss it while he was so angry. To change to a safer topic, she added quickly, 'Barbara not only brought the flowers, she brought a written apology from Mike. I threw it away unopened.'

'It's all it deserves. And yes, we'll talk after dinner. What time are we eating?'

His smile was an effort but perhaps it was a sign that his anger was dying down. 'It'd be better if the casserole had another half-hour in the oven, but whenever you like after that.' She pressed her lips together to stop herself babbling on, though it was tempting to try to fill the heavy silence.

'I've time for a shower, then. Is that convenient, Jessica?'

'Of course.'

He stopped as he was leaving the room and spoke more naturally. 'Your hair looks pretty and it's nice to have dinner waiting, but don't overdo things, will you? These viruses can hang around for months, even years, if you don't allow yourself time to recover properly.'

With that, he was gone, and she was left to finish setting the table and figure out what she needed to ask him. After a while she shook her head, picked up the newspaper he'd brought back with him and began to leaf through it.

As they ate, Jivan gradually relaxed, telling her about his day. 'The scientist was very useful. His work fits in well with an idea I have for my next book. After I left him I did some personal shopping, then I walked along the Swan River foreshore. Perth is a stunning location! I don't know why I haven't been here before. I think I'll set a story here.'

A little later he said casually, 'I nearly forgot. I just heard that they're going to release the film of *Shere Murder* earlier than originally planned. Maybe, if things go well, you could come to the Australian premiere with me. Or even the UK premiere. I shall definitely have to go to that.'

'I'm looking forward to seeing it. It's such a powerful story. I hope they haven't spoiled it.' She studied him, head on one side. 'I think you're trying to be like Sam.'

He grimaced. 'I sometimes wish I were like him, that's for sure. Life might be easier if one could be totally ruthless about other people's feelings. As it is, I was brought up not to create waves and to maintain a calm public face, whatever my personal feelings.'

'My mother was a bit that way. She always used to say, "What will the neighbours think?" as if that was crucial to any situation.' Jessica saw him relax still further.

'Did she really care about the neighbours?'

'Oh, yes! And she hasn't changed. She still worries about them and the people at her church, too.' She hesitated, then couldn't help adding, 'The press goads you into losing your self-control sometimes, though, don't they?'

'Unfortunately, yes. And certain members of the press are particularly good at it. There's a man called Frenton, a friend of my ex, who seems to take great delight in treading on my tender spots.'

'I'm not trying to be inquisitive, Jivan, but if I decide to accept your offer, if we're going to live together, I'll need to understand how you really feel about things, if only so that *I* won't tread on your toes.'

He looked at her, his face expressionless suddenly. 'And the same applies to me. But I've been able to talk to you more easily than to most people. I think we'll both gradually learn where to tread lightly.'

And although she admired the hero he'd created, the totally self-contained Sam Shere wasn't the sort of man who would ever have attracted her. Underneath the public Jivan, she rather suspected there was a badly hurt boy who had hungered for love all his life, and then married a cold-hearted woman who had ripped his feelings to shreds. The wounds might not show, but they were there nonetheless.

Jessica remembered how she'd retreated into herself when she'd been dragged back to England as a child. She'd become more an observer than a participant at the family gatherings.

That sudden loss of her sunny childhood had set her on the path she was now following. Tomorrow's path might take her in another direction entirely – well, it definitely would if she took up Jivan's offer.

She spoke without thinking. 'I'm glad you're not like Sam Shere, Jivan. He's too hard, too perfectly in control of himself. A person like that would be impossible to live with.'

'I'm not sure sometimes that *I* am possible to live with,' he said in a low voice.

'You seem very reasonable to me.' She could feel her cheeks grow warmer as he stared at her. 'And you can't get much closer quarters than this small unit to test that out.'

A reluctant smile spread across his face, '*Merci du compliment, chérie*.' He blew her a mock kiss. 'Turning to a more mundane subject – may I have another helping? You're obviously a talented cook, as well as a brilliant writer. This sauce is not from a packet.'

She smiled. 'No. It's an old family recipe. Auntie Ida's Beef Pot. I'm glad you like it.'

There was a sudden banging on the door.

Jivan frowned at her. 'Expecting someone?'

'Definitely not.'

'I'll answer it, then.'

'Thanks.' She turned to face the door. Something told her that this interruption did not bode well.

'Press.' A camera flashed.

'*How dare you*!'

The anger in Jivan's face and voice made her rush across the room before he could do something the press could twist the wrong way. 'Darling!' She clutched his arm. 'Don't get upset! We knew this was bound to happen.'

The man stared through the fly screen door, his eyes flickering from her face to Jivan's. 'I could keep your address secret if you give me an exclusive interview. How long have you known one another?' The way he said 'known' was an insult in itself.

Jivan set Jessica firmly aside and spoke to the reporter. 'I'm about to close the door. I shall not open it again.'

Jessica stared at him. Years of aristocratic breeding suddenly seemed to radiate from him. Not to mention powerful anger.

There was a moment's absolute silence, then he started to close the door. The camera flashed again, through the window this time. She came out of her shock and ran to draw the curtains.

When she turned back, Jivan was still standing with his back pressed against the door, hands clenched by his sides. He looked so bitter and unhappy, she walked across and laid her hand on his shoulder.

With an inarticulate murmur, he pulled her into his arms, resting his cheek against her hair, as if he needed comfort. 'I'm sorry, Jessica. I shouldn't let them get to me like that. But nowhere seems to be safe from their prying, not even here, where I felt as though I'd found asylum.'

'It is annoying to have them poking their noses into our lives like that.' She could have stayed in his arms for ever, but when he moved his head away from hers and stepped back, she forced herself to follow suit.

'Did the public "darling" mean that you're going to accept my offer?' he asked, his voice so low that she could barely hear him.

'Yes, I am. If you haven't had second thoughts.'

'It's definitely what I want.' He looked into her eyes, his own very serious, very beautiful and very sad. 'Are you sure, Jessica? It's *your* reputation that'll suffer, for I have none left.'

'I'm sure.'

'I feel I'm taking advantage of your troubles and that doesn't seem at all fair.'

From somewhere she managed to summon up a smile and say calmly, 'Don't be silly! I'm old enough to be responsible for my own life decisions and you're offering me a golden opportunity to write full-time.'

'Then I'm honoured, Jessica, and I can't resist accepting. I think we'll deal very well together, don't you?'

'It won't be my fault if we don't. What do you want to call our relationship in public?'

He ran a hand through his hair, rumpling it. 'People have *partners* all the time these days. Would that term suit you?'

'Fine by me. And if they ask about the future, why don't we just smile and insist we're getting to know one another better?'

'Yes. What will your family say? Your mother particularly.'

'She won't be pleased, but it's my life, my decision. I'll phone them in a day or two. Better if they hear the news from me. Um – I'd prefer to let my family think we're in love, if you don't mind.'

'What will your parents think of my being part Indian?'

Her smile was rueful. 'I don't think my mother will mind that aspect. It's the *living in sin* that will upset her.'

'You don't mind my background at all, do you?'

'What, after all the aliens I associate with?' Then she saw that he was in no mood to turn something so important to him into a joke, so she added softly, 'No, I don't care one way or another, Jivan. I'm more concerned that you're a nice person to be with.'

'I'm not sure I'm even that. When I'm writing, I lose touch with the things and the people around me for days on end and become totally immersed in my tale.'

'How wonderful! Can I do that, too? I've never had the opportunity to lose myself in a story for hours on end, let alone days.'

His smile became warm and friendly again, and he leaned across to clasp her hand. 'Then it's agreed. Do you have any champagne? I think our decision calls for a toast.'

'Only some cheap Aussie champers.'

'Cheap Aussie champers will do very well, thank you.'

'It's in the fridge. Barbara got it for me when she did the shopping. She knows it's one of my favourite drinks.'

'Talk about the lucky country.' He laughed as he crossed the room. 'Only in Australia would champagne be regarded as a cheap drink, one to be apologised for.' He returned a few minutes later with two brimming glasses. 'You're not having more than one glass tonight, young lady. You're only just starting to recover.'

She raised the glass in a toast. 'Here's to us. And thank you, Jivan. Thank you for everything.'

He clinked glasses with her and his eyes held hers for a moment. 'Here's to our friendship, Jessica!'

And with that she had to be content. It was all he had to offer. Or all he *thought* he had to offer. She didn't know whether there was hope for more, but she intended to find out.

Thirteen

By the weekend, Jessica was feeling a lot better. She felt they both needed a break, so suggested a drive out and lunch somewhere. They wound up in Mandurah, the holiday town an hour's drive south of Perth that she visited occasionally, and stopped to explore it.

As they strolled along the foreshore in the autumn sunshine, they saw dolphins frolicking in the water. One had a baby with it, swimming next to its mother's side as if held in place by elastic. Jivan stopped, his face alight. 'Oh, look! How gorgeous!'

They exchanged glances. 'Are you thinking what I'm thinking?' she asked cautiously. He'd told her on the way down that it was time he changed houses.

He nodded. 'Yes. Let's find an estate agent.'

There were plenty of ordinary houses to let, but Jivan insisted they needed a larger than average place, and that was more difficult. The third agent they spoke to, a laconic man called Ed, who didn't seem particularly interested in helping them, shrugged and said dubiously, 'You might look at some of the canal properties, but all the best ones on our books are for sale, not to rent. I've only got a couple of houses to let there and the rents are high.'

'We'd like to see them,' Jivan said. 'My – um, employer won't mind.'

'Easier if I drive you.' Ed heaved himself out of his chair and led them out to the back, where a late model Mercedes was parked out of the sun. He clearly hadn't recognised Jivan.

They visited the two rental houses but weren't satisfied. They were on small blocks of land, very close to the nearby houses.

'Pity you aren't buying,' Ed said. 'I've got a cracker of a house going for a bargain price.'

'Show us,' Jivan said. 'It won't hurt to look.'

Within ten minutes they were there. Ed eased himself out of the car and gestured to a large white house in a very modern box shape. 'Owner built it for his retirement and died of a heart attack before it was finished, poor sod. His wife doesn't want to live here on her own. She's not short of money, so she just wants to get rid of it as soon as possible. Any decent offer will secure it.'

Jessica didn't think much of the outside, but was delighted with the inside. All the main living areas overlooked the water and were large, airy rooms. The two main bedrooms upstairs had en suite bathrooms and also overlooked the man-made canals. Pelicans swam past, moving this way and that in a perfectly synchronised ballet.

Jivan had to nudge her to continue their inspection of the house, which had five bedrooms in all, a games room, huge casual living areas and elegant formal entertaining areas.

When they'd finished the tour, Ed said, 'Why don't you two go round again? Take your time. I've got my iPad with me.'

Jivan turned to Jessica as the door closed behind Ed. 'Your face has already given you away. He knows perfectly well that you love the place.'

'Oh, dear. I'm sorry.'

He chuckled. 'I like it, too. Let's walk round again and decide how we could divide it up if we lived here.'

'But you didn't want to buy a house, just rent.'

'I can afford it.'

'What about the press?'

'The street side of the house is the rear, and the whole place is like Fort Knox, so there's poor access unless people come past on the water. And even from there I don't think they'll be able to see into the rooms on the canal side. Didn't Ed say they have some special sort of glass on the windows to keep the sun out?'

'Yes. Do you really, truly want to live here? Since you're paying, it has to be your decision.'

'I'll buy it, then.'

She gaped at him. 'Just like that?'

'Exactly like that. There are some advantages to being a best-selling author. But my agent will complete the sale for me so that my name isn't on any of the papers people see.'

'That's wonderful.' She couldn't resist it. She twirled round, spreading her arms out and making happy noises, then realised how silly she must look and stopped, blushing.

He stepped forward and held out his arms. 'May I have the next dance?'

She walked into his arms. 'Certainly.'

He began to hum a waltz tune and they circled the room solemnly, then he let go of one of her hands and pulled her towards him. Without hesitation she lifted her face for a kiss. It was only the lightest touch of his lips, but it seemed to set the seal on a very happy day.

When he moved away and offered his arm, she tucked her hand in it and they went round the house yet again.

'Now, let me see if I can still drive a hard bargain,' he said. 'I'm pretty sure I get that skill from my father.'

When they got back to Perth, Jessica was still radiating happiness and Jivan watched her in both surprise and amusement. He had never met a woman who took so much pleasure in simple things.

The fact that he was becoming fond of Jessica was beginning

to worry him a little. He realised she'd said something and was waiting for an answer. 'Sorry. I was miles away.'

'How soon can we move in?' she repeated patiently.

'I'll have to go back to Queensland and sort things out there first. Not to mention getting a removal firm in to transport my personal effects a few thousand miles.'

'We can move down to Mandurah as soon as you get back and camp out on my furniture to start with.' She looked round her villa and pulled a wry face. 'That house makes this seem even more poky, doesn't it?'

'Mmm.' He hesitated, then gave in to temptation. 'Will you come across to Queensland with me, Jessica, and help me decide what to keep and what to sell? Apart from anything else, a holiday would do you good.'

'Are you sure?'

'Yes.'

'Well, I've never been to Queensland, so I'd like that. Only I don't want to cause you too much expense.'

He laughed and pulled her towards him for a hug. 'Jessica, you are the least expensive female I've ever met. It'll be really good to have your company.'

'Then I accept.' She moved out of his arms. 'I'll have to pack up my own things as well. I've bought a few pieces since I came here, because it was so minimally furnished. We could use my furniture in the unimportant rooms like my office, to save a bit of money.'

'Would you be offended if I said I'd prefer to get new furniture? I don't like rooms to look . . . ad hoc.'

'Isn't that a bit of a waste?'

'I'm not exactly short of money and I feel I more than earn my creature comforts.'

'I'll give the things to my favourite charity, then. And I'll resign from my job tomorrow. I'll keep my car, though, so that I have transport of my own in Mandurah.'

He hesitated, then shook his head. 'I'm afraid you can't do that. They'll be able to trace your car. I'll lease one for us.'

He hated to see her pleasure fade. 'I did warn you there would be downsides to living with me.'

* * *

To Jessica's astonishment, cameras began to flash at Brisbane airport and a small group of reporters barred their way. She looked sideways at Jivan and saw him frown, as if he hadn't expected this either.

The reporters, she noticed, were not in the friendliest of moods. It was as if they took Jivan's hostility so much for granted that they were annoyed by it before the questions even started.

'Are we going to be hearing wedding bells again, Jivan?' one of them called mockingly.

'Does she know about your temper?' asked another.

Jivan's hand tightened on Jessica's arm and she pressed closer to him. 'I don't like this!' she whispered.

'Do you think I do?'

The anger on his face worried her, so she decided to try to divert his attention. 'All right, JC, let's see who can look the most smoochy and loving. Bet you I win!' She draped herself against him and gazed soulfully into his eyes. To her relief, he chuckled and then gave her a hug and a warm, sexy look.

Of course the cameras caught it.

A microphone was thrust near their faces. 'Tell us about your wedding plans,' said a man with an acne-scarred face and a cynical expression.

Jivan's hand jerked in Jessica's, but his smile stayed more or less put. 'I didn't know you were in Australia, Frenton.'

'Oh, I like to get around. Well? When's the wedding?'

'We just want to – er – get to know one another better first.'

'You seem a lot more relaxed today, Jivan,' someone else called out. 'Is that a woman's magic touch?'

Jivan was staring down at Jessica so intently that the noise around them seemed to recede for a minute. Then the long furry microphone waggled for attention right under their noses and he took a deep breath. 'You could say that.'

A woman's voice called, 'How did you meet? Jessica, how about *you* answering some questions? Give us a woman's point of view on the great Jivan Childering.'

'Did you fall madly in love with him at first sight?' It was the sneering voice again.

'Jivan presented me with a prize. That's how we met.' She was immediately angry with herself for sounding so feeble.

'Jessica was the winner of the British *Write A Bestseller* competition a couple of years ago, a major coup. Her book *One Small Planet* is brilliant. She also won the Australasian Star-Writer Award recently with the ongoing series.'

A woman's voice exclaimed, 'That's where I know her face from. I covered that function. It's Jessica Lord, isn't it?'

She nodded.

'So it's a meeting of minds, as well as bodies?' the hostile voice sneered.

'Indeed it is. As usual, only *you* can phrase things with such delicacy, Frenton.'

'Is she moving in with you?' The woman's voice again.

'Yes. Jessica is doing me the honour of sharing my life and home.'

'Heaven help her!' Frenton's voice again.

Jessica was already beginning to dislike that man. She turned back to Jivan and linked her arm with his, smiling up at him again. 'Shall we go, darling? I'm looking forward to this holiday.'

The cameras began flashing as they walked away.

'Do try to keep smiling, Childering!' came Frenton's voice. 'It'll shock the TV viewers rigid.'

Jivan muttered something under his breath and Jessica clutched his arm as he sped up, striding across the airport concourse to a waiting limousine.

Behind her, she heard someone say, 'Never seen the Bengal Tiger so tame and friendly. He didn't even rise to your baiting that time, Frenton. You must be losing your touch. What do you think of *her*?'

'No class. She won't last long, but she'll give us a headline or two.'

'She must be a good writer to win those awards—'

The voices cut out abruptly as the driver closed the limousine's door.

'Who was that horrible man with the sneering voice?' she asked.

'That's the one I was telling you about. Don Frenton is a scheming gutter-crawler, and you must never believe a word he says or a promise he makes.'

'He seems to enjoy goading you. Is – is there a reason?'

'Sort of. He was a friend of my ex, probably her lover as well. Since we broke up, he's been helping her rake the dirt. But what the hell is he doing in Australia? And how did they find out we'd be at the airport?'

'Someone must have seen us boarding the plane, I suppose. Anyway, that's broken the ice about us, given me my first taste of press attention.'

'You mean, the vultures have had their first feed on your reputation. Unfortunately they'll be back, Jessica. In the meantime, we'll be turning into the garage of a hire company and changing limousines.'

She looked at him in puzzlement.

'To make sure no one follows us. I always do something to make sure I'm not followed. I'll be even more careful when we move to Western Australia. I don't want word getting back to my ex that we're there. Frenton is bound to tell her he saw me in Brisbane.'

Was Jivan being paranoid, she wondered, or were people like Frenton and his ex really as bad as he said? She certainly hadn't liked the look of the man. The other journalists hadn't been nearly as intimidating.

Without warning, Jivan took her hand. He didn't say anything, so she didn't either. She hadn't expected him to touch her when they were out of the public eye. She liked to hold his hand, though. It was warm, with long, elegant fingers.

As the new car, not a limousine this time, swung out of the garage by a side door, they slumped down out of sight in the back. This driver wasn't wearing a chauffeur's uniform, but was dressed casually. He kept a careful eye on his rear-view mirror.

After a while, he said, 'I think we're clear now, sir. But I'll keep a careful watch. If you like, I'll put some music on the front speakers to give you two a bit more privacy.'

'Thank you.' He turned to Jessica. 'You coped well today. More than well. It wasn't half as bad for me as it normally is because *you* defused the situation with some humour. For which I'm grateful.' He took her hand and raised it to his lips, kissing it gently, then stared at her and pulled her closer, kissing her on the lips before holding her close. 'You once told me you weren't the stuff of which heroines were made, but you were wrong. You are most definitely heroine material and showed it just then.'

A shiver ran through her. She had to stop this or she'd give her feelings away. She moved back a little and said brightly, 'What a nice thing to say. But *your* heroines are always raving beauties. Except for your first, Catherine Grey. She's one of my favourite fictional characters of all time.'

'I was new to the genre then, didn't realise that luscious heroines were expected in my sort of book. They're caricatures, really, there to decorate the story.'

'That sounds dreadfully chauvinistic.'

'I suppose so. Someone told me the same thing once on a television programme, but I refused to pay any attention to what they said and—'

He broke off abruptly, staring at her. 'It was *you*! You were the viewer who said that on Sally Mennon's show! Why did I never realise it before?'

She could feel her cheeks getting warmer. 'I was hoping you wouldn't remember. Does it matter now?'

'No, of course not. But the kiss we just shared does matter. I shouldn't have given in to temptation.'

'Why not?'

'Because it was part of our agreement that we wouldn't be lovers and that's because I want no more romantic entanglements – *not even with you*! I made that as clear as I could when we were discussing our arrangements.'

She gathered together the shreds of her pride and fought back. She wasn't going to be a doormat. 'That kiss, Jivan Childering, was not a crime, but a very spontaneous and enjoyable physical connection between two people. And it was *you* who initiated it, not me. So what the hell are you complaining about?'

'I'm not complaining, I'm . . . putting a stop to it.' He drew in a deep breath, and added, 'And I'm also apologising. For an error. For the kiss. It definitely won't happen again.'

'You still haven't told me why not.' She tugged at his sleeve. 'Look at me, damn you, when we argue!'

He looked and the chill in his eyes froze the remaining fire within her.

'You know why not. We're going to write, *not* have a sordid little affair.'

'Any affair *I* choose to have will not be sordid!' She wiped a tear from her cheek. 'Only you can dirty it – as you just dirtied that perfectly nice, n-normal kiss. Well, don't worry, Jivan. If I have any more impulses to act *normally* with you, the memory of your ridiculous reaction today will kill them stone dead!'

'Fine.'

A little later he said suddenly, 'There's something I need to emphasise, something you must always bear in mind.'

'Oh?'

'My ex. You must always be careful of where you go, what you do. I've not lived with anyone else and I'm still worried that she'll come after you as well as me.'

Jessica looked at him in surprise. 'You do think she's gone over the edge, don't you?'

'I'm convinced of it. So we'll both be careful.'

She fumbled in her bag for a tissue, wiped her eyes and blew her nose. 'Fine. Careful it is.'

And she would be equally careful not to let him know she loved him.

Watching Jessica, Jivan felt guilt trickle through him. As she had said, it was only a kiss. Why the hell had he made such a fuss?

He was filled with disgust at himself. And uncertainty. She was right. He had spoiled the mood. In his panic. Yes, panic. She was too easy to kiss. Too easy to like. He was afraid of losing control.

He hoped the driver hadn't overheard them, wouldn't mention that they'd been kissing in the back.

As they drove along in silence, Jivan came to the conclusion that it was up to him to mend the bridges between them, but he wasn't quite sure how to begin.

Jessica pulled a book out of her handbag and stared down at it, turning a page from time to time.

Only when the road started climbing up through some low hills did she notice she'd been holding the book upside down. She shut it hastily, hoping Jivan hadn't noticed.

'Was it an interesting book?' he asked.

'Yes, very.'

'Not many people can read upside down.' His face was perfectly expressionless, but his eyes had lost their chill.

She scowled at him, then the humour of it struck her and she couldn't help smiling. 'Trust you to notice that!'

'Friends again, Jessica? I'm truly sorry if I upset you. You're right. I did over-react.'

'I never hold grudges. Let's forget it. Where are we?'

'We're about thirty kilometres north of Brisbane, and we'll be at my place in a quarter of an hour or so.' Jivan pointed. 'Over that way.'

Ten minutes later, they turned off the main highway. Another five minutes and they turned on to an unmarked road and stopped at the only gateway.

'Is this it, sir?' the driver asked.

'Yes.'

As the car moved forward, Jessica gazed around them in delight. 'What a beautiful setting for a house! I could have been perfectly happy living here, you know.'

'I was due for a change. Got to keep the press guessing.'

The driver came to a halt and got out their luggage.

Jivan gave him a generous tip, then turned to Jessica. 'Let's go inside.'

The car pulled away and they were alone, with only the gentle sounds of nature around them.

Fourteen

The interior of the house made Jessica feel sad. It was furnished in what she mentally labelled minimalist executive style and there were no personal touches. Yet Jivan had been living here for a good while.

'Are you tired? No? Then let me give you a tour.'

In the rooms he used, the furniture had been set up to suit one person – one very solitary person. It was obvious which rooms he didn't use, because they were full of elegant, dusty furniture.

Why had he bothered to rent such a large place?

When they went upstairs, she was shown into every room, including the master bedroom. He dropped his suitcase in there and they continued.

'Choose which bedroom you want.'

She chose one with a balcony which had a beautiful view down into a valley.

'I'll bring up your suitcase in a minute. There's one more layer to show you, since the house is built into a hillside.'

Below the ground floor was his office. It was well equipped and she guessed he must spend most of his time in there. It had every piece of equipment you might consider necessary and there were three desks plus a long trestle table full of piles of papers.

A huge picture window led out on to a patio looking out across the same valley. There were a few pieces of comfortable outdoor furniture and she could imagine him sitting there, alone, frowning slightly, as he often did when he was supposed to be relaxed.

'I hadn't realised how bare it was,' he said as they stood on the patio. 'Even your little villa has more . . . more . . .'

'Signs of life,' she said, without thinking. 'Ornaments, books, mementoes, life's normal clutter.'

'Yes, signs of normal life is a good way of summing it up. When Louisa and I split up, she took all the furniture – even that in my office. She took all the ornaments and paintings we'd chosen together, too – every single one. Except for the two vases she broke over my head.'

'Was there nothing you loved, wanted to keep?'

'She made a point of specifying the things I'd loved.' He shrugged. 'I didn't argue, because all I wanted was to be free of her. When I moved into this house it came with all I needed, except for office equipment.'

He spread his hands wide in a helpless gesture. 'All I thought I needed. Perhaps you'll help me with the indoor décor in Mandurah? Make it feel more like a . . . home.'

'I'd be delighted to do that.' Her heart ached for him. How many layers of unhappiness were there behind his public mask?

'I'll only be taking the things from my office with me.'

'Let's go and look at the contents of the kitchen, then. I'm hungry. We might have to go out for a meal.'

He flung open the kitchen door. '*Voilà*!'

It was as sterile as an operating theatre.

'Is anything yours?'

'No. There was enough crockery and so on to manage. I use a lot of frozen meals, but I buy fresh fruit and vegetables in the nearby town. They have a good farmers' market.' After a pause he added slowly, 'It's not like your kitchen, is it? You might have run out of food when you were ill, but you had all the trimmings – herbs, spices, and even an electric mixer.'

'I like to cook.' She tugged his hand – anything to remove his frown – and pulled him across to the fridge and freezer. 'Let's investigate.'

By the time they had assembled the makings of a simple meal, she was feeling tired. It had been a long day.

He noticed, of course. 'Sit down, Jessica. I'll finish this. I don't expect you to wait on me.' He took a bottle of red wine out of the rack and opened it expertly, pouring her a glass and then one for himself. 'Here's to a speedy farewell to this place!'

'Here's to our future together,' she corrected. 'I'm not drinking negative toasts.'

He stood perfectly still, as if this comment had taken him by surprise, then nodded.

'No negative anythings,' she added.

'I can't imagine you being negative.'

'I try not to be.'

His words were so low she had to strain to hear them. 'So will I from now on.'

The following morning Jivan supplied Jessica with basic office stationery, and set her up with his old laptop in the formal dining room, then vanished into his office to start packing up.

She got out her thumb drive and plugged it in, then logged on to her server and went through her emails. She sent one to Barbara at home. After that she felt too tired to work on her book, so began to put together a letter to her parents. But it was hard. Very hard.

Jivan came to join her mid-morning. 'If you're busy, I'll leave you in peace.'

'Not really.' She hesitated, then confided, 'I'm just trying to draft a letter to my parents to tell them I'm going to be living with you. I ought to have done it before now, with the press taking such an interest in us, but I doubt there'll be anything in the English newspapers.'

'A letter not an email?'

She sighed. 'My mother prefers real letters.'

He rolled his eyes.

'Um – have you told your family about us?' she asked.

'I see no need to. They won't care who I'm living with – though they would care very much if I were re-marrying. They have a lot of foolish ideas about the right sort of person for a Childering to wed – even a Fitz-Childering.'

'Did they think Louisa the right sort of person?'

'Yes. She was and still is good at putting on the correct act to suit her company.'

A taut silence stretched between them. His smile had faded. She should never have asked about his ex, Jessica decided. 'Did you want something?'

'I need a break, so I'm going to pick up the mail. Would you like a walk round the gardens?'

'I'd love it!'

The gardens were lovely, neat and tidy near the house with a couple of seats to enjoy the views. The natural vegetation had been left in the rest of the grounds, with paths cut through it.

'Fancy having to pick up your mail from the end of such a long drive,' Jessica said. 'And what an address! Road Mail Box 197. It's fine in weather like this, but what do you do in the rain?'

'Drive to the mailbox.'

When he opened the padlock, they saw that the box was quite full. 'I may have to hire a virtual assistant when we get to Mandurah, someone who can work for me at a distance. So many readers now email me and I like to make sure they all get replies.'

'I could help out with that.'

'Most certainly not! You're going to write masterpieces, woman, not do secretarial work. Besides, whoever does it will probably be glad of the extra money. There are always dozens of applicants for part-time jobs. Gina's going to miss the work I gave her here. There aren't a lot of jobs going in a small town like Sharra Creek.'

'It's hardly a town. Population five hundred and twenty-three, or so it says on the sign I saw. We'd consider that a tiny village in England.'

'Allow me to point out a serious error in your calculations. The population is five hundred and twenty-four while you're here.'

She chuckled, glad to see him relaxing. 'Yes, but I'm not exactly a permanent inhabitant, am I? So I don't count. Any more than I'll count in Mandurah. You won't want me to hang around for ever.'

He stopped walking to stare at her. 'You're not thinking of leaving already?'

'No, of course not, but I do understand that this isn't a permanent arrangement. It's a wonderful breathing space for me, but I won't stay when I'm no longer wanted.'

'You've only just started living with me. Who's talking of you leaving, for heaven's sake?' He sounded a bit huffy.

Without waiting for an answer, he turned away to cram the letters into the leather satchel he was carrying. He was about to refasten the padlock on the mailbox when a car drew up on the other side of the road. 'Oh, hell, I don't believe this! How did they find us?'

He glared at the car and the two men getting out of it as if he'd like to pound their heads in.

'Press,' Don Frenton said, quite unnecessarily. The other man had his camera at the ready.

Jivan didn't react, beyond a tightening of the lips and a clenching of his hands into fists.

'How's the love-life going, Childering? Wedding bells, patter of tiny feet – there must be something happening here? I mean, the two of you can't be spending *all* the time writing! Or can you? Perhaps you put all your emotion into your books.'

Jivan's expression was granite hard. 'You're wasting your time, Frenton. Go and crawl back under your stone.'

'It's a public road. There's no law against stopping the car here. And the scenery's pretty good, too.' His eyes raked Jessica's body as they had once before. 'We can all enjoy the view, can't we?' He paused, his eyes very obviously on her breasts, then added, 'Even if we don't scale the peaks.'

There was such a depth of anger in Jivan's face that, once again, Jessica was terrified he might do something foolish. She linked her arm in his. 'Performance time,' she said in a low voice, then continued loudly enough for her words to carry clearly in the still afternoon air. 'Darling, I've got something in my shoe. Can I just hold on to you while I get it out?'

She clung to Jivan's arm and slipped off her sandal, hissing, 'Stop scowling at him and look lovingly at me, you idiot! No one would believe you even *liked* me at the moment.'

He blinked in surprise and supported her while she pretended to tip a pebble out of the sandal. When she slipped it back on, his arms tightened around her and he looked down into her eyes, smiling.

'Shall we give them a real run for their money? Another kiss would make a nice shot, don't you think?'

Before she could answer, he bent his head and kissed her, then moved his head a few inches away and stared at her. Then he muttered, 'Oh, hell!' and leaned in again to bruise her mouth with a passionate kiss.

She wanted to cry out, to beg him not to kiss her like that when he didn't mean it, but her cry of protest was still-born, and she couldn't help kissing him back.

Afraid he would see her feelings reflected in her face, she rested her head against his shoulder. 'D-don't let me go! If you do, I'll fall over. That was a kiss and a half.'

'I'll not let you go.' His voice was a warm soft breath in her ear, so quiet that she wondered afterwards whether she had really heard those words or only imagined them.

The sound of a car engine starting broke the spell. Jessica felt Jivan turn his head, then he said, 'They've gone now. We shall no doubt feature as a devoted couple on the gossip page of that rag. Not as much news in a kiss as in a quarrel, but it'll fill a column or two and Frenton will manage to make it sound dirty.'

As they started walking, he added, 'I don't want him popping up under our feet in Western Australia. We must take great care how we travel there.' A moment later he stopped and frowned. 'I've got to find out how he got to us so quickly.'

'Perhaps he had someone following us?'

'No. Not possible. But perhaps he paid someone to plant an electronic tracing device on our luggage.'

She gaped at him. 'Is that possible?'

'Oh, yes. If I can't find it, we'll buy new luggage. And . . . I'm sorry the kiss got a bit out of hand.'

She wasn't going to pretend. 'I'm not. I enjoy being kissed by someone I like.'

'You're a very attractive woman, Jessica. I hadn't made allowances for that.'

'Allowances?' Her voice came out husky.

'I'm trying to apologise for my lack of self-control just now.'

'I just said it was all right.'

For some reason that answer didn't please him. 'Do you react so strongly to any kiss, then?'

Already she was tired of treading on eggshells, of considering every word before she spoke. 'No, I don't, and it's extremely rude of you to suggest that. What am I hired as? Palace Virgin and Ice Princess? Well, it's a part I can't play. And kissing isn't exactly a major crime.'

She turned on her heel and started walking briskly towards the house, then paused and tossed a final shot back at him. 'Do we have to get psycho-analysed every time we touch each other? Why can't we just enjoy each other's company, for heaven's sake, like we did in Melbourne?'

She didn't turn to look at him again and he didn't try to catch her up.

Nor did he mention the kiss again.

But *she* couldn't forget it.

Louisa saw that she'd got an email from Don Frenton with a file attached. About time too.

She opened the email and saw only a few words: 'Will ring to discuss attached photos.'

She clicked on the attachment and found three photographs: Jivan holding the hand of some fat, saggy female wearing glasses, Jivan smiling at the same female, and Jivan kissing her.

Louisa growled under her breath. She wasn't having that. No way. He was coming back to her, whatever it took, and if that female got in her way, she'd teach her a sharp lesson.

Trust Don to use photos like this to torment her. He loved stirring people up.

No doubt he'd want paying again for the rest of the information. If she had to keep paying people at this rate, she'd use up all her money.

On the other hand, by the time she'd finished, she'd be back with Jivan and *he* had plenty of money, with more rolling in all the time. He'd turned out to be one of those rare authors who make a fortune from their writing. She hadn't expected that or she'd have been more careful. She couldn't wait to get her hands on it and live as she deserved.

He'd be grateful to her one day for persisting. She'd make sure of that. She knew how to keep men happy.

And she'd be a hell of a lot more careful who she played around with next time, since it was obviously a sore point with him.

Three days later Jivan put down the phone and looked across at Jessica triumphantly. 'That's it! All arranged. Let's take a holiday before we fly back!'

'What do you mean, "take a holiday"?' she demanded. 'The past three days have felt like a holiday to me. This is a beautiful spot.'

'Well, I fancy a proper holiday. And you still aren't looking a hundred per cent. You fall asleep on the balcony each afternoon and you're in bed by nine o'clock at night.'

For him, it would be a relief to get out of this house. He'd have to make sure they occupied bedrooms at opposite ends of the one in Mandurah. Lying in bed, he could hear her settling to sleep next door. Every single night he had wished she were sleeping with him, filling the emptiness of the bed as she filled the daytime emptiness.

He frowned as he asked himself yet again what there was about her that made the world a brighter place simply because she was with him? He couldn't explain it. What he'd had with Louisa in the first happy months was a pale shadow of this.

If he made love to Jessica, gave in to temptation, would he be sowing the seeds for an eventual breakdown of their relationship? Because he didn't want to lose her.

Nothing would make him get married again, but perhaps if he and Jessica didn't become lovers, they'd be able to stay friends. He'd like that. He really would.

He smiled at her. 'I'm not taking no for an answer, Jessica. Just put yourself in Uncle Jivan's hands and pack your things for a quick getaway tomorrow. Be ready to party.'

She looked at him ruefully. 'I don't think I'm a party animal. I always have trouble staying awake after ten o'clock and I'm shy with strangers. Where do you want to go?' She would much rather have gone straight to Western Australia. She had really taken to Mandurah.

'Where we're going is a surprise.' He took her hands and pulled her up from the sun lounger on the balcony. 'Go and pack, woman, while I finish making the arrangements!'

'But what about the rest of the furniture – and all those wonderful gourmet frozen meals?' She grimaced at the thought. They were full of salt and who knew what else, and to her they barely tasted OK. She had insisted on buying some proper food in Sharra Creek. 'You can't just dump them in the bin when we leave.'

'I'll give them to Gina, then. Will that satisfy you?'

'Yes. I can't abide waste.'

'I've noticed. Oh, and we'll stop off on the way to buy some new suitcases.'

The removal firm was late, which meant that it was noon before they could leave for their holiday. As they waited, Jivan paced up and down with an irritated expression.

Jessica, sitting patiently under a tree in the garden as the last of the things were carried out, laughed as he strode across towards her. 'No wonder they call you the Bengal Tiger! If you had a tail, you'd be lashing it.'

'Who calls me that?'

'The press. I heard them say it at Brisbane airport.'

'Well, they're wrong, as usual. My father's family comes from the north of India, not Bengal.'

'Whereabouts?'

'Agra is probably the nearest place you'd recognise.'

She smiled ruefully. 'I know the name, but I doubt I'd be able to find it on the map. Though I have seen the red fort on a travelogue. It must have been very grand in its day.'

'It's still amazing. My father took me there once when I was a child. It was the only time my mother let me go to India. We went to the Taj Mahal, too. It was so beautiful it made me shiver.'

He snapped his mouth shut. He had been on the verge of offering to take Jessica there one day. How stupid could you get? He had no intention of visiting his father again. None whatsoever.

As they drove off, Jessica twisted round to stare back at the house, but Jivan kept his eyes on the road ahead.

'Aren't you at all sorry to leave that lovely house?' she asked.

'No.'

'Well, I am. I'd have liked to stay there for longer.'

'I don't stay anywhere for long.'

'You've *bought* the house in Mandurah.'

He shrugged. 'I can sell it again when I tire of it.'

That made her wonder if he would get rid of her as easily when he tired of her. Would he not look back on their relationship, such as it was, if they split up?

She would never be able to forget him, she was sure. Each day seemed to tie them more tightly together.

Well, it felt like that to her.

Louisa picked up the phone. Who was calling at this hour?

'Darling, how are you?'

'Don?'

'None other.'

'At last. What do those photos mean?'

He sniggered. 'Straight to the point, as usual. I've seen your ex.'

'Obviously. Where is he?'

'Here in Australia. Shacked up with a rather pretty woman.'

There was dead silence at the other end, then, 'She isn't all that pretty. Who is she?'

'Her name's Jessica Lord and she's a writer. Jivan can't keep his hands off her. Want his address? He's in Australia.'

'We thought he might be. Whereabouts in Australia?'

'Wouldn't you like to know?'

She sighed. 'All right, Don. How much?'

He named a sum.

'That's daylight robbery!'

'I could be persuaded to help you more cheaply next time if I get a ringside seat at any blow-ups between you and Childering. Such scenes sell rather well to certain newspapers.'

'As long as you keep your sharp tongue off me in any article.'

'Have I ever bad-mouthed you in public, Louisa?'

'No. Thank goodness. What the hell are you doing in Australia anyway?'

'I was offered a rather good short-term contract. It was a chilly winter day with snow forecast and it seemed like a good idea at the time to go somewhere sunny.'

'Give me your contact details. If I decide to come out to Australia to visit my dear ex-husband and get rid of that new woman of his, I'll come and visit you as well.'

'Louisa, is Childering really worth all this hassle?'

'He is to me. He's extremely rich now and I want my share. I helped him get started, after all. I should never have agreed to that damned settlement.'

'You won't get any more money out of him legally.'

'Then I'll have to find another way to get it, won't I?'

Frenton put the phone down and sat thinking for a while. He'd always thought Louisa too intense; she'd been more obsessed by Childering than she'd wanted people to know.

Money was always useful and Louisa had been paying him well to keep an eye on her ex, but he'd expected her to have moved on from her failed marriage by now.

Oh well. If *she* blew up in public that'd be another story to sell for a nice fat profit.

He mentally rehearsed a few headlines. *Famous novelist's ex-wife revealed as stalker.* No, too long. *Obsession and revenge among the glitterati.* But you couldn't really call Childering glitterati, could you? *Novelist's ex-wife stabs him to death.*

He shocked himself with that one. Where the hell had the idea come from? Louisa wouldn't commit murder.

Or would she?

No, surely not. But he'd have to keep an eye on things. He wasn't getting involved in the heavy stuff.

Fifteen

Jivan took evasive action on their journey again. After a while he pretended to receive a phone call saying a family member was ill. He got the driver to drop them at the Sunshine Coast airport.

Only when he was sure the man had driven away did he go and buy some luggage. They unpacked in a quiet corner and asked a security man where they could dispose of the old suitcases.

Then 'Mr Simpkins' hired another car. Jivan even produced a credit card in that name to pay with.

The car was a late model, medium-sized, nothing special about it.

Jessica was about to ask to be put on the insurance as a co-driver, but Jivan gave a quick shake of his head and she put her purse with its row of official cards away.

'Your name might be recognised,' he said as they walked away from the counter.

'No wonder you write thrillers,' Jessica said in amazement. 'How did you get that credit card? I hope it's legal.'

'Yes, it is. To set it up, I had to go through a lot of red tape and bring the bank and the police in on my problems. I have a driving licence in that name too.'

'I didn't realise you'd had your problem officially registered.'

'Anna insisted I sign up with a security company specialising in protecting celebrities. I doubt Louisa has a clue that they've been keeping an eye on her. They'll alert me if she leaves the UK. I've already reported the latest incidents and Frenton turning up at my house to them.'

'You're more like Sam Shere than I'd realised.'

'Am I? Well, sometimes it's necessary. Money brings problems as well as advantages.'

Once they were clear of the airport, they both relaxed. The road stretched ahead of them like an invitation, the sun bright in a cloudless sky, and suddenly the constraints of the last few days were gone. Within a short time they had joined a stream of traffic heading north.

'Do you fancy some music?' At her nod, Jivan reached for the radio controls.

When he began to hum in time to the music from a programme of golden oldies, she began to sing along as well. To her surprise he slipped into the harmonies, his soft baritone matching well with her contralto.

'That was great!' she exclaimed when the song ended. 'I didn't know you could sing that well.'

'I was in the school choir. I didn't dare admit to the other boys how much I enjoyed it.'

A Beatles song came on. 'One of my favourites,' she said.

'Mine too.'

And they were off again, singing at the tops of their voices.

Three songs later they turned off the highway.

'Caloundra?' Jessica queried, looking at a road sign. 'Is that where we're going?'

'First stop, yes. If we like it, we'll stay. If not, we'll move on.'

'Sounds like a plan.'

The town attracted them so he stopped outside the tourist office. 'Wait here and I'll find us somewhere to stay.'

When he came out he drove them to a huge hotel complex. 'They said this beach resort is the best place to stay and rang through to book us in. It looked very nice in the brochure, I must say.'

It was more than nice – it was gorgeous: exquisite gardens, a swimming pool as big as a lake to one side, and beyond the hotel, the beach, a gentle curve of white sand.

'Will a two-bedroom suite be all right with you?'

'Whatever.' She was starting to worry about how much this was going to cost.

An attendant came and collected their luggage, while another held the door open for them. Jivan dropped the car keys into the woman's hand without even glancing sideways.

At the reception desk, Jessica stood back and let him do the booking. He didn't even ask how much the suite cost, but made it plain that he wanted the very best facilities – and anonymity. 'If anyone finds out I'm here, we'll leave immediately.'

'We pride ourselves on our discreet service, sir, though it'll cost a little more.'

'That's all right.'

Within minutes they were being shown to a lift away from the public ones and were given a key to it. When they got out on the top floor, they were escorted to a suite by a woman in a white linen suit with a small hotel logo on the jacket pocket. The man who'd taken the luggage was already waiting for them there.

Jivan strode inside, checked the lounge area and bedrooms, then nodded. 'Yes, this will be fine.' He slipped a generous tip to both of them.

When they were alone, Jessica wandered round the luxurious rooms, even more worried now about the price.

'Is something wrong? Don't you like it?'

'Of course I do, Jivan. But I'm just a – a bit stunned by how you behaved.'

'I booked a room and asked for privacy. What was so unusual about that?'

'You sailed into the hotel like royalty and within a minute had them all bowing and scraping in front of you. It was amazing to watch.'

He looked startled. 'Did I really do that?'

'Mmm. And then, well, you didn't even ask the price of the room.'

'Does it matter? Do you want me to find out?'

'No, of course not. But you must let me pay my share.'

'Certainly not. This holiday was my suggestion and it's my treat, a little self-indulgence, if you like.'

'I don't intend to sponge off you.'

'You're not sponging. Please, Jessica – I've not had anyone to share things with for a long time, and – well, it will make me very happy to give you a real holiday.' He put his arm round her shoulders. 'Come on! Choose which bedroom you want.'

Later, unpacking her brand new suitcase in a large, airy room with green and white curtains and matching green bedcover, she had to tell herself to calm down. He was being – well, if not loving, definitely warm and friendly. But what made her accept his generosity more willingly was that his air of sadness had completely disappeared. She felt she really was doing him good.

The trouble was, he was devastatingly attractive in this mood.

'Haven't you finished unpacking yet?'

His voice from the doorway made her jump in shock. 'Sorry. I was miles away.'

'Would you like to go for a swim?'

'Oh! I – um, didn't bring my swimsuit.' On purpose. It was elderly and faded, not something she wanted him to see her in.

'There's a shop in the lobby. We can buy you one there – or better still, a bikini.' He grinned. 'I bet you'd look great in a bikini.'

'I couldn't possibly!'

'What? Buy a swimsuit? Or wear a bikini?'

'Both.' She was far too big for a bikini. She'd lost a lot of weight during her illness, but still wasn't the size or shape to wear a bikini. Too many curves.

'Then I'll have to go and buy some bathers for you.' He stared at her, head on one side, assessing. 'Size fourteen? C cup?'

She was sure her face must have turned bright scarlet. 'Jivan, it's one thing to live with you – I mean, I won't be costing you rent or anything, and I can help out with the cooking. And I'll also accept this holiday as a one-off. But I don't expect you to buy me clothing.'

'It's because you don't expect anything from me that I'd like to spoil you a little. Don't stop me, Jessica. I've got a lot of money sitting in the bank doing nothing.'

'But—'

He tried to look menacing and failed. 'Do I go and choose a swimsuit on my own or are you coming with me?'

She gave in. 'I'm coming.'

She told herself it was to prevent him returning with a bikini.

The shop had some beautiful clothes and they found a one-piece swimsuit which was superbly cut, the material subtly patterned in shades of turquoise.

Jivan insisted on buying her a matching sundress to go over it.

'This must be the last thing you buy me,' she whispered. 'I love the dress, but you have to stop. I'm not the sort of person who needs presents to keep her happy.'

'That'll do for the time being, then. Let's go and get changed.'

They spent the rest of the day in idle luxury: a swim; a poolside drink in a private area to one side of the pool, for the use of the guests from the top floor only; a wonderful dinner – seafood as fresh and tender as anything she'd ever tasted, vegetables presented like works of art, all followed by crêpes Suzettes flamed in style at their table.

It wasn't until they started walking back to the lift that Jessica realised she was more than a little tiddly. 'Oh!' She clutched at Jivan. 'My head's gone all swoozely.'

'Here, hold on to me.' Then he smiled. '*Swoozely*? I don't think I've met that word before.'

'I made it up the first time I ever got tiddly. It sounds like I feel. Oh dear! I didn't think I'd drunk all that much.'

'You haven't. But you've been ill. I should have realised and stopped you drinking more than one of those cocktails.'

'I didn't want to stop. The cocktails were luscious.' She flung wide her arms. '*Everything's* been lovely today, one of the nicest days of my whole life.'

He tugged her through the doorway of their suite.

'Oh. Are we here already?'

He tried to guide her towards the sofa, but she resisted.

'Isn't this place gorgeous? The only other time I had a posh hotel room was when I won that prize in London.'

He chuckled. She was adorable like this, absolutely adorable. 'When your books become bestsellers, you can have any room you want. Whoops! This direction.' He tried to turn her towards her own room, but she giggled and evaded him, kicking off her sandals and pattering towards the balcony in her bare feet.

He followed quickly, afraid of her falling over the edge, but she stood quietly now, content to gaze across the floodlit grounds towards the beach. When he put his arms round her from behind, she snuggled up to him and, heaven help him, he didn't try to stop her, couldn't.

As they turned to go back inside, she twirled round, twining her arms round his neck.

'Jivan, I don't know how to thank you. You've done so much for me, nursed me better, offered me a real chance to write, and now this wonderful holiday.'

Her face was beautiful in the moonlight. He could no more have resisted the temptation to kiss her than he could have flown off the balcony and soared away across the starry sky.

And Jessica, utterly relaxed and off her guard, didn't even hesitate, but returned his kiss with all that was in her.

He would have stepped away then, but she murmured a protest and pulled his head towards her again. 'Don't stop. Oh please, don't stop!'

'But Jessica—' Her lips sought his, so soft, so warm that he had to taste them again, and after that he didn't want to stop either.

They shed their clothing piece by piece as passion flared in them both. Tentative touches became caresses, igniting a tide of urgent need.

As they lay down on her bed, he retained just enough self-control to whisper harshly, 'Are you sure you want this, Jessica? Are you quite sure?'

'I've never been more sure of anything. Oh, Jivan, don't turn away from me this time. Please . . .' Almost in a whisper, she added, 'I can't bear it if you don't want me. What's wrong with me? I've never made love properly before. No one wants me.'

He stilled at those words, but couldn't bear the utter anguish in her voice. How could she think herself anything but desirable? He stopped her words with a kiss and after that his common sense fled, as did the cynic who normally sat on his shoulder, mistrusting the world.

Wonder took the cynic's place, and with it the utter tenderness and joy that only she had ever roused in him. Step by gentle step he led and she followed, kissing, caressing, teasing until they had both crested a warm golden wave of happiness.

And afterwards, lying with her head on his shoulder, her soft, even breath fanning his chest, he couldn't find it in him to regret what had happened. Or to spoil it for her. 'It really was your first time, wasn't it?'

'Yes. And it was beautiful. Thank you, Jivan.'

He lay there and listened to her breathing in the quietness of the room, and as the soft sounds deepened into sleep, he found a lump in his throat. She had given him a very precious gift. Too precious.

He almost wished he hadn't met her, because she made him feel vulnerable. No, he didn't wish that. It had been a wonderful evening, one of the best of his life, too.

But since Frenton had come to Australia and traced them so easily, he couldn't help worrying about what might happen if Louisa found out about Jessica and took exception to their relationship.

She'd sent threatening anonymous messages to a couple of women he'd dated after his divorce and they'd backed away.

He doubted Jessica would back away, so he had to protect her. He'd get on to the security firm again and see if they could help him find a way to stop Louisa once and for all.

But his ex was very clever, and it wasn't going to be easy.

Avoidance hadn't worked. What would?

He looked sideways at the gentle, loving woman beside him. He wasn't going to let anyone hurt Jessica.

He'd just lie down for a few moments, because he was tired now, then he'd escort her to her own room. He didn't spend the night with women, not any more.

So much for his resolution. It was morning when he woke to find Jessica snuggled up against him, her hair a glorious tangle, her body so soft and feminine he had to kiss her just once more.

Jessica woke slowly, blinking at him short-sightedly. He guessed she could only see him as a blur without her glasses.

'Oh! It wasn't a dream, then.' Her smile was utterly radiant. 'And you stayed with me all night. How wonderful to wake up together.'

'You're a witch. You've enchanted me. Last night was – was—'

Only then did it occur to him that they hadn't taken any precautions last night. He had *never* done that before. He sat bolt upright in the bed. 'Oh, hell!'

'What's the matter? What did I do wrong?'

'You did nothing wrong. It was me. I didn't use any protection. You're not on the pill by any chance?'

'No. Let me work it out . . . I think – yes, it ought to be in the safe time of my cycle – just.'

He relaxed a little. 'I'd better buy something today.'

Her eyes were very clear and honest. 'Then you want it to continue between us?'

'Oh, yes. But, Jessica, we have to get things straight – I'm very fond of you as a friend, but I'm not looking to fall in love. Nor do I ever intend to get married again. I most particularly don't want children, as I've told you before.'

'I understand that.'

'You must realise by now, I'm not an easy person to live with.'

She smiled. 'I had guessed.'

'If you can accept those parameters, I think we can live happily together for a while, until . . . well, until you've had enough of me.'

She took a deep breath and summoned up all her courage. 'Let's just see how we go, shall we?' And that was enough of the deep stuff. 'I'm hungry. Shall we call room service or do you want to go down to the dining room? And whichever it is, can we do it quickly, please?'

He relaxed again. 'We'll call room service. I'm hungry too, but I'd prefer the pleasure of your company without interruptions. If someone recognised me, it'd spoil everything.'

'How sad that you always have to worry about that. Are your readers such a problem?'

'Most of them aren't, no, but occasionally one oversteps the mark. And then there's my ex. I don't want her to find out where we are.'

'What exactly does she do?'

'Follows me wherever I go, sits at the back during my talks and stares at me.' He ticked the points off on his fingers. 'Tells lies to other journalists about our life together, blackens my name in subtle and not so subtle ways, signs me up for subscriptions to porn magazines, books caterers to turn up and provide for a non-existent party.'

'That's terrible.'

'And she's getting worse.' He hesitated, then added in a quiet voice, 'I worry that she's mentally ill.'

'Oh, you poor thing.'

'I'm telling you because I don't want you to think I'm paranoid about not being recognised, and because you may have to face her at some stage, simply because you're with me. If so, don't trust her an inch.'

She was looking shocked so he tried to speak more cheerfully. 'Now, let's order some food. A lot of food.'

Five golden days they spent in Caloundra, making leisurely trips to places of interest nearby. Jessica could feel herself getting better almost by the minute. Her favourite place was Buderim, where they strolled round some of the most beautiful gardens she had ever seen, and visited the Serenity Falls, her idea of a perfect waterfall.

Jivan preferred the hinterland. 'I love the Glass House Mountains. They're so incongruous in the softness of the landscape, obstinate lumps of rock defying nature to wear them down.'

When they got back to the hotel on the fifth day, he said abruptly, 'I think we should leave tomorrow and fly back to Perth. My agent emailed to say the house sale has been completed. It's a lot easier to push one through quickly in Australia than in England. And although this break has been wonderful, I have a book to write.' He sighed as he added, 'Also, I haven't been recognised so far and I'm afraid to push my luck.'

'So what travel precautions have you taken this time?'

'We'll leave the rental car to be picked up here and get a limo to the airport. It'll save a lot of fuss.' And it would offer fewer chances of them being recognised.

'Whatever you like.'

'Let's pack, then.'

He could tell Jessica was disappointed at the abrupt ending to their holiday, though she tried to hide it. But it was safer this way, emotionally as well as physically.

He had woken up before her today and lain there worrying. He was getting altogether too fond of her. And that wasn't safe for either of them.

He had to protect her till something could be done about Louisa.

Sixteen

As Jivan and Jessica left the hotel, holding hands and laughing, a man entering stopped dead and spun round. 'What the—' He fumbled for his mobile phone, but by the time he'd got it out to snap a quick photo, they were being driven away in a limousine.

He went to the reception clerk. 'Wasn't that Jivan Childering?'

'Who?'

'Childering, the famous novelist.'

'I couldn't say, sir. I wasn't looking.'

Her very reticence made him even more suspicious.

It took him several attempts to find a member of the hotel staff willing to be bribed. When he showed the woman a photo of Childering, she hesitated. He pulled out a hundred dollars and pushed it into her hand. 'Have you seen him?'

She nodded.

'Do you know where he's going now?'

'No, but . . .' She looked down at the money.

He added another hundred.

'The limo driver might be able to help you. He was from Avenney's.'

'Thank you.'

'You won't say anything about this, will you? I could lose my job for talking about guests.'

'No. I won't mention this to anyone.'

He waited till she'd left to make a phone call. 'Frenton? I have some news that will interest you.'

'About?'

'A certain writer. You put the word out that you were looking for him. Well, I've just seen him.'

'Ah. Where.'

'It'll cost you to find out.' He named a sum.

Frenton sighed. 'It'd better be worth it.'

'I want the payment first.'

'Time could be important. We don't want the trail to go cold. You know how clever he is at slipping away.'

'Transfer the money to my bank account online and then I'll tell you.'

'Don't you trust me?'

'No.'

Frenton let out a huff of annoyance. 'Oh, very well. Give me the details of your account. I'll transfer the money straight away.'

Half an hour later, the payment appeared in the man's bank account, so he made a second phone call and shared the information.

He thought about it afterwards. From what Frenton had said, it seemed that someone else was very eager to track Childering down as well. Well, no prizes for guessing who. It had to be that ex-wife. Weird. It must be several years now since their divorce and she was still hounding him.

He wished suddenly that he hadn't told Frenton. Money wasn't everything and this wasn't a huge amount. He didn't like stalkers.

Too late now. It was done.

Jivan and Jessica flew to Perth first class. He'd phoned in advance to explain his problem to the airline staff, who had arranged for them to board and disembark privately, at a cost, of course.

At the other end they got straight into a limo while the other passengers were still waiting to leave the plane. The driver was directed to a place where an official would bring their luggage.

'Talk about doing things in style,' she teased as they were driven towards Perth.

'It's safer.' He reached out to hold her hand, surprising her.

They spent two days at Jessica's unit. She refused Jivan's help as she sorted through the smaller personal possessions she had collected since she came to Australia.

He spent most of his time at the dining table, frowning thoughtfully as he worked on his laptop, hardly saying a word, so lost was he in his new story.

The only time he used the phone was to arrange a hire car for the final day.

Jessica contacted Barbara to say goodbye, sure her friend wouldn't tell anyone where they were. During the discussion, it came out that Barbara's eldest son was leaving home and moving into his own unit, so she offered him her unwanted bits and pieces.

'You've been so kind to me, Barbara, I'm not going to charge your son.'

'Well, thank you, then. I do understand Jivan's need to stay hidden, so I won't ask where you're going, but you will drop me an email now and then, won't you? Or phone me for a chat?'

'I'll definitely keep in touch.'

'Is there any way we can help you get away?'

'I'll ask Jivan. It's his show.'

Jivan jumped at the offer of help, so Barbara arranged to come round with her son to collect the furniture and say goodbye the morning they were leaving. They'd load up his trailer and he'd leave his mother to drive Jessica and Jivan to the car rental place in Jessica's car, then deliver the car to the vehicle auction centre.

'Your Jivan is being very careful,' Barbara commented.

'Tell me about it. I go along with it, to stop him worrying, but I wonder sometimes if things are as bad as he seems to think. After all, his wife isn't in Australia.'

'Well, he knows her better than you do, so take his warnings seriously.'

'I will.'

Jivan woke up the final morning sneezing and with red eyes. He had got up in the night to hunt for his hayfever medication and not found it. He fumbled through his toiletries again, just in case, but there was no sign of it.

He muttered in annoyance and went to find Jessica, who was in the kitchen, packing the last few groceries they were taking with them. The unit looked bare now, more like one of the places he usually lived in.

'Have you got a cold or is it hayfever?' she asked as he announced his presence with another sneeze.

'Hayfever. I only get it intermittently. I don't know what's come into bloom, but whatever it is, it's hit me hard. I need to buy some more medication. If I catch it early I can usually stop it in its tracks. Can I borrow your car?'

Barbara and her son turned up as he was speaking.

'Look, I'll just nip out to the pharmacy.' He winked at her. 'I have other things I need to buy as well.'

'Stay and have a coffee,' Jessica said to Barbara when her son had left with his new possessions. 'I know the furniture has gone, but we can sit on those packing cases. Well, we can till the courier comes for them.'

Barbara frowned as she took the battered old mug of coffee. 'I'm going to poke my nose in because I care about you. What gives? Are you and Childering lovers or not?'

'Well, yes, but then . . . not exactly *lovers*.' Jessica blushed. 'It started as a business arrangement, us living together, I mean.'

'Strange sort of business arrangement.'

'He's lonely and I needed time to write.'

'Hmm. I've heard some lame excuses, but that one takes the cake. Go on.'

Jessica couldn't resist the opportunity to confide in her friend. 'Things got out of hand on the holiday, though, and we slept together.'

'You're deeply in love with him, aren't you? I know you. You'd not have got into bed with him otherwise.'

'I am, but please don't say anything to him about how I feel.'

'Why on earth not?'

'Love is the last thing he wants. Or long-term commitment. I think he was pretty badly hurt by his failed marriage.'

Barbara sipped her coffee, frowning. 'That's as may be, but why are you going to live with him if he doesn't love you? You're only torturing yourself.'

Jessica clasped her hands round her mug, comforted by its warmth. 'I'm doing it because I think he's fonder of me than he realises. Living together may give me my only chance of forging a real relationship with him, so I have to take it.'

Barbara groaned. 'Jessica, what sort of reasoning is that?'

'Pretty poor, I know. I'm a dreamer. Unrealistic. Reaching for the moon.'

'I agree with all of those except the last. He's not the moon; he's just a man.'

Jessica tried to smile, but couldn't manage it. 'Whatever.'

'And if it doesn't work out?'

'Then I'll leave him. But at least I'll have something to

remember. I see a different side of him when we're alone, you know. He's charming and fun.'

'I still don't like what you're doing. Not at all. You're acting like a grateful doormat. Jessica, he's *using* you.'

'I'm using him as well. I'll be getting some real writing time. If Jivan continues to deny himself love, that'll be beyond sad.'

'Well, don't say I haven't done my best to make you see sense.'

'You haven't said anything I haven't told myself. But at least I'll have given it my best shot.'

'I wish you luck, but Jessica, if you ever need to get away from him, you can come to me any time of the day or night.'

'Thank you.'

Jivan came back just then, and at the same time a phone began ringing.

Jessica jumped up. 'That's my mobile. I think I left my handbag in the bathroom. Excuse me for a moment.'

Barbara greeted Jivan with, 'Look after her. She's more fragile than you realise.'

'I shall try not to hurt her.'

She waggled one finger at him. 'You do more than try, buster. You make sure you don't hurt her, or you'll have me to deal with.'

'I care about her happiness.'

'Can't you even say you love her?' she threw back at him.

'I don't believe in romantic love. It's a dangerous myth.'

'Ha! That's like saying you don't believe the sun will rise tomorrow.'

'I am as I am.'

Barbara shook her head. 'You are as you choose to be. You're living behind high walls, literally and mentally, Jivan. You should come out from behind them and join the rest of humanity. Most of us are worth getting to know.'

There was silence for a moment as they eyed one another like two adversaries unsure whether to start a fight.

In the end he handed her Jessica's car keys. 'I heard what you said. Now . . . I believe you're driving us to pick up the hire car.'

The phone call was a wrong number and Jessica overheard the conversation between her friend and Jivan. Trust Barbara to come straight out with that. Still, it was nice to have a friend who cared.

Since their return from Queensland, Jivan had withdrawn into himself. Was this because he was back into his writing or because he was afraid of getting too close to her? She suspected the latter. Even when they made love, she could sense him holding something back, which made her feel as though she had to weigh each of her own words before she released it. And yet, he was thoughtful and considerate as a lover and companion. Was he *showing* the tenderness he never put into words, or was she imagining that?

If she let him see how much she loved him, would he send her away?

Oh, stop worrying, you fool! she told herself, and went to join the others. What will be, will be.

'I'll just use the bathroom,' Barbara said.

Jivan smiled ruefully at Jessica. 'I was having a little chat with your friend. If I ever write a thriller with a female protagonist, she'll be like Barbara.'

'Like Barbara?'

'Mm. She's a strong woman, though she looks and acts like the universal mother. That could throw a few interesting twists into the tale.'

'You're right. She has mothered me, as well as becoming a good friend. She says I'm too soft. I know that, but I can't seem to change it.'

'It shows in your stories. I think your readers like that about you.'

'Good. I hope they go on liking it. Will you help me do an idiot check to make sure I've not forgotten anything? You go through all the cupboards and drawers in the kitchen and I'll do the bedrooms. Let's hope the courier gets here soon for our boxes. I'm more than ready to go.'

He watched her walk out. Barbara was right. Jessica was one of the most gentle people he had ever met, though she knew how to stand up for herself. He loved living with her. He frowned. No, that sounded too romantic. He *enjoyed* sharing a house with her, working with her. That was a better way to look at their relationship.

Was it a relationship now? He had meant it only as a short-term business arrangement, beneficial to both of them for a few months, but not permanent. He frowned again. Why did he keep focusing on the end? Their time together was just beginning and it promised to work well, thanks mainly to Jessica.

He hoped it'd last for longer than a few months, because he had no doubt whatsoever that she wasn't like Louisa and could be trusted implicitly.

There was the sound of water flushing from the bathroom and Barbara came back, followed shortly afterwards by Jessica.

The courier turned up and then the villa was left bare and impersonal.

'Let's go,' Barbara said.

Jivan watched Jessica stand in the doorway of the unit. 'Something wrong?'

'Not really. I'm just saying goodbye to my past then I'll join you on tomorrow's path.'

'I think I've heard that phrase before. Is it a quote from a poem?'

She laughed. 'No, a hymn, though I don't think it's a well-known one. I heard the phrase when I started university and it's stuck. My goodness, I expected so much of the future in those days.'

'You've done pretty well, won awards and so on, achieved your main ambition in life.'

'I suppose so. But it took a lot longer than I'd expected.' She stared into space for a moment, then locked the front door and put the key into an envelope, which was already stamped. 'There you are. Final task about to be accomplished. Can you stop at the postbox on the corner, Barbara?'

He wondered why her friend had thought it necessary to warn him not to hurt Jessica. As if he would ever do that!

Frenton drew a blank with the limousine. It was a very exclusive company and no one at the head office would talk to him about their customers.

So he went to keep watch on Jessica Lord's unit. She'd have to come back here from Queensland, surely? He sat at the end of the little cul-de-sac under a tree, slouched down in the car.

There was no vehicle in front of her place so he waited. And waited.

When a car eventually drew up in front of the unit late in the afternoon, he sat up a little straighter, camera at the ready.

But a strange woman got out, accompanied by a couple. She used a key to open the door of the unit and ushered them inside, talking and gesticulating. If he'd ever seen a sales pitch, this was one. Then he saw the sign on her car door and used his binoculars to read it: a real estate agency.

If this woman was trying to let the villa, Jessica and Childering must have left. But where had they gone to now?

Childering had done it again, damn him, slipped away. Well, Frenton wasn't going to the expense of hiring a private investigator. He'd leave that to Louisa. He had other things to do in Australia than act as her minion.

That evening he contacted her online to bring her up to date.

'He's been in Australia all this time!' she exclaimed. 'Where?'

'He was in Queensland, but I think he came across to Western Australia which is where his new partner lived. Where he is now is anyone's guess.'

'Who's the woman?'

'I told you: Jessica Lord, another writer. Look, isn't it about time you let him go, love?'

'No. It bloody well isn't. I shan't stop until I get what I'm owed, my share of his money.'

Her voice had a strange edge to it, and not for the first time he wondered whether she was losing it. Well, you had to have a few screws loose to stalk someone as she had been doing. It had amused him to help her at first, but now he'd had enough.

He'd have cut the connection sooner if she hadn't been paying him to keep his eyes open. But she might get annoyed with him if he stopped helping and she could be a nasty, spiteful bitch when she took against someone.

'I did my best, Louisa. Look, I'll be in touch if I hear anything else while I'm in Australia.'

She switched off the link without a word of thanks.

When he switched on the TV, they were forecasting another hot day. Frenton scowled at the presenter. He'd had enough of Australia's interminable summer heat, and this project wasn't nearly as interesting as he'd expected. Once it was over, he'd probably head back to Europe. He was actually old enough to retire, and could afford to if he lived carefully, but who wanted to be frugal all the time?

Besides, what would he do with himself all day if he wasn't working? Write his memoirs? Ha! No one would want to read them and anyway, there were certain things better forgotten.

He'd definitely stay out of Louisa's way when he went back, though.

Seventeen

Jessica stood up and stretched her aching shoulders. She always forgot where she was while she was writing. As she gradually brought herself back to the real world, she went to the window to gaze out at the sparkling expanse of man-made canal, a view she never tired of.

Even as she looked, a dolphin curved out of the water and another followed. She and Jivan had both rushed outside the first time this happened, and even after four weeks and many sightings, she still felt her heart lift when she saw a sleek grey back or heard the sound of air being blown out as a dolphin surfaced. Where else in the world could you have free-swimming dolphins thirty metres away from where you sat eating breakfast?

She went back to sit at the computer, but couldn't settle. It was late afternoon and she needed a break from her story.

Guilt made her read through the letter she'd been trying to write to her parents, a difficult task. This time she'd finish it, and if it wasn't perfect, too bad.

Fingers clicking on the keys, she persisted through two more awkward paragraphs, trying to explain that she was living with Jivan. The letter reflected her mental turmoil! She couldn't send it till she'd shaped it into something that made sense.

The door opened behind her. 'Your mail, Jessica. I didn't bring it in earlier because you were lost in your work.'

'Thanks.'

He looked at her searchingly. 'Something wrong?'

She shrugged. 'Just trying to write to my family and tell them about . . . you know, us.'

'I thought you'd done that ages ago!'

'I've tried several times. I was determined to tell them last time I phoned. But I just can't seem to – to find the right words. My mother is so old-fashioned about that sort of thing and ever since her cancer, I don't like to upset her.'

He put a letter on the desk beside her and she stared down at the ominous air mail sticker.

'Oh, no!'

He had started to leave but turned when she spoke.

'This is from my mother. I got her monthly letter last week, so why would she be writing again so soon?' Her voice faded away, but she still didn't open the letter.

'Aren't you going to read it?'

'I suppose so. Could you, um, let me do it on my own?'

'Of course.'

As she reached for a paper knife she heard the door click shut behind him. Please, she prayed silently, please don't let them have heard about us. I should have told them. I *will* tell them. I'll phone them today as soon as it's morning in England. I don't know why I didn't phone before.

Taking a deep breath, she opened her mother's letter.

Dear Jessica

I'm writing to your old address and hoping that this will still reach you. When you phoned last week, you didn't say anything about moving, so we're a bit puzzled about what's going on.

A few days ago, we received a letter, a dreadful letter, from someone signing it 'an anonymous well-wisher'. It said you'd moved away from Perth and were living with Jivan Childering. He's the writer whose books you like so much, isn't he?

The letter said he was a dreadful man, who'd beaten his first wife, and you were putting yourself in danger living with him.

There the paper was bubbled and the ink smeared. Jessica drew in a shaky breath. Her mother must have been weeping as she wrote. But how dare this person say Jivan was a wife beater? She'd stake her life on it being a lie.

Was this . . . could it be his ex-wife trying to cause trouble? Mopping her own eyes, she turned back to her mother's letter.

> *The person sent some newspaper cuttings showing you at the airport with him, so it must be true that you're living together. We were very upset that you hadn't told us.*
>
> *I don't know if it's true that this Childering beats women, but you should be very careful if he shows the slightest sign of violence.*
>
> *Your father said I should phone you but I couldn't say this clearly. I'd have been too upset. It's taken me several goes to write this letter.*
>
> *Jessica, will you please phone and tell us what's happening? Please! Whatever it is, it's better than losing touch. We love you so much and worry about you living so far away.*
>
> *If you ever need help, need anything, don't forget that we're always here for you.*

The handwriting changed at the bottom, where her father had added a bit, in his large, slashing script, with several underlinings:

> *Whatever you're doing with yourself, Jessica, I'm not happy that you haven't let us know about your move and your new living arrangements.*
>
> *Your mother is worried sick and I'm angry that you've upset her, but I can't see you falling in love with a violent man and I do not trust writers of anonymous letters. They're only trying to cause trouble.*
>
> *Ring us up as soon as you receive this letter.*

Jessica drew in another quivering breath and more tears fell as she re-read the page and added a blister or two of her own. How could Jivan's ex have known her parents' address? They weren't celebrities.

It didn't take her long to guess what must have happened and work out who had sent this anonymous letter. When she worked for the government, she had given her parents as next of kin.

Their address would still be on record at the department. Only two people could have accessed that information: Mike Larreter and Barbara.

She knew it couldn't be Barbara, so it had to be Mike who'd done it out of sheer spite.

'You'll get yours one day,' she muttered. 'And I wish I could be there to see it.'

She tried to stop crying but couldn't. She reached for a tissue and blew her nose. You're being unreasonable, she told herself. You knew what you were getting into when you accepted Jivan's offer, and you knew how it would hurt Mum.

But she hadn't thought of Mike playing such a nasty trick.

She went to stand by the window. It was no good. She'd have to phone them, though heaven alone knew what she'd say to them.

She glanced at her watch. It was nearly tea time, so would be early morning in England. They would be up by now. Best to get it over with. It wouldn't grow any easier with keeping.

And she'd better tell Jivan before she phoned home.

She went along to his office. He was standing by the window, staring at the water. His computer screen was unlit and the desk was a tangle of papers.

'I'd like to phone England.'

'You didn't need to ask that, surely?'

'I feel better if I ask, since you won't let me pay my share of the bills.' She turned to leave, but he strode across the room and stopped her, catching hold of her arm and swinging her round gently to face the light.

He studied her face for a moment, then folded her in his arms. 'What's happened to upset you? Tell me.'

For a moment she leaned against his chest and let him hold her. 'The letter was from my mother. She was very upset because an anonymous well-wisher had written to tell them about us.'

'It'll be my ex.'

'I can't see how your ex would have my parents' names and address. I think it's more likely to be Mike Larreter.'

'Would he do that?'

'Yes.'

'Do you want to cancel our arrangement?'

'*No*!' It was out before she could stop herself. 'Um – that is – not unless you do. Perhaps me being here is spoiling your writing time.'

His voice was firm. 'I definitely don't want to cancel our agreement. Of course I don't!'

'There's no "of course" about it. You can be hard to understand at times, Mr Childering.'

His eyes softened into a real smile. 'Believe it or not, Jessica, I'm aware of that. I promise you that far from regretting your presence, I'm enjoying your company.'

'Are you really?'

'Yes. And it's not because we're sleeping together. I'm constantly surprised at how easy you are to live with and how pleasant our life is. I'd expected more difficulties, more . . . well, moods. Are you always so even-tempered?'

'You call *this* even-tempered?' She dashed away the moisture still trickling down her cheeks and blew her nose into a crumpled mess of soggy tissues.

His hand touched hers fleetingly. 'Compared to people I've lived with before, yes. I'm not talking only about my ex but about my mother and her family as well. You don't play games with me and you say what you think – most of the time, anyway. No one can be totally honest about their feelings and thoughts, but you come close.'

Heavens, if he only knew how she'd been trying to conceal her love – and now had to conceal another secret till she worked out what to do about it.

'And you've started writing properly here. I love to see that. Where are you up to now, chapter ten of book three?'

'Nearly finished it.' This time she didn't have to force a smile. She had never before enjoyed this freedom to create, to pour out the words when they welled up inside her. One day she had written solidly from ten o'clock at night till four o'clock the following morning, gripped by a sudden surge of inspiration. Afterwards she had taken a leisurely hot shower in the spare bathroom, grabbed something to eat and propped a note on the kitchen surface asking him not to disturb her. She had then slept until noon the following day, waking to a feeling of exhilaration.

Jivan hadn't seemed to think her behaviour strange, but greeted her with a smile when she eventually got up, and asked her how it was going.

Her mother would have had hysterics at the mere idea of sitting up all night writing, and would have been knocking on the door, insisting she stop work.

'It's wonderful having the freedom to write when I choose,' she said, seeing he was still waiting for a response. 'I can't thank you enough for that, Jivan.'

'That at least I can give you.'

'I still feel guilty at taking so much from you.'

'You give just as much in return.' He planted a quick kiss on her cheek. 'And not only in bed.'

She nodded, but her mind wasn't on their conversation. 'I think I'll go and make that phone call. I'll use the living room phone.'

Jessica sat staring at the telephone for a moment, then dialled, trying to keep calm. 'Mum?'

'Jessica! Oh, thank goodness!'

'I'm sorry I didn't write. I was . . . I didn't know how to tell you.'

'That you're living with Jivan Childering?'

'Yes.'

'They all seem to do it these days. Are you in love with him?'

'Yes.'

Maureen Lord sighed. 'And is he in love with you?'

'I—' She couldn't lie to her mother, never had been able to. 'I don't know.'

'Oh. Is that enough?'

'For the moment.'

There was a silence, then, 'Give me your new address and phone number before you forget. And Jessica, love, your father says anonymous letter writers are scum, and I'm to listen to *you*, not this person.'

'Is he there?'

'No, he's in the shop and it's the morning rush.'

'Tell him thanks for believing in me, then.'

The conversation that followed was stilted, but not nearly as difficult as Jessica had expected and there were no recriminations.

'Well, I'd better let you get on now, Mum.'

'Just a moment. There's one more thing I want to emphasise, Jessica. Your father and I both do. Don't forget that if you're ever in trouble and need help, we're here and always will be. And – and I hope you find happiness with this man. We'd like to meet him sometime if things go well.'

When she put the phone down, Jessica wept again. She had never cried so much in her life and she could guess why. She'd missed two periods now, but hadn't taken a pregnancy test, because she'd been hoping . . . hoping what? That her body was lying to her? It wasn't likely. She was usually very regular. Or that Jivan would talk about love and a future together? That was even less likely.

As for the test, there was the small problem of keeping it secret. They usually went out together, because they only had one car.

The phone rang again and she picked it up, thinking it was her mother calling back because she'd forgotten to say something.

But the female voice on the other end of the line was brisk and impersonal. 'Jessica Lord?'

'Yes.'

'Would you be interested in doing a survey about your shopping habits?'

'No, thank you.'

She heard the sound of the connection being cut at the other end. That was strange. If it was a survey, how had these marketing people found out her name?

It couldn't be . . . No, surely it wasn't Jivan's wife.

When she went to look for him, she heard the sound of fingers tapping on a keyboard in his room. It was such a busy sound, she left him to it. No reason for both of them to stop work early. She could tell him about the phone call later.

No reason to upset him quite yet about her pregnancy, either. There were still seven months to go, after all, and she wasn't showing yet. Some people didn't show early on, apparently.

But, oh dear. She loved living here with this more relaxed Jivan, loved this beautiful house too, hated even to think of leaving.

She promised herself that she'd buy a test within the next month. But she had no doubt about what the test would show.

And after that?

His reactions would dictate her next step.

Eighteen

A week later, Jessica woke up in the early morning to find Jivan fast asleep beside her. He'd been writing until late last night, so she'd come to bed on her own.

She lay studying his face. Since they'd been living here, he seemed happier. They got on so well together. He made her laugh and their backgrounds were so different he made her think about life differently sometimes, and she felt pretty sure she did the same for him.

They had watched some of their favourite movies together, taking it in turns to choose and discussing them vigorously afterwards. She didn't always agree with him, and didn't pretend to, nor he with her.

And they talked – oh, how they could talk! About anything and everything.

Only when the press did something to upset him did a black mood come upon him, and she didn't blame him, because she'd seen one or two ridiculous articles that were supposed to be about his womanising lifestyle. She knew for a fact that the journalists were lying: he hadn't been with anyone else since she'd come to live with him, couldn't have, because he'd been with her all the time.

He didn't stir as she got out of bed, so she went to take her shower in the spare bathroom, studying her body in the mirror and finding no signs of what was happening to it. Thank goodness she didn't suffer badly from morning sickness; just a slight feeling of nausea when she woke up.

She made a cup of tea and went into her office to check her emails, because most of those from the UK came in during the Australian night.

There was one from her sister-in-law, which was unusual. Kerry usually left it to her mother-in-law to keep in touch. Some sort of document had been attached.

Feeling apprehensive, she began to read the email:

Dear Jessica

Last week Dad showed us the letter they'd received about you. Mum was upset even though she tried not to let that show. You know how old-fashioned she is about people living together before marriage.

It's bad enough that you're shacking up with this man, but how could you let your family find out about it this way?

That's not the main reason for me contacting you, though. I've scanned in an article from one of those scandal rags some of the customers at the shop ask us to stock. Horrible things, they are.

This one came out yesterday and Mum hasn't seen it, thank goodness. She'd have a fit.

*The headline says **'Writers' Sizzling Love Affair Down Under'** and it's about you and Childering. That's bad enough, but it also says he's known for hooking up with women for a few months and leaving them – or they leave him. It hints that he's violent towards them.*

If you care about Mum, you'll phone home as soon as you receive her letter, and set her mind at rest about how he's treating you.

Kerry

PS Peter here. If you have any worries about your safety, you should leave Childering straight away. Trust you to get your life into a public mess. You always did have your head in the clouds. But you're my sister and families should stick together, so if you need help, money or whatever, let me know.

Trust Peter to believe she'd landed herself in trouble without waiting to hear her side of the story, she thought. Her brother would be the last person she'd turn to for help.

She studied the attachment again, feeling sick at what the article hinted at. Mike Larreter couldn't be responsible for this. The byline under the article simply said 'Pennyman'.

Whoever had written it should be ashamed of himself . . . or herself. Was it Jivan's ex? If so, how could she have got hold of a photo taken in Australia?

That horrible Frenton person must be involved.

She suddenly remembered someone phoning her up, pretending to be doing a survey. And she'd been dumb enough to confirm her name.

Jivan had believed Louisa didn't know where he was in Australia, but she must know now. He said she seemed to find out very quickly when he was in the UK. She had a lot of contacts in the media and among people he used to know, people who didn't know what a lying bitch she was.

Who was the contact in Australia? That horrible Frenton person or Mike Larreter? Or both?

When Jivan got up, it was nearly lunchtime. Jessica tried to keep her news to herself, but as he drank his morning cup of coffee, he studied her thoughtfully.

'Something's happened.'

'I was waiting till you'd had breakfast to tell you.'

'Tell me now. It's obviously upset you.'

'My sister-in-law emailed me and attached a scanned article from an English scandal rag. It made me feel sick.'

'Show me.'

She led the way to her office and opened her email program. 'There.'

She shuddered every time she saw the words ***Writers' Sizzling Love Affair Down Under***. 'That photo of us was taken in Melbourne, wasn't it?'

'Yes. Frenton was hanging around. I'd bet it's one of his photos. How the hell did they find out where I was in Australia?'

She told him about the recent phone call.

'Damn!' He looked round. 'Just as I was feeling I had a real home.'

'I'm sorry. I shouldn't have confirmed my name to the caller, should I?'

'You haven't had the practice I have at being suspicious. We'll change the phone number.' He gave her a quick hug. 'They'd have found out some other way, believe me. They're nothing if not ingenious. I'd hoped to escape notice for a while longer, though, by moving here. I shall have to do something about her.'

'Isn't it best just to ignore this?'

'Did ignoring the harassment stop someone writing an anonymous letter to your parents?'

'No. That's upset my whole family.'

'I think it's time for me to fight back much more seriously. I'll get those private investigators into a more active mode.' He came across and put his arms round her. 'I'm sorry, Jessica. I shouldn't have brought you into the firing line.'

'It was my own choice to live with you. You did warn me. But I agree you should do something. You can't spend the rest of your life hiding.'

He hesitated, then added, 'Your brother's tone in that email isn't exactly . . . loving?'

'No. Peter always sees the worst in anything I do. You should have heard what he said about me trying to become a novelist. Well, who cares about him? Come and get some breakfast.'

'I'll just grab a quick sandwich. I'm not really hungry. I need to think things through. And I need to ring Anna about my new story as soon as our time zones mesh, see what she thinks. I sent her the first three chapters. Sometimes it drives me crazy trying to work for an English publisher from Australia.'

'Maybe you should go back to live there, then.'

'I like Australia and I don't like the English winters, though I love the summers there. It's the perennial migrant's dilemma, isn't it, torn between their old and new countries. Do you miss England?'

'In some ways, yes, especially English springs and my family. But it's not only the sunshine here that I like; it's the different feeling in the air, the energy, call it what you like. Maybe that's because it's a younger country. I'm beginning to wonder if I'll ever settle completely in either place, though.'

'You can come back to the UK with me next time I visit. We'll hire a serviced flat for a month or two. Well, we'll do that if I can put a stop to this harassment. I'm not having you put at risk.'

He put his arms round her and they stood close together for a while, then he pulled away and went upstairs. She heard the shower, then his footsteps as he came down. But he went into his room without looking for her and shut the door firmly.

She'd never seen him so grim. This wasn't the time to tell him about her pregnancy, though the worry of it was keeping her awake at night. She went back to her computer and fiddled around, then got angry at herself for letting that article stop her working. She made herself write, and if it wasn't her best story-telling, well, she could always polish the scenes tomorrow.

How many tomorrows would she have here once Jivan found out?

They met briefly mid-afternoon and agreed to share an evening meal, so Jessica got some steaks out of the well-stocked freezer. Barbecuing usually seemed to relax Jivan.

When he joined her, he said, 'I've sent that article to my lawyer to see if it's libellous. I'm hoping my ex and Frenton will one day cross the border into suable territory.'

He finished his coffee, then studied her. 'You should rest for a while now. You look washed out. I'm going to the post – do you want anything at the shops?'

'Some fruit. Doesn't matter what. No, on second thoughts, I really fancy some strawberries.'

'All right.'

It was an hour before he came back with the shopping. Then he vanished into his room and closed the door firmly. She thought, from the expression on his face, that he was up to something other than writing. She could tell.

He had his window open and she could hear the faint murmur of voices.

But even though they spent a pleasant evening together, sitting out looking at the house lights reflected in the canal as he barbecued their steaks, he didn't tell her what he'd been doing.

The next morning he said curtly, 'I need to do some research. I think I'll drive up to Perth. Do you want to come? I'd have to drop you at the shops for a couple of hours, though.'

'No. I'll stay here.'

It was the opportunity she needed. She waved him off then called a taxi and went out to buy herself a pregnancy test kit.

When she got back, she was so nervous she dropped the box and all its contents spilled out, the instructions fluttering across the bathroom floor. She didn't even want to touch them. Oh, she was being silly. Taking a deep breath, she picked them up carefully and found out what to do. Not rocket science!

The test was positive. She sat on the edge of the bath, staring at the indicator for a long time. She'd known she must be pregnant, and yet having it confirmed was still a shock.

Then she straightened her spine, literally and figuratively. Two of them had made this baby, so why was she blaming herself?

She'd never particularly wanted children, but suddenly she wanted this one. How could you not? She was worried that the child's father wouldn't, though. But perhaps Jivan would change his attitude, as she had?

She hid the test at the back of a drawer and went to sit on the terrace and think.

The phone rang several times before the sound registered and she rushed to pick it up, worried that whoever it was might hang up. Jivan could let a phone ring itself out if he was busy, but she never could.

'Yes?'

There were some long-distance beeps, then, 'Is that Jivan Childering's residence?'

'Yes.' The word was no sooner out than she realised she shouldn't have said it. But she hung on in the hope that she might find something out about who was calling.

The voice had a sing-song intonation and the words were hesitant, as if the speaker was using a foreign language.

'Please don't hang up,' the man said. 'I am not trying to sell you anything. I'm a cousin of Jivan and my name is Barlal. Could I speak to him, please?'

She didn't know why she believed him, but she did. 'I'm sorry. He's out for the day.'

Silence, then, 'Are you the housekeeper?'

'No. I'm a friend of Jivan's. We, um, live here together.'

'Ah. Then you will be able to give him a message, please. The matter is very urgent.'

'Yes, of course.'

'His father has had a heart attack and is asking for him.'

'Oh dear! I'm so sorry. I hope it's not serious.'

'We are not sure at this stage, but my uncle Ranjit has recovered somewhat and is very upset at the thought of dying while he's so . . . at odds from his eldest son. Could you ask Jivan to call me as soon as he gets back. It really is urgent.'

'I'll give Jivan the message as soon as he returns.'

'Thank you. This is my number . . .'

Only when she had put the phone down did it occur to her that the person hadn't asked her name. Nor had she asked for any checks about the caller.

But she still thought the man had been genuine.

This was a crazy way to live, worrying about every phone call. Why had she thought she could accept this way of life? It was upsetting her already, and they'd only been together for two months.

And she still had to tell him her news.

Jivan didn't get back until late afternoon. When she told him about the phone call, his lips tightened.

'I rang the travel agent,' she wound up, holding out her notes to him. 'They can get you on a plane to Delhi tonight and from there—'

'You presume too much. I'm not likely to be going to India.'

She blinked in surprise at the harshness of his tone. 'But your father is—'

'He hasn't tried to contact me for a long time. Not since he got married. I was only nine years old and it hurt me very badly that he stopped seeing me, didn't even phone, let alone invite me to stay with him. My mother told me he'd gone back to India and that was that. She was married by then with twins but she still seemed angry at Ranjit.'

Jessica put the piece of paper down on the coffee table. 'Well, here's your cousin's phone number. He's called Barlal, by the way. You should at least ring and check the situation.'

'Thank you.' He made no move to pick up the paper. 'I think I'll take a shower now. Would you like to go out for dinner tonight?'

'I've got a sauce simmering on the cooker and salad in the fridge. I only have to cook some pasta.'

'Very well. We'll go out somewhere tomorrow.' And he was gone without another word.

Something was wrong between the two of them. Was it he who was creating this distance, or was it her?

She certainly didn't like him ignoring his father's message.

Feeling sad, she walked back into her office. She was tired of always having to think before she spoke. Tired of him keeping his distance. Why had she thought she could change him? Because she was stupidly naïve, that's why . . . and besotted with him.

Over dinner, Jivan kept up a flow of trivial chat until she could have screamed at him. He didn't mention his father. It was like chatting to a stranger.

After the meal, he said, 'Let me clear away. You look exhausted.'

'I am.' She went into her office, switched on the computer but was too tired to do anything but play games on it.

An hour later, he poked his head in the door. 'Shouldn't you get an early night? I'm going to bed soon.'

The hard knot of anger dissolved a little inside her, but not completely. 'I probably should.'

'Would you rather sleep on your own tonight?'

The anger came back with a vengeance. 'No, I wouldn't! But if *you* want to, you have only to say so. It's *your* house, after all.'

'Jessica, don't say things like that.'

She glared at him across the room. 'One of us has to talk frankly. If something's bugging you, then you ought to bring it out into the open. I feel as if I'm treading round the edge of a volcano with you sometimes. I never know whether it's going to flare up and scorch me or not.'

'I . . .' He stared at her, then looked down. 'You're right. Come and talk to me, will you? There is something we need to discuss.'

She switched off the computer and marched into the lounge, flicking off the bright ceiling lights and putting on the softer wall lights. She flopped on to the smaller couch, leaving no room for him. 'Well?'

He sat down opposite her. 'I ought to apologise first. Yesterday morning, I went to look at the newspaper cutting again and I read the email that came with it. I should have asked permission, but I did have a good reason. I was trying to keep that from you for a while.'

'Oh?' She wasn't going to give him any help to get rid of her, which was presumably what he was leading up to.

'Your sister-in-law said that you must be in love with me to be living with me.' He drew in a long, slow breath. 'And I realised that she was right. It's been staring me in the face all along.' He looked up at her. 'You are, aren't you?'

She nodded.

'How long?'

'Since Melbourne.'

'So long!'

She shrugged. 'Lightning will strike in the most unlikely places.'

'But you never said a word about your feelings.'

'You don't love me. You didn't want my love, so I didn't offer it. I took the only thing I could get – some time together.'

'I do care about you, Jessica. Greatly. But I made it clear that I didn't want any permanent involvement.'

'Yes. Only I didn't realise at the time how much in control of your emotions you were, how *impervious* to other people's feelings. I doubt it would have made any difference to me if I had known. I've always been a fool to myself, as my brother doesn't hesitate to tell me.'

Scorn filled her voice as she added, 'You needn't worry. It won't make me cling to you. I can leave tomorrow if you prefer to be alone from now on. I won't make a fuss.'

'I don't want you to leave. I like living with you.' He ran one hand through his hair, leaving it looking untidy, for once. 'I can't promise you happy ever after, but surely we can go on as we are?'

Could she? She stared at him, then shook her head. 'No. I can't do it. But you needn't think I'll walk away empty-handed.'

'What do you mean?'

'I thought there was something wrong with me – as a woman.' She looked at him coolly. 'Now I know I'm a normal woman, capable of pleasing a man, physically at least.'

'But—'

She took a sudden decision. 'Don't say anything until I've told you the rest.'

He waited.

She didn't try to soften the blow. 'I'm pregnant.'

His gasp was raw and his expression horrified. 'Caloundra?'

'Yes.'

'But you said it was the safe time!'

'It was, in theory. But you can never be truly certain, can you?'

His lips moved as he tried to count up the weeks. 'It's still early days yet. Are you quite sure, Jessica?'

'Yes. I went out and bought a pregnancy test today. It came up positive.'

'They're not infallible.'

'No, but taken in conjunction with my more emotional state, occasional morning nausea and a slight thickening of my waist, I don't think there's any mistake.'

'Then we must get you to a specialist immediately.'

She glared across the room at him. 'I'm not terminating.'

'I didn't think you would. Don't put words into my mouth.'

He turned to stare out of the window, his back to her. 'I didn't want children.'

'Tough. You've got one on the way.' Her heart felt as if it had fractured, but she held her head up as she looked across at him. 'Or rather, I've got one.'

He spun round. 'I'm not repudiating my child.'

'But you are repudiating your father. What sort of man refuses to go and see his sick father, maybe for the last time? What sort of father would *you* make for my child?' She stood up. 'I love you, but I don't like you very much at the moment, Jivan. So I'm leaving you.'

'You can't.' He intercepted her by the door. 'We have to talk this through, work out what to—'

She shook his hand off her arm. 'No, we don't. I know what you want and it's not what I want. Don't worry, though. I won't make any claims on you. I'm not after your money.'

'But—'

'The good thing about us not being married is that you have no hold over me.' She swayed, dizzy suddenly, and had a fear that this upset might harm the child. She had to end this agony. 'You're right about one thing. I am exhausted, Jivan. We can talk in the morning.'

'Yes, and— Oh, hell, no we can't! I have an appointment in Perth. I can't break it.'

'Why did you come back today, then? You could have stayed

up there.' She moved towards the door. 'I have to lie down. I didn't sleep much last night.'

He took a step backwards and allowed her past.

'I'll sleep on my own tonight.' She didn't turn to look at him as she spoke.

'Jessica—'

Her control broke and she was sobbing as she walked away. 'For heaven's sake, leave me alone, Jivan! I've had enough for today. I'm too tired to see straight, let alone talk sensibly.' She ran into the spare bedroom and slammed the door shut.

Part of her hoped he would follow, but she knew him too well for that. Just as he demanded his own space, so he allowed others the same privilege.

Even when they didn't want it.

He would wait for her to come out.

As the dark hours of the night passed, she slept very little, just lay there staring up at the ceiling, her thoughts quiet and sad. Their relationship – whatever that was – hadn't lasted very long, had it? She'd been naive to think it would. And she might be able to please the man she loved in bed, but he didn't want to stay with her, did he?

Well, she would walk away with her self-respect intact, at least, because when Jivan got back from Perth the next day, she'd have left. She'd take the decision out of his hands.

If she couldn't find a seat on a flight out of Perth, she'd go to Barbara's then back to England as soon as she could.

Ironic, wasn't it? She'd achieved her big ambition, come back to Australia. But it had all fallen apart. Perhaps she wasn't meant to live here.

One thing she was sure of was that her parents would help her. Hell, even Peter would help her if necessary. The Lords were always there for family members in trouble.

Hearts don't break, she thought, as dawn began to lighten the room. At least, mine hasn't. It's just turned to ice. Like his.

Only then did she fall into an uneasy sleep.

Nineteen

The next morning Jivan peeped into the bedroom, but Jessica was sound asleep and the tangled bed gave evidence of a restless night. He stared across at her, feeling guilt tug at him, and something else, something he didn't dare acknowledge.

He sighed as he turned away. He'd seen the raw pain on her face last night, hadn't meant to hurt her so badly, but he'd been shocked.

The news about the baby couldn't have come at a worse time, because Louisa had moved to a different and far more dangerous level of harassment. She seemed to be increasing her efforts to force him to go back to her. As if he would ever do that, even if he hadn't met Jessica.

On top of that, his father had chosen to get in touch with him for the first time in many years. Well, Ranjit would have to wait . . . as Jivan had waited. The most important thing was to protect Jessica.

And protect his unborn child, too.

He was shocked by that thought, still wasn't used to the idea.

Let's face it: he was no good at relationships, let alone families. With Jessica, he'd almost got it right, but still there was something inside him refusing to let go, refusing to unbar the doors of his – what? – call it his 'soul' for want of a better word. The longer he spent with her, the more aware he was of this. And yet, he couldn't bring himself to act.

However, that must wait. The most important thing at the moment was the danger to Jessica. The private investigators had uncovered recent links between Louisa and an illegal organisation specialising in harassment on demand, HOD for short.

HOD's website was hard to find, but once you convinced them you were serious about wanting their services, you could get through. As his investigators had done. HOD apparently guaranteed that it could annoy anyone without leaving a trace of any link to the client.

It grew worse. Apparently 'annoy' was a euphemism covering HOD's willingness to do anything at all, including having someone murdered, if you were prepared to pay for it. Due to HOD's recent activity, this matter was being investigated officially by several governments, so his people were liaising with a special branch of the UK police force.

But international investigations took time and could be rather delicate, so they advised him to take every precaution possible to stay safe and to keep Jessica safe, but not to say anything to her about HOD yet.

He'd thought he could do that if she lived with him, if they changed where they lived in Australia and kept out of public view.

How could he have been so stupid? As had been pointed out to him in the past two days, she was with the same publisher as him, a large publisher with many employees. It wouldn't be too hard for a determined person to find someone at Meridian or one of its subsidiaries who was willing to earn money by giving out information on either of them.

And this was all happening at a time when Jessica was more vulnerable than ever.

No, however little he wanted to do it, he had to send her away from him. But where could he find somewhere safe? And what if she refused to go?

He was used to being lonely, had faced it before, could face it again. But she needed her family till this was settled. Would she be safe with them, though?

His security company was investigating that for him and he didn't care how much it cost.

And afterwards? He didn't dare hope that Jessica would want to be with him again after he'd sent her away.

He closed the bedroom door quietly behind him and went to the kitchen but didn't feel like eating, so scribbled a note.

I didn't disturb you, because you were sleeping soundly and you looked utterly exhausted yesterday. Take it easy today. I don't want you falling ill again.

I'll cut today's meeting short and be back as soon as I can – by early to mid-afternoon. We'll work something out then.

Jivan

He left the note propped up against the kettle and on an afterthought picked up the piece of paper with his cousin's name on it, a cousin he'd met the one time he went to India with his father. Jivan remembered a chubby boy of his own age called Barlal. He remembered too much sometimes.

As he got into the car in the garage, he blew a kiss towards the house, then thought how stupid that was. As if she'd know that he'd blown her a kiss.

He nearly turned and went back, then reminded himself that there were three lives to protect now, not two.

He had to keep his appointment this morning.

As soon as she heard the garage door roll up, Jessica opened her eyes, but she didn't try to get up until she heard the car drive away and the garage door roll right down.

The minute she sat up, nausea washed through her and she ran for the bathroom, barely reaching it in time. She had only felt slightly nauseous before, but this had been a close call. Was it because she was upset, or was this the next stage of her pregnancy?

Once her stomach had settled down, she looked at herself in the mirror, dismayed to see how white her face was. She had to take better care of herself and her precious child from now on.

She washed her mouth out, recalling yesterday's scene with Jivan. It was no good. She'd never get through to him, never gain his trust. Would anyone?

She rang Barbara at work. 'Can I come and stay with you for a day or two while I sort out a flight to the UK? And will you not tell anyone, especially Jivan, that I'm there?'

'Oh, Jessica! I'm so sorry. What happened?'

'I'll tell you later. How do I get a key to your place?'

'Ring me when you're setting off and I'll contact my son. You'll be about an hour getting there, so he can nip across and be ready to let you in. He's not working this week and he owes you a favour for the things you gave him.'

'Thanks.'

After that Jessica didn't weep. There was too much to do. She took a quick shower, made some toast and forced it down a small bite at a time as she put together a list and prioritised the jobs. Even with strawberry jam on it, the toast tasted like cardboard, but she was determined to feed her body.

She had to toughen up, she told herself as she cleaned her teeth again. In a few months she would be responsible for another life, and the thought of that made her feel stronger.

She tried to remember whether she'd ever given Jivan her parents' address. No, she didn't think so. He knew which town she came from, of course, so he'd be able to find them, but his need to search might win her more time to move on before he got there.

First on the list was a plane ticket. She rang a travel agent and asked them to get her the first cancellation on any airline flying to the UK.

'Give me your number, Ms Lord, and I'll get back to you within half an hour max.'

She took her mobile phone with her as she started packing. It rang ten minutes later.

'There's a cancellation for this afternoon.'

'Oh my goodness! I'll take it.'

'Let me get your details and your credit card number . . .'

She was unable to believe she'd be in England the next day.

She rang Barbara again. 'Change of plan. There's a cancellation and I fly out this afternoon, so I won't need your help, but thanks.'

'What time do you fly out?'

'Two thirty.'

'You have to book in early, so you'll be at the airport by lunchtime. How about we meet for a coffee? I'd like to say goodbye properly.'

'That would be good.'

One hour later Jessica had packed everything she needed. She'd have to leave her desktop computer and reference books behind, but she had her tablet which contained her backup files, and she was taking all her work on a thumb drive as well. She'd buy a cheap computer and printer once she was settled somewhere.

Then came the hardest task of all: writing a note for Jivan to tell him she was leaving permanently. It took several attempts and in the end was very brief.

Jivan, I think it's better if I leave now. We've said all that's needed. I can manage with my family's help.

Don't try to come after me. I've got a seat on a plane this afternoon.

Thank you for everything.

Love

Jessica

When she carried the luggage out to the taxi, there didn't seem to be very much. Was this all that was left of her life in Australia? That made her feel deeply sad.

The driver put her suitcase into the boot and she put the hand luggage containing the precious tablet on the back seat next to her. All the time she kept glancing along the street, terrified Jivan might return before she left.

But he didn't.

She tried to tell herself she was relieved about that.

The drive up to Perth was an anti-climax. It was another sunny day, the traffic was light and the driver wasn't talkative, thank goodness. She didn't think she could have made sense at the moment. He switched on the radio and let a talk show take over. She didn't hear a word anyone said, but the sound of voices and the occasional musical interlude were vaguely comforting.

At the airport, she confirmed her booking, checked her luggage in, then went to wait in the coffee shop.

Fifteen minutes later her friend arrived and they exchanged hugs, neither needing to say how they were feeling.

'Want to talk about it?' Barbara asked as they sat down.

Jessica shook her head. 'No, not really. What good would that do? But there are a couple of things you should know.' She managed a wobbly smile. 'The most important one is I'm pregnant.'

'How on earth did that happen in this day and age?'

'First time we made love in Queensland. We were in too much of a hurry.' Jessica gave a bitter laugh. 'The irony is, it should have been the safe part of my cycle and we've been really careful ever since.' She gave her companion a very level look. 'Don't worry about me. I won't let it stop me writing and I will get on with my life. I realised on the way here that I won't be alone from now on. I'll have a child to love. That's such a comfort. I never wanted children before, but I do want this one. Very much.'

'I'm glad for you, then.'

'That's enough about my woes. Tell me what's been happening at the department.'

Barbara chuckled. 'Mike's got himself a job over in New South Wales. Heaven help them! We're going to have a big farewell party.'

'Does he deserve one?'

'Oh, he won't be coming. It'll be after he's left.'

And to her surprise, Jessica found herself laughing. Then she glanced at her wristwatch and stood up. 'Thank you for coming. I need to go through to the waiting area now.'

Barbara gave her a fierce hug. 'All right. Keep in touch. One day I'll come to England and descend on you for a visit. I'm due long service leave in two years. Three wonderful months away from the office. Or you might come back here for a visit one day, in which case you're invited to stay with me.'

'I don't think I'll be coming back to Australia in the foreseeable future. What I need at the moment is my family. Oh, hell, if I stay one minute longer I'll weep all over you.'

Jessica hurried off and didn't dare look back.

Barbara watched her until she was out of sight then bought a sandwich and another coffee. She got out her laptop and started work on a little job she'd been meaning to sort out. No one would be able to interrupt her here.

When she looked at her watch, two hours had passed.

She glanced at the notice board. Jessica's plane had taken off a while ago.

As she was walking across the airport car park, she saw a figure she recognised getting out of a car parked crookedly in a corner, as if it had been hastily dumped there. She marched over to intercept Jivan. 'You've got a nerve, following her here. Can't you even let her go in peace?'

His gaze was filled with as much pain as Jessica's had been. 'I wanted to say goodbye properly.'

The professional in Barbara saw a man in extreme emotional crisis. 'Her plane took off over an hour ago. You look upset. Come and have a coffee with me.'

He let her settle him in a corner and fetch him a coffee, all without a word, so she knew she was right to speak to him. She decided to use shock tactics.

'Have you told her you love her?'

'I don't—' He broke off and stared at her with such anguish on his face that she found herself taking his hand.

'How long are you going to go on fooling yourself, Jivan? Of course you love her. And she loves you.'

'I daren't love her.'

'That's a strange word to use. Tell me why not.'

'My ex-wife has been stalking me for years, but I think . . . no, I'm fairly sure she's crossed some sort of mental boundary. To put it bluntly, I think she's gone mad. And . . . Barbara, I'm pretty sure she'll try to kill me if I won't do what she wants, which is marry her again. If she sees me with Jessica, she'll attack her too.'

'Are you sure of this? Have you told the police?'

'Yes, I'm sure. And I've hired a specialist company in the UK to pursue the matter. They've registered the problem with the police, but they can't do anything without proof and . . . there are some other things happening that I can't talk about. Unless we can catch Louisa out and get her locked away, I daren't go back to Jessica. I don't know why I even came here today. She's safer away from me.'

'You came because you love her.'

He nodded. 'And to tell her I'll support her and the child. That at least I can do through our mutual publisher without raising my ex's suspicions. Will you give me her parents' phone number and address?'

'I'll think about it. In the meantime, I'm going to ring and ask them to meet her plane. She shouldn't arrive on her own. She looked rather fragile today.'

Barbara gave his hand a pat, then let go of it and wrote down the Lords' number. After all, he was in Australia, so there wasn't much he could do from here.

'If you need to talk, phone me. Any time. I mean it.' She gave him her business card. 'I have your home phone number. What about your mobile?'

She put it on her phone then walked out to the car park with him. Impulsively, she gave him another hug, which clearly startled him. He gave her a quick hug in return, a hug so tentative she hugged him again.

She hadn't expected to feel sorry for him. If he was telling the truth, and she was pretty good at knowing when someone was lying, he was caught between a rock and a hard place.

As she got into her car, memories hit her hard. She'd had a couple of encounters with stalkers during her former career as a psychologist. One had ended badly in the death of her client, and was part of the reason she'd changed career track.

She wouldn't give him Jessica's address in the UK and she'd try to persuade him to stay away from her.

It would be better by far for her friend to be unhappy than dead.

Jessica trudged slowly out of the luggage pick-up area in Manchester airport, feeling so exhausted it was hard to put one foot in front of the other. When she saw her parents waiting for her, she blinked, thinking she'd imagined it, but no, there they were, waving.

Her father had lost a little weight and her mother had put some on in the years she'd been away. Only a few years, but both were greyer than she remembered. They were looking at her uncertainly, as if wondering whether she was glad to see them.

She abandoned the luggage trolley and ran into her mother's arms. 'How did you know I was arriving today?'

'Your friend Barbara phoned us.'

'I was never so glad to see anyone in my whole life. I was just wondering about hiring a car and—'

Her father, who had retrieved the trolley, pushed his wife gently aside. 'Don't I get a hug, too, Jessica?'

'Of course you do!' She flung her arms round the solid warmth of him. 'Dad, you look so well.'

'I'm feeling well. Our Peter is managing the shops now – not that I don't help out – but I haven't got the worries and responsibilities. *He* loves it. Eh, what am I talking about that for when you've just got off a plane? Let's get you home.'

In the comfort of the car, she leaned her head back and closed her eyes. 'I can't believe I'm in England again.'

'We hope you're going to stay here this time,' he said severely. 'Your mother's been worried sick about you. Family belong together.'

She blinked away a tear. She mustn't keep crying all over everyone. 'Maybe I had to go all the way to Australia to realise how much I needed you.'

'Do you want to talk about it – what brought you back?' her mother asked hesitantly. 'You don't need to, if you don't want. Your friend said to leave that up to you. But if that man has hurt you and comes anywhere near me, I won't be held responsible.'

'Barbara didn't tell you the rest of it, then?'

'No.'

'Then I'd like to.' And very quietly, she explained the situation.

There was a long silence, then her mother said softly, 'It's bound to be a beautiful child, with a mother like you and a father like that. I've seen photos of him. He *looks* good, even if he doesn't act it. And we've always got room for another little one in the family.'

'We certainly have,' her father echoed.

'Oh, Mum! Dad! You're absolutely wonderful.' And for the first time in her life, Jessica truly felt a part of the Lord clan, there at the warm centre of their circle, loved and loving.

When they got back, even Peter was more friendly than ever before. 'You did right to come home, Jess,' he said gruffly. 'We won't let you down like that fellow did.'

Twenty

Jivan left Perth airport feeling as if he'd made a friend. He now had Barbara's mobile number and could ask her advice if he had trouble with persuading Jessica to accept his help.

At first he had a dream run home, hitting every traffic light at green and getting on to the Roe Highway more quickly than he'd expected.

Then a traffic light changed just before he reached it and when he braked, the car was sluggish in responding. He made a mental note to have the brakes checked. You couldn't be too careful about such things.

When he turned on to the Kwinana Freeway the traffic was much heavier, with a line of big trucks heading south, so he changed to the central lane. It was then that he noticed the big silver four-wheel drive, which had been travelling behind him for a while. It had started moving closer and tail-gating him.

'Get back, you fool,' he muttered. In this patch of heavy traffic, coming so close was sheer lunacy. To his dismay, it crept even closer, so he sounded his horn. But its driver took no notice and suddenly accelerated, nudging Jivan's vehicle sharply from behind.

He cried out in shock and tried to brake, but his car was even slower in responding this time.

Before he knew what was going on, the silver vehicle had thumped into him again, far harder this time, not hitting him squarely but catching the left rear corner. When his brakes failed completely, Jivan was helpless to prevent the front of his car swinging round towards the vehicles in the fast lane.

As he fought for control, a truck in the fast lane just managed to accelerate out of his way and he missed it by inches. The car behind it braked just enough to avoid him narrowly. By some lucky freak, he was able to steer towards an emergency stopping area for some roadworks.

The brakes weren't working at all now and he couldn't even slow his car, so it crashed hard into a temporary fence of huge plastic containers filled with water. Air bags ballooned up around him, cushioning the impact, and his car shuddered to a halt, among sounds of tortured metal.

But he was still alive!

Stomach churning, he punched the deflating air bag out of his way and bowed his head over the wheel for a few seconds, then realised he might still be in danger. He looked all round to make sure his attacker hadn't followed him, but there was no sign of the big silver car.

Traffic droned past next to him, the drivers gawking at him.

The truck and car that had managed to avoid him had pulled up in the same emergency lane, one further ahead and one behind him. The truck driver was running towards him.

'You all right, mate? I saw in my wing mirror how that bastard shoved you into our lane. Good thing *he* braked in time.' He pointed to the younger guy next to him who had now joined them.

'You two did brilliantly to get out of the way,' Jivan said. 'I probably owe you my life.'

'In my job, you learn to keep your eye on what's going on around you. It was you sounding your horn that made me look and realise what was going on,' the truck driver said.

'I've called the police,' the younger man said. 'And I've got the number of that car. You're *sure* you're not hurt?'

'I've probably got a few bruises but that's all.' He brushed futilely at the white powder from the air bags which was all over him.

'You've got an enemy,' the truck driver said thoughtfully. 'I mean, that wasn't an accident.'

Jivan shrugged. 'Only my ex, but she's in England.'

'Did she catch you playing the field? Good-looking fellow like you wouldn't have any trouble finding women who're up for it.'

'No. I caught *her* out, actually.'

'Then why the hell would she send someone after you in Australia?'

Jivan shrugged. 'Who knows? Perhaps it's not her.' He suddenly began to shake and couldn't stop for a moment, so had to lean against the car. 'Sorry. Reaction.'

The man patted him awkwardly on the arm. 'Not surprising. Take your time.'

The police arrived ten minutes later and it was two hours before Jivan was free to go. He was glad he had two witnesses, because when he first told his tale, they looked at him suspiciously and whipped out a breathalyser.

'Nothing,' the officer reading the results said.

They took him more seriously after that, questioning the two other drivers in more detail.

As soon as the police let him go, the truck driver took off. After they'd questioned Jivan about the failing brakes, the police insisted on taking the car away to be examined. It was badly crumpled and not drivable anyway.

They offered him a lift, but the younger driver, who seemed to have quite enjoyed all the fuss, offered him a lift down to Mandurah, so he took that.

'I recognised you straight away,' the young man said as he waited for a break in the traffic. 'I've got a couple of your books.'

'Oh. That's nice.'

'Bloody good stories, they are.'

'Well, when we get to my place, I'll give you a copy of my latest, if you like. As a thank you.'

'Great! I've always wanted to ask where you get your ideas.'

Jivan patiently answered the same old questions all readers asked. He was relieved when the man dropped him off and left with his book.

The first thing Jivan did was make a cup of strong coffee, then phone Barbara and tell her what had happened. 'There's no doubt it was done on purpose. I need to contact Jessica and get her a bodyguard and a safe place to stay ASAP.'

'You think your ex will go after her? Even now Jessica has left you?'

'Who knows what Louisa will do? I'm not risking anything. Only, I don't think Jessica will speak to me.'

'Phone me if she won't and I'll call her and tell her to listen to you. I already gave you her parents' phone number. This is their address.'

He scribbled it down. 'Thanks for taking me seriously, Barbara.'

'Make sure you continue to protect yourself as well as Jessica.'

The next day, feeling rested after a good night's sleep in her old bedroom, Jessica went downstairs to find her mother and father. They plied her with food and a big mug of tea, then sat down one on either side of her at the kitchen table.

'You had a phone call last night,' her father said. 'About an hour after you'd gone to bed.'

'I did come up to tell you,' Maureen added, 'but you didn't stir, not even when I put the light on. You looked so exhausted I didn't wake you up.'

'Who was it?'

'That writer fellow, Childering.'

'Oh.' She frowned as she stared down at her piece of toast. She swallowed what she had in her mouth and put the piece down, adjusting it to sit neatly in the middle of her plate.

When she thought she could control her voice, she asked, 'What did he want?'

'First he wanted to know if you were all right,' her father went on. 'He sounded really worried, so that's a point in his favour, at least. I said of course you were all right and I told him straight out that we Lords look after our own.'

Grim satisfaction sounded in his voice as he added, 'He didn't like that, I could tell, but I'm not pussy-footing around when someone hurts my lass.'

'Mmm.'

'He said he'd ring back at a more convenient time.'

'If he rings again, I don't want to speak to him.'

She was beginning to find a fragile peace because she was surrounded by love. She'd have to think carefully about her future, how to support herself and her child, and she'd make sure that child was surrounded by people who loved it. Family.

It would be folly to look back. She didn't dare talk to Jivan. If she did, she might weaken.

When Barbara rang a little later, Jessica was happy to take that call.

'Have you forgiven me for telling your parents you were coming, Jessica?'

'Forgiven? I was grateful. They were waiting for me at the airport and I was never so glad to see anyone.'

'That's good. Look, I'm ringing about something else today. Jivan phoned me and said—'

'I don't want to know what he said. It's over between him and me.'

'Not yet it isn't.'

'What on earth do you mean by that?'

'His ex is on the rampage and you may be in danger.'

'She's been causing trouble for a while. I still don't want to speak to him.'

'You have to. We're talking about real danger, as in someone trying to murder you.'

'*What*? Why would anyone want to murder me?'

'Because you and Jivan love each other.'

Jessica was silent, then said, 'He doesn't love me.'

'He does. And he's starting to face it. Look, he had a car accident yesterday.'

'Jivan did? But he's the most careful driver I've ever met. Was it a drunken driver? Is he all right?'

'He's OK, but only thanks to some very skilled driving by two other people who got out of his way as he crashed on the freeway coming back from the airport.'

'He was at the airport?'

'Yes, wanting to say goodbye to you properly. But he was too late. He and I had quite a chat. Then he rang me later to tell me about the accident and ask me to warn you to be careful.'

'I can't believe what you're saying.'

'Someone must have got at his brakes while he was talking to me at the airport. Then, when he started driving back to Mandurah they used a big four-wheel drive to shove him out of his lane on the freeway into the fast lane. He jammed on his brakes hard but they failed. Luckily he was near some roadworks, so had somewhere to spin off the road.'

The words seemed to echo in Jessica's head and she could only whisper, 'Someone tried to *kill* him?'

'We don't know if they were trying to kill him or frighten him. After all, he was driving a modern car with top safety features.'

'Did the police catch them?'

'No. It was a stolen car. No sign of the driver.'

'It can only be his ex-wife.'

'Yes. That's what he said.'

'Dear heaven! What will she do next? He's got to go into hiding straight away.'

'He's taking precautions. And he wants you to take them too. She may go after you next.'

The silence on the line was filled with faint crackling sounds as Jessica tried to get her head round that.

'Talk to Jivan when he calls, Jessica. Let him help you find somewhere safe to hide till this is over. If you stay with your parents, you won't be safe enough *and* you'll endanger your family.'

Jessica put the phone down and stared at it for a long time before she raised her head and looked at her parents. She didn't want to leave them, felt as if she'd only just found them properly.

But she didn't want to put them in danger. Definitely not. Or her unborn child.

'What's the matter, love?' Her father took the buzzing phone gently out of her hand and set it down.

Jessica was still so shocked, she blurted it all out. 'Jivan thinks my life's in danger. His ex-wife seems to have . . . gone crazy.' She explained about the car accident and some of the nasty harassment he'd faced over the years.

'We need to get you away, then,' her father said at once.

'Where to?'

The phone rang just then. They looked at one another.

'If it's him, you'd better speak to him.' Her father picked up the phone, his expression grim. 'Ah. Mr Childering. Yes, she's here. I'll put her on.' Without asking, he pressed the speaker function on the phone and put it down between them so that he could listen in.

'Jessica, I'm so sorry I wasn't there to say goodbye and help you make suitable arrangements.'

'Are you? But you wouldn't have stopped me going?'

'Of course I'm sorry. And no, I'd not have stopped you, for your own sake, because I'd found out from the security company I've hired that you were in danger. I was coming home to persuade you to get away that very afternoon. Look, did Barbara explain what's happening? She said she would.'

'Yes. I find it hard to believe. It's like something you see at the movies.'

'I'm still trying to come to terms with it myself. But the security people say it seems likely that Louisa's totally lost all sense of morality. The trouble is, she's hired a hit firm to harass me, which as it happens is also being investigated by the international police.'

'How do they know what she's doing?'

'She's not as clever about hiding her tracks as she thinks she is.

And my company always checks the situation out with the police in serious cases like this. They've been asked to work with the police and inform them about every step they take from now on, because the police team investigating don't want anything to happen till they're ready to pounce. It's rotten luck that you and I have got involved.'

Instinctively, Jessica placed a protective hand over her belly and glanced at her father. 'I'll find somewhere to go, Jivan. You're right: I can't stay with my parents. It's probably better if you're not involved in hiding me, either. I'll rent a furnished bedsitter somewhere and I'll be extremely careful, I promise you.'

'Unfortunately, we think it's gone past that. You need a trained bodyguard 24/7.'

'*What*? Surely not.' The situation seemed to be getting more and more surreal.

'Don't fight me on this, Jessica. If Louise finds out about the child, who knows what she'll do?'

'I don't know what to say.'

'Say you'll do as I ask.'

Her father nodded vigorously.

'Very well.'

'Give me a couple of hours to organise it and stay near the phone. And Jessica, once this is over, can you and I talk about ourselves?'

'Will we have anything to talk about?'

'I think so. But for the time being, we need to get you into hiding. You'll have to change your appearance and stay away from everyone you know.'

'But your ex doesn't even know me.'

'She knows you were living with me and I'm sure she hates you for that. It'll be easy for her to find out what you look like, because there's a photo of you on the covers of your books and your photo's been in various newspapers. Talk to your friend Barbara if you don't believe me about the urgency.'

'All right. I will talk to her. Do you have a photo of your ex?'

'I'll send you a link to her online business site. There's a photo of her on it.'

'Thanks.'

'My investigators will work with the police team to help you change your identity as well as your appearance, and find you a place to stay.'

'This'll cost you a fortune.'

'You're worth a fortune, Jessica. Look. Time is of the essence, so I have to go. I'll phone back soon. 'Bye.'

His voice sounded choked. He was hinting at the things she'd longed to hear, but did he mean them?

She switched off the phone and looked at her father.

'You'd better do as he says, love.'

'I suppose so.' But then she'd be on her own again. And so would Jivan. Would he be well protected?

She got online and they all studied the face of Louisa Parry, who was thin and glamorous.

'Does she look like a killer to you, Dad?' Jessica asked doubtfully.

'Who knows what a killer looks like? Better safe than sorry, love. I'm glad Childering has hired professional help.'

She hugged her father, suddenly needing the human contact, and stayed with her head against his chest for a while, letting him stroke her hair as he had done when she was a little child.

Her mother came to sit at her other side and held her hand.

Oh, she didn't want to leave them! She didn't! She'd only just got back.

Jivan put down the phone and took a moment to pull himself together. Then he started making phone calls and it was two hours before he got back to Jessica.

'A man will be coming to pick you up. He'll introduce himself as Samuel Shere. He'll take you to a safe house and stay with you until further notice.'

'Oh. Right.'

'If you have a laptop you'd better take it with you. You may be there for a while. But even if you can get on the Internet, don't do it. Don't contact anyone, especially me or your parents.'

'But how will I find anything out?'

'Your bodyguard will do that. Jessica . . . take care.'

'You too.'

He glanced at his watch and ran up to his bedroom where he packed a suitcase and picked up his own laptop.

By that time the taxi had arrived, so he switched on the electronic security system and left the house. He looked back, sighing and hoping he'd be able to return to Mandurah one day. He had enjoyed living on the water.

He had especially enjoyed living with Jessica, missed her dreadfully.

Barbara was right. Why had he been so reluctant to commit?

After Louisa had listened intently to the report from HOD, she asked, 'Wasn't that a bit extreme? I didn't ask you to kill him.'

'You did request a strong warning and he was in a modern car with several air bags, so he wasn't likely to be killed. Our operative took advantage of a sudden opportunity. They're all trained to think on their feet.'

'Hmm. What next?'

'We'll contact him and ask him to get in touch with you, then you can deliver your ultimatum to him, as you've requested.'

'Good.' She was looking forward to that. And to living with him again. See if she didn't charm him into her bed.

The woman rang back just as Louisa was getting ready for bed. 'He's left Australia, so we couldn't get through to him. He could only be on one plane going to the UK from Perth, so we'll have someone at Heathrow watching out for him.'

'What about the woman who was living with him? You said she'd gone back to live with her parents.'

'Yes. Did you know she was pregnant? Her mother phoned some members of the family to tell them.'

The room seemed to spin around Louisa. 'That bitch is expecting his child?'

'Yes.'

'How the hell did you find that out?'

'Modern surveillance gadgets are very sophisticated and you did ask us to investigate her and her phone calls as well.'

'Yes. But I didn't expect . . . Look, can you continue to keep an eye on her? I don't want them getting back together.'

'He chased after her to Perth airport, remember.'

'I won't forget that. And listen, I want to see him face to face to deliver my ultimatum. I'm not doing it on the phone.'

'Very well. It may cost more.'

'He's got plenty of money. He'll pay me back later.'

After the call ended, Louisa sat by the phone, drumming her fingers on the table top. It was taking longer than she'd expected and costing more. Far more. She'd had to sell her flat to pay for this, but she'd got a good price for it and now had plenty of money in hand.

It'd all be worth it in the end. She'd make sure of that.

And that child would never be born. She'd make sure of that, too.

Jivan Childering didn't need children; he just needed her.

Twenty-One

A man came into the shop, ignored the young woman behind the counter and approached Richard. 'I believe you're expecting me, Mr Lord.' He lowered his voice. 'I'm Samuel Shere. Don't repeat my name, please.'

'No. I understand.'

'I'll come back around two in the morning to pick up your daughter and take her to a safe place. Tell her not to put any lights on anywhere in the house while she's getting ready to leave. I checked out this district before I came into the shop. It'll be best if she leaves by the warehouse gate in your back yard.'

'How do we know we can trust you?'

'You'll get a call shortly from a lady who phoned you from Australia before. She'll confirm my name. Mr Childering can't do that himself because he's in the air at the moment on his way to the UK. Tell your daughter not to mention any names during this phone call, and it would be helpful if you and your family didn't talk about this on the phone.'

Richard studied the man's face but it gave nothing away. 'All right.'

'Now, it'd look better if I bought something. Act as if you're helping me find it.'

'The assistant's been with us for years. She won't worry if you're with me.'

'Nonetheless, humour me.'

The so-called Samuel Shere walked out of the shop a couple of minutes later having paid the young assistant for a set of school mathematical instruments, which were in a brightly coloured paper bag.

It was usually quiet at this time of day, so Richard waved to his employee and indicated that he'd be nipping into the house for a few moments. It was so convenient living on site.

He told his wife and daughter what had happened and Maureen looked at him in dismay. 'I've already mentioned Jessica on the phone to some of the family.'

'Well, let's hope no one was listening in.'

Five minutes later the phone rang and the assistant transferred the call from the shop. Richard again switched over to speaker, so they could all hear it.

Barbara's voice sounded clearly. She didn't greet Jessica by name, though. 'How are you going, dear? Is England warming up at all?'

They chatted about the weather for a couple of minutes, then Barbara asked, 'Did you enjoy your visit from that friend you were telling me about? He was due today, wasn't he?'

'Yes. He only left a few minutes ago.'

'Sheer pleasure, seeing old friends. You'll see him again soon, no doubt, now he's back in England.'

'I hope so.'

'Have a nice day, then.'

Richard picked up the phone and set it in its cradle. 'So that's that. I wonder where your Jivan is heading.'

'To a good hiding place, I hope. With a bodyguard of his own.'

'These people suggest someone's bugging our phone. I can't believe it.'

'Better safe than sorry. Don't say anything important on the phone from now on. I'll go and pack. Thanks for lending me your laptop, Dad.'

'You'll like it. It's a new one, with all the bells and whistles, including an anti-theft program. I hope you manage to do some writing. You may have a lot of time on your hands.'

'I hope not.' She doubted she'd get any writing done till she was sure Jivan was safe.

She went up to her bedroom to sort out her clothes. But she

stood there lost in thought for quite a while before going down to wash and tumble dry the garments she'd been wearing. Who knew when she'd be able to do that again?

This all felt totally surreal. How could she possibly have got mixed up in an international investigation into murder?

Jessica woke when someone shook her. 'Go away!'

Her mother's voice penetrated the fog of nightmarish dreams. 'Jessica, love, you need to get up. Remember not to put the light on.'

Then it all came back to her and she sat bolt upright, glancing at the bedside clock whose green numbers were glowing brightly in the darkness. 'Oh! Thanks for waking me, Mum. I didn't think I'd get to sleep.'

'I'm glad you did. Do you want a quick cup of tea?'

'Better not. I don't know how long I'll be travelling for.'

'I'll leave you to get dressed, then.'

Her clothes were ready to slip into and she tucked her pyjamas into the backpack her father had found for her. She'd found a rounders bat in the bag and had left it there, more for luck than because she expected to use it. He'd kept that old bat behind the counter of the shop for years in case someone tried to rob him, but had never had to use it, thank goodness.

When she went downstairs, her parents were waiting for her and they each gave her a big hug.

'Don't come outside with me. I know my way across the yard.'

'I have to come out to unbar the gate then lock it after you've gone. We're going to be very careful too.' Her father picked up the backpack and handed her the laptop in its carrying case.

The yard was dark and then grew suddenly bright as the moon sailed out from behind some clouds. It was like an old black and white movie.

Her father opened the tall wooden gate just enough to let her through and she heard a man's voice.

'Samuel here.'

'It's him,' her father whispered, handing her the backpack and giving her shoulder a quick squeeze. 'Watch how you go, love.'

She took a deep breath and stepped outside.

* * *

When Jivan got off the plane in the Middle East, he saw a young man holding a sign that read 'Mr J. Chandler', his assumed name, and signalled that he was the person.

His guide led the way across the vast airport without looking back and Jivan followed him into a side corridor then a small office whose door had no sign on it.

A woman at a desk looked up, studying Jivan. 'I'm sorry you're having such trouble, sir. We've booked you through to Frankfurt instead of London, and under the name Chandler again. If you'll just hand me your ticket?'

He passed over his documents.

'And your passport?' She studied it, held it under a machine and nodded. 'Please go through that door. Someone will take you on board when the time comes.'

'Thank you for your help.'

She nodded, still not cracking a smile, so he went out of the rear of the office and was passed through machines that scrutinised both him and his hand luggage.

The police team was certainly taking no chances with his safety.

He was shown into a small but comfortable room and offered refreshments, which he declined. He seemed to have lost his appetite completely today.

'I'll come back for you in about an hour, sir,' the attendant said. 'Don't hesitate to ring if you need anything in the meantime.'

With a sigh, Jivan sat down for another wait, unable to settle to reading, unable to do anything but beg whatever fates were out there to keep Jessica safe. He hadn't admitted to himself how important she was to him till this happened.

He was only too aware of it now.

He was also aware of the danger they were both in. He hoped these present strategies would ensure that he could slip into his own country safely and secretly.

He'd known organisations such as HOD existed from researching his story backgrounds, but now he knew what it felt like to be a target, to have those you cared about in danger. Money, he decided, could be a curse as well as a blessing.

He'd been wrong about one thing in his books. The stakes

would have been considerably higher for his character, Sam Shere, if he'd had loved ones to protect.

'Damn you, Louisa!' he muttered at one stage.

If there had been room, he'd have paced up and down, but the cubicle was only two and a half strides long.

At last the door opened and the attendant beckoned to him.

He was whisked out to the plane in a covered vehicle and taken on board with the food supplies. Then he was back to sitting in a comfortable seat and enduring another period of waiting as they flew towards Frankfurt.

The journey seemed to have been going on for ever already and he was only about halfway there.

At Frankfurt Jivan was again led to an inconspicuous office. They searched him and his luggage carefully, then drove him out in an airport runabout to a small private plane.

A man in a smart uniform was waiting for him. 'I'm your pilot, Mr Chandler. Call me Fred.'

'Pleased to meet you. Any news on my friend? Is she safe?'

'I couldn't say, sir. They'll bring you up to date on the situation when you get to England.'

It was night now so all Jivan could see below them were lights. He was suddenly overcome by tiredness, so gave in to the desire to take a nap.

Someone shook his arm and said, 'We're nearly there, sir.'

He awoke with a start. They were flying over a dark landscape and seemed to be heading towards a small cluster of lights. Dotted around were bigger clusters of lights, presumably larger towns.

Fred cleared his throat. 'I've been asked to remind you that your security company is now working with a government initiative to catch HOD and you'll be answerable to our operatives. HOD have been increasing the range of their so-called services and have lately taken out a couple of people our government and that of another country would rather have kept alive. Your security company has been most co-operative and has an excellent record. You chose them well.'

'I bet they're regretting taking me on as a client. Are you with them or the police?'

'I'm not with your company but we're all working together to put an end to this and keep you safe.'

Which made Jivan realise that this man was a government operative of some sort. 'I'm glad to hear that. Is Jessica caught in the middle of this or have you got her away?'

'I'm afraid you're both involved, sir. We'd rather have kept you out of it, but you'd become targets. We've got one of our best agents looking after your friend. If anyone can get her through it, Mary can.'

Jivan sighed but didn't ask for more information. It was like living through one of his own stories. Not at all pleasant.

When they left the plane, they were checked by a customs official, then Fred handed Jivan over to another operative, Chas, who took him to a medium-sized car and handed him a bullet-proof jacket. 'If you'd just put this on, sir.'

'Is that really necessary?'

'We hope not.'

He hoped not, too. 'Where are you taking me?' he asked as they set off.

'To one of our special safe houses, a farm near Haworth, in Bronte country. We don't like to have our little confrontations in crowded public areas or they might take hostages or kill bystanders, not to mention alert the public. There'd be hell to pay if that happened.'

'You think it'll come to a confrontation?' Jivan asked in surprise.

'I hope not, sir. But you'll be quite safe in the cellar there. It's been specially built to withstand attacks.'

'Is Jessica in the same place?'

'I couldn't say, sir.'

'Oh, dammit, can't you see I'm worried sick about her?'

'I still can't tell you anything, sir. This has escalated into a major operation and information is on a need to know basis only. If we don't stop HOD we might find terrorists using their services and we do not want that.'

He added quietly, 'You'll be brought up to date when you arrive, I'm sure.'

Jessica stopped outside her father's yard, wondering how she was supposed to know that this man really was a friend.

He whispered, 'Samuel Shere', and she nodded, but he could

be anybody for all she knew. No, she wasn't going to think like that. She had to trust in the system Jivan had set up to protect her.

'Samuel' opened the front passenger door of a small car and shut it on her quietly, then came round to the driving seat. 'I'll drive slowly till we're away from the houses. If at any time I tell you to duck down, do it instantly.'

Once they were out of the town he sped up and proved that the car was nippier than it looked. After about half an hour, he turned off the road at an isolated group of houses, where he drove round to the rear.

'We're just changing cars, Jessica. It'll be safer.'

They transferred to a four-wheel drive that was standing with a key in the ignition. There was no sign of anyone else, but she felt as though someone was watching her.

They left the rear area by a different exit, bumping down a rough dirt track. Some time later, after following several twisting country lanes, most of them hidden between drystone walls, Samuel pulled up at what looked like a farmhouse.

He ushered her inside the dark hall, dumped her bag on the floor and left without another word.

When she heard the car driving away, Jessica's heart began to thump. Had she been delivered into a trap?

A woman materialised out of the darkness and said quietly, 'I'll shine a torch on the floor to show you the way, Jessica. We'll be using the cellar.' She picked up the bag and walked towards the rear of the house.

All Jessica could do was follow the woman.

The cellar seemed very bright after the dimness of the entrance hall. Her guide had short iron-grey hair and was dressed in dark trousers and top. She had a gun in a holster on her belt. She gestured to some chairs. 'I'm Mary. And no, this isn't a trap, it's a safe house. We want to keep you alive.'

When they were seated, she went on in the same abrupt tone, 'I'm afraid you've got caught up in a major international operation. The authorities of several countries are now after an organisation that's started killing people on demand.'

Jessica nodded.

'Childering's security company wasn't aware of the full situation when they took on his case, but they're now working with the authorities to help catch the hired assassins.'

'Is Jivan all right?'

'As far as I know. He should have arrived in England by now and will be joining us here – well, he will if they can get him through without being spotted. If not, he'll be taken to another place of safety.'

She waited a moment, then asked, 'Any questions, Jessica?'

'Would you answer them if I asked you?'

This time she did win a fleeting smile from her bodyguard.

'I might. The best thing you can do for the moment is try to grab some sleep. I'll show you the facilities and the safe space you can retreat to if things get really sticky, though I doubt it'll come to that.'

She showed Jessica how to get into and out of a hidden room behind a cupboard in the cellar. When you were inside, it felt claustrophobic, like a large cupboard. Jessica hoped she'd not have to use it.

How had she and Jivan got mixed up in all this? It could have been one of his stories.

She prayed he was safe.

Jessica woke up some time later slumped in an armchair. She felt disoriented for a few seconds. When she heard footsteps above her head, she realised she was alone in the dimly lit room.

Feeling vulnerable, she got the rounders bat out of her backpack and tucked it into the back waistband of her trousers. They were elasticated and easily accommodated both her expanding waistline and the bat.

Mary came back and put the kettle on. Before Jessica realised what she was doing, her bodyguard had moved round behind her and taken the bat out of her trousers.

'What's this for? Don't you trust me?'

'My father put it into my bag and it didn't seem a bad idea to have it handy.'

Mary shrugged and handed it back. 'If it makes you feel better, carry it. But don't keep touching it or you'll alert people to its presence. And don't try to use it unless I give you permission.'

'Oh. Right.'

When they heard a car outside, Mary got up. 'That'll be our reinforcements. Stay at the top of the stairs. Shut and lock the door into the hall if there's any trouble.'

She opened the door and her voice sounded clearly. 'I haven't worked with you before.'

'Call me Tom. I'm taking a break from the US, as you'll see from my papers.'

'Go first and don't draw your gun.'

Back in the safe room, she checked his papers, asked for tonight's password and then nodded. 'Want a coffee?'

'Later perhaps. You might like to grab some sleep while you can.'

'Yeah. Good idea.'

Jessica was left with another stranger. She didn't like the look of this Tom, though there was no reason for her feelings.

Mary lay down on a couch and went straight to sleep.

Tom paced up and down, seeming very much on edge. He went upstairs a few times, presumably checking the house. He hardly said a word to Jessica.

Time passed very slowly. She sat at the table, pretending to read, unable to sleep.

While Tom was up in the main part of the house, she put the laptop and her luggage into the secret room in case she had to hide in there.

Did he know about it? Mary hadn't mentioned it to him and the entrance faced away from the steps leading into the cellar, which was very uneven in shape.

She suddenly realised Tom had been gone much longer this time and went to the bottom of the stairs to listen. It sounded as if there was more than one person upstairs.

She went to wake Mary, explaining in a low voice what she thought she'd heard.

'Damn! I didn't recognise him, but he had all the right paperwork and the latest password, so I assumed he was all right. I must be more tired than I thought. You'd better get into the secret room, just in case. And don't come out until I open the door, whatever anyone threatens or does. I mean that. It's bullet proof.'

Jessica nodded and went inside the narrow, claustrophobic space.

This time she noticed a little glint of light and found it was a spy hole into the main part of the cellar. So she watched what was going on outside.

Tom came back. Alone.

'Where is she?'

'Lying down in the inner room.'

'You'd better show me how it works.'

'I'll just grab a coffee first.'

'I'll make it. I'm thirsty, too.'

Mary accepted his offer but continued to sit on the other side of the table from him, watching carefully what he did.

When he brought the coffee across, she asked for sugar, and as he went to get it, she quickly dropped something into his cup.

Such a simple, old-fashioned trick, Jessica thought. If Jivan wrote it in one of his books, people would complain and say it wouldn't work in this day and age.

Only it did work. Within a couple of minutes of drinking the coffee, Tom's eyes glazed over. He tried to stand up but couldn't. The way he glared at Mary as he slumped said it all. He was definitely not on their side.

Through the spy hole she watched Mary run lightly up the stairs and lock the cellar door from inside, bolting it top and bottom for good measure. Then she pulled a small lever that Jessica hadn't even noticed.

When she came down, she opened the door of the secret room. 'You might as well come out while we wait. That place is too small for comfort. The lever sends out a warning signal and calls for backup,' she explained.

Even as she spoke, Tom groaned.

'I'll just make sure lover-boy here can't hurt us if he regains consciousness.' She produced some thin rope and used it to tie his hands behind his back, then fastened his feet to the chair legs. 'I'd like to know how they found out about this place and our password,' she muttered. 'We must have a leak somewhere.'

She took out a very small phone and when it rang she identified herself with some numbers, then said, 'Chief, we're stuck in the cellar with one captive.' She explained what had happened then listened intently. When she ended the call, she turned back to Jessica. 'They want us to stay here till it's safe.'

Someone tried the cellar door. 'Open up or we'll break the door down.'

'Here we go,' said Mary, not seeming worried about the threat.

The lights went out suddenly.

There was a click and one dim light went on. 'Emergency lighting,' Mary explained.

Something crashed against the cellar door.

'Good luck,' Mary said. 'That door's got a steel core to it.'

'What if we can't get out again?' Jessica asked nervously.

'There's another exit, but that's not the best solution at this stage. We'll be safer staying here.'

After that they listened to the crashing sounds as the intruders tried to force open the door. These stopped after a while. From then on they sat in silence, listening to some thumping on the floor above.

'They're trying to break through the ceiling,' Mary said with another of her not-quite smiles. 'There's a layer of steel there, too. So unless they've brought an acetylene torch, they're stymied.'

Tom seemed to be conscious now, but since he had a gag in his mouth, he wasn't able to say anything. When he started trying to rock his chair to and fro, Mary poked his chest with her gun. 'Sit – still – you. Or I'll have to knock you out.'

He slumped against his bonds and the silence resumed.

Jessica still found it hard to believe this was happening – until she looked at Mary's grim expression and saw the gun held steadily in her hand.

Twenty-Two

'We're five minutes away from the safe house now, sir,' Chas said.

A minute later, a red light began to wink on the dashboard. Chas cursed under his breath and pulled up abruptly by the side of the road.

'What's the matter?' Jivan asked.

'Something's gone wrong. That's our warning signal broadcasting from the safe house. How the hell did anyone find out about this place?' He picked up the phone from its hands-free cradle and pressed a button.

Someone answered his call immediately and they had a rapid conversation. He cursed again.

'They don't know how it's gone wrong but somehow HOD have found out where Jessica and you are being taken. They've got inside the house, but not inside the safe room. Jessica is there already but they've mistimed it and you're not there, thank goodness. Heads are going to roll for this.'

He started to turn the car round and Jivan stopped him. 'Are you going to leave Jessica in danger?'

'My job is to protect you, sir. Other people are on the way and in the meantime—' His phone rang again.

After only a few words, he put it down. 'I'm to go and help. The helicopter has been delayed. *You* are to stay here. I suggest you go behind that wall, sir.'

'No. I'm coming with you.'

'You are *not* a trained operative. You'll get in the way.'

'I've had training in unarmed combat and if you've got a spare gun, I'm a fair shot, too.'

'I thought you were a writer?'

'I write thrillers. Action research helps me get them more realistic and also keeps me fit in a sedentary job.'

The man looked at Jivan and made a quick movement as if to pin him to the seat, but Jivan stopped him and twisted his arm to prevent follow-up.

'You've got damned good reactions.'

'So I'm told. Look, if you leave me here, I'll only follow you.'

Chas sighed. 'Very well. But you are to obey my orders. And here!' He unlocked the glove compartment and handed a gun to Jivan.

'Thank you.'

'Do not do anything rash.'

He drove off slowly, without headlights, stopping in a dip in the rough lane. 'The car will be out of sight from the house and we can cut across the fields. I've been here before so I know the layout. Stay a couple of yards behind me.'

They crept forward slowly across the field, stopping every few yards. Another car drove up to the house from an easterly direction as they got within a hundred metres of it. 'Get down!' Chas threw himself to the ground as he spoke and Jivan followed his example.

Chas moved close enough to whisper, 'No one is supposed to be getting here yet, so it's not one of ours.'

'What do we do?'

'Stay back and watch. Intervene only if it seems worthwhile and *I* will decide what's worthwhile. Got that?'

'Yes.'

The car stopped in front of the house and a man got out, turning to help a woman out.

As the moon emerged from behind the clouds, Jivan whispered, 'That's my ex-wife!'

'Are you sure?'

'Oh, yes. I've got very good eyesight.'

'She doesn't look to be a captive.'

'She probably hired them to deliver me into her power and has come to gloat. She's after my money.'

There was the sound of a helicopter in the distance and Chas made a low, satisfied sound. 'Here come our lot.'

The people from the car were just starting towards the farmhouse when they heard it and the two men spun round, staring into the sky and gesticulating to one another.

Louisa tried to go back to the car, but one man dragged her into the building.

The helicopter lights were getting closer.

'Come on. Let's get a bit nearer,' Chas said.

'What about Louisa?'

'Your ex is the least of my worries. She helped cause our current trouble and fed money to a criminal organisation so she's going to be in big trouble when we pick the HOD operatives up. Also, she came here voluntarily, so her safety comes second to yours. By a long way.'

Louisa heard the helicopter and turned to her guide. 'You didn't say you were bringing in a helicopter.'

'It's not ours.' He turned to his colleague. 'How the hell did the police get on to us?'

'Is that the police?' Louisa asked. 'We have to get out of here!'

'We have to get inside, you mean.'

'I'm not staying to be caught, even if I have to *walk* back to civilisation.'

'I thought you wanted to see your ex?' the man said sarcastically.

'I do. But *you* promised the police would know nothing about this.' She turned to leave and he yanked her inside the house.

She yelled and kicked, and he cursed as she bit him. He dumped her on the hall floor.

'Shut up, you!' the other man said. 'We've heard more than enough from you on the way here.'

Another man came to join them in the hall.

'Where are they?' Louisa's guide asked.

'They've locked themselves in the cellar.'

'Well, break the damned door down.'

'It seems to be steel-lined.'

'Shit! This must be one of their prime safe houses, then. We shouldn't have come here. They're not going to let us go easily.'

'We do have one card to play if things get tough.' He gestured towards Louisa.

She gaped at him. 'What the hell do you mean by that?'

'You'd make a useful hostage if push came to shove. You can always pretend we kidnapped you, so you'd not get into trouble with the police.'

'No way am I acting as hostage. Hostages can get shot. All I want is to see my husband. Leave me out of the rest.'

'If you mean your ex, he's probably locked in the cellar with the others.'

She looked towards a window. 'Well, if that's the police, I'll see him another time.'

One man wagged a gun at her. 'Stay where you are and shut the hell up.'

He went to the window of the front room to look out. 'They're landing in the field.' He slapped the flat of his hand against the wall several times, cursing.

Spotlights suddenly shone on the outside of the house and a voice called, 'This is the police. Come out with your hands up.'

'We'll go out behind her. Better tie her hands.'

Louisa began screaming and yelling, trying to beat them off, but they had little trouble subduing her. She continued to yell at the top of a very shrill voice.

'Stuff a gag in that big mouth of hers. We don't need that racket. Now, open the door and stand her there.'

He waited till this had been done, then yelled, 'We have a hostage. If you don't let us go, we'll kill her.'

There was silence, then the disembodied voice from near the helicopter asked, 'Who is she?'

'Louisa Parry, ex-wife of the novelist Jivan Childering. If you let us go, we'll release her when we're away from here.'

'No deal.'

In the field to one side, Jivan was listening to this. 'Are they going to let these people kill her?'

'Still got the hots for her?' Chas asked sarcastically.

'No. But I don't want to see her killed.'

'They're just playing for time. Those thugs wouldn't keep their word. They'd definitely kill her after they leave. Our side is actually trying to save her life. It should be quite easy to track them. Someone will have crept forward to put a tracer on the car while they're talking.'

'The HOD people will find that surely?'

'They don't have time to check it.'

They listened to some arguing and negotiating and, in the end, it was agreed that the police would let the men and their hostage go.

Chas's phone buzzed.

He answered it.

'Where are you?'

'In the field between the house and the main road.'

'Can you block the road with your vehicle if we delay this lot a bit longer? We want to get them away from the house before we act.'

'Yeah.'

'Do it, then.'

He turned to Jivan. 'This time you stay here. I'll move the car.'

Jivan nodded and crouched there, looking towards the house, which was still brightly lit by the spotlights. Where was Jessica? Was she all right?

After some more arguing, the men came out of the house holding Louisa in front of them, and got into the car.

As they started to drive away, there was an explosion inside the house and it burst into flames.

Mary's phone rang and she listened intently. 'Oh, hell! Yes, sir. We'll do that.'

'What's wrong?'

'They set the house on fire as they left. We have to get out of here before the steel panels buckle in the heat and trap us inside.'

'How?'

'The other exit.' She went over to another wall and fiddled around. A panel slid aside and she nodded in satisfaction, then turned to Jessica. 'Still got that rounders bat?'

'Yes, of course.'

'Hold it ready in case *he* gives us any trouble.' She marched across to Tom. 'We have to get out. You too unless you want to be fried alive. Your friends have set the house on fire. If you give us any trouble, she'll hit you good and hard.' She paused to study him. 'In fact, I wonder if we'd better knock you out first then drag you out of the house.'

'I'm not stupid enough to get myself burnt alive,' he snapped.

She undid the ropes tying him to the chair and the ones tying his feet together, leaving his hands still bound. 'Let's go. You can walk between us.'

The tunnel was low so that they had to bend, and after a while it began to slope upwards.

They got to the exit and Mary dealt with the door. As it opened, Tom suddenly shoved her hard and kicked the gun out of her hand. He tried to scramble over her, in spite of his bound hands, but Jessica thumped him good and hard over the head with the rounders bat. She hit him again for good measure, terrified he'd turn and fight her.

He fell unconscious across the threshold of the exit.

The two women dragged him out of the tunnel and away from the house. Flames were spreading rapidly through it now. Mary tied his feet again and fastened him to a fence post away from the fire. 'Thanks, Jessica. Let's find out what they're doing.'

Another short phone conversation ensued. 'They want us to go into the field on this side. They've got a hostage situation but they daren't let the HOD fellows go. Unfortunately, the land team has been delayed. Keep hold of that bat, just in case.'

Jessica nodded, surprised to find herself smiling. Well, this was the first time she'd ever found a rounders bat useful. She'd spent years as a child completely failing to hit the ball with such a narrow piece of wood.

Bending low, the two women crept across the field, in time to see a big four-wheel drive roar round the house and disappear into a lane on the other side.

There was the sound of a crash and they ran forward to look down to where the road dipped.

'Well placed!' Mary said with satisfaction.

But one of the men managed to get out of the car and he was holding a struggling woman in front of him. There was enough light to see the blood pouring from a cut in her head.

'That's Jivan's ex-wife,' Jessica whispered. 'He thinks she's gone mad.'

'She's got a loud voice. Oh, no.'

The man shook Louisa like a rat and tried to force her to walk. As she sagged down, he took out a gun and threatened her.

When she continued to scream and struggle, he raised it.

'He's going to kill her!' Mary raised her own gun. 'Hell, I'm too far away to risk a shot.'

At almost the same moment, Jivan and Chas also saw what was happening, from the other side.

Jivan was much closer.

'Fire near him, see if you can distract him,' Chas called in a low voice.

Jivan raised his gun, aiming it carefully. He didn't want to fire, but he could see the moment when the man focused his gun on Louisa. So he fired two shots at the fellow.

The man stood very still and for a moment Jivan thought he'd missed. Then his target crumpled to the ground, dragging Louisa with him.

Chas raced past him and approached the two figures with caution.

'You got him! You *are* a good shot.' He bent over the figure. 'Good. He's dead.'

Jivan suddenly felt sick and bent over, vomiting helplessly.

Chas dragged the woman away. 'Come and hold her while I check out the other men in the car.'

Jivan moved forward, reluctant to face Louisa under any circumstances. But he needn't have worried. She was unconscious. Blood was still pouring out of the cut on her forehead and out of another one on her arm where his second shot must have hit her.

He picked her up and turned towards the house. The firing there had stopped. He trudged forward.

'Stop where you are!' a man yelled into a loudhailer.

He stopped. 'I'm with Chas.'

'Don't move.'

'She's bleeding to death.'

Two men approached and one took her off him. The other said, 'Get down on the ground.'

He obeyed, not liking the look in their eyes.

Chas came running up. 'He's on our side. Let him up.'

'You sure?'

'Certain. He just killed a man who was about to shoot her.' He gave Jivan a hand up.

'She was their hostage. I knew we couldn't trust them to spare her life.'

'Well, he's dead and so is one of the other men. He died in the crash. The third one is trapped in the car.'

'The house is a goner,' the other man said. 'Pity. It was a useful place. Let's go and see if Mary and her charge are all right.'

As they approached the brightly lit area at the rear of the house, Jivan saw Jessica standing beside an older woman. Her face was covered in smuts and she was muddy and dishevelled, but she didn't seem to be injured, thank goodness.

'Jessica!' he yelled.

She swung round. 'Jivan? Oh, you're safe! Thank goodness.'

He began to run towards her and she cast aside the bat and ran straight into his arms.

Mary stood with arms folded and a fond smile on her dirty face. 'I love it when they get soppy,' she said to Chas as he joined her.

He turned to look at them and gave her a friendly nudge. 'He certainly does care about her, never stopped pestering me for news of her. He's a crack shot, too. It was he who killed the fellow holding the other woman hostage.'

'*She* is feisty too, hit our captive over the head when he tried to escape. Knocked him out cold with this.' She bent to pick up the rounders bat.

'A damned rounders bat!'

'Yes. I used to be good at rounders when I was at school.' Mary took a hit at an imaginary ball.

Jivan held Jessica close and smothered her face with kisses. 'Thank goodness you're safe. I was terrified I'd lost you.'

She held his face still between her hands and kissed him back thoroughly. 'This time I'm not going to let you push me away.'

'I wouldn't have let you go away from Mandurah if it wasn't for being warned about this lot.' He gestured around them. 'I thought you'd be safer away from me with your family.'

'We might both have been safer if we'd stayed in Australia. Well, safe from everyone except the press.'

Someone coughed nearby and they turned to see Mary and Chas smiling at them.

'The ambulances will be here soon. We'd like to get you two checked out.'

'I'd rather go and have a long shower,' Jessica said.

'We'll let them check you and the baby,' Jivan said firmly.

'She's all right,' Jessica said at once.

'She?'

'I have a feeling it's a girl.'

'With your eyes and hair, I hope.'

'There they go again,' Mary muttered to Chas. 'They've got it bad. Sweet, isn't it?'

The first ambulance arrived just then and took the unconscious Louisa away, sirens screaming.

'I hope she makes it,' Jivan said softly, and shuddered.

Jessica studied him. 'What's wrong?'

He bent his head. 'I killed a man tonight. Shot him. That makes me feel sick.'

'Did you have any choice?'

'Not if Louisa was going to have any chance of surviving.'

A fire engine turned up just then, but it was too late to stop the fire from consuming the whole house.

'It was an unhappy place, that house,' Jessica said. 'I hated the feel of it.'

Only after the paramedics in a second ambulance had checked out Jessica and Jivan were they allowed to go home.

Before they left there was a phone call from the first ambulance.

The paramedics came across to Jivan. 'I'm sorry. They thought you should know. Ms Parry didn't make it. She'd lost too much blood and she wasn't in very good health. Undernourished they call it in developing countries. Anorexia when it's done on purpose.'

He stared at them in shock. 'Louisa's dead?'

'I'm afraid so.'

Jessica put her arm round him, thanked the two paramedics and walked a short distance away with Jivan. 'You did everything you could.'

'I suppose so.'

'You know so.'

He nodded. 'It's just . . . sad that her life ended like that.'

She stood in his arms, not saying anything but feeling he was finding it comforting to hold her.

A short time later more operatives arrived and he pulled himself together.

Chas came across to collect them. 'Where to?'

'My parents' house,' Jessica said without hesitation. 'About time you met them, Jivan.'

'Will they want to meet me?'

'They're dying to.' She put her arm round his waist. 'They've always got room to love one more. And Jivan . . .'

'Yes?'

'I want to meet your father and mother, too.'

'My mother is easy. She's bound to come to England when she hears about all this.'

'And your father isn't easy? Find out. After all, he contacted you, didn't he?'

'Are you going to boss me around?' he demanded, but couldn't keep up the pretence of anger for more than a few seconds.

'Yes, I am. But only for your own good. You have to learn to trust people and you can start with us Lords. You're going to be part of the family for the rest of your life, after all.'

'What a wonderful thought.'

Epilogue

The wedding was arranged for a month later, to allow Jivan a quick visit to India to see his father. Jessica insisted on that but refused to go with him.

'This is between you and him,' she said firmly. 'But I'm not marrying you till it's sorted out.'

He came back to England with a more peaceful expression in his eyes, Jessica thought, when she met him at the airport, but he didn't say anything till they were alone that night in the refurbished bedroom that had been hers as a child.

'OK. What exactly happened, Jivan?'

'I had several long talks with my father, who is, incidentally, a lot better than they'd expected. He'll need an operation, but they think he'll be good for a few more years.'

'Great. And . . .?'

'My father did write to me after he went back to India permanently. Several times. And sent presents. I never received them. When he tried to phone, he was told I didn't want to speak to him.'

'Ah. Your mother's doing, do you think?'

'Yes.'

'That's sad.'

'I don't think I can forgive her for it. I was too young to be that unhappy and she didn't attempt to comfort me. Just stuck me in a boarding school. I don't want her messing up my child's life.'

For a moment his face looked sad, so Jessica kissed him until he smiled at her.

'Oh, you make my world so much brighter,' he said huskily, tears in his eyes.

'Good. Go on.'

'I'm to take you to visit my father as soon as possible. This won't be his first grandchild but—'

She put a hand over his mouth. 'Granddaughter. I was right.'

'They found out what sort it is already?'

'Yes. I have a blurry image of what looks like an alien being.' She pulled it out of her handbag and gave it to him.

He looked at it and raised it to his lips to kiss the image. Then he hugged Jessica all over again.

'Meeting you was the best thing that ever happened to me.'

'I feel the same way about you.'